THE ARKS OF ANDROMEDA

THE IMPERIUM CHRONICLES
BOOK ONE

W. H. MITCHELL

Cover design: Steven Novak (NovakIllustration.com)

Published by: Willbot Books, 2020

ISBN-13: 978-1-7351189-0-1

Works by W. H. Mitchell

The Imperium Chronicles Series

The Arks of Andromeda, Book 1 (2017)

The Dragons of Andromeda, Book 2 (2018)

The Robots of Andromeda, Book 3 (2020)

Humor

A Little of Me Goes a Long Way (2015)

To my wonderful wife, who puts up with me
when no one else will.

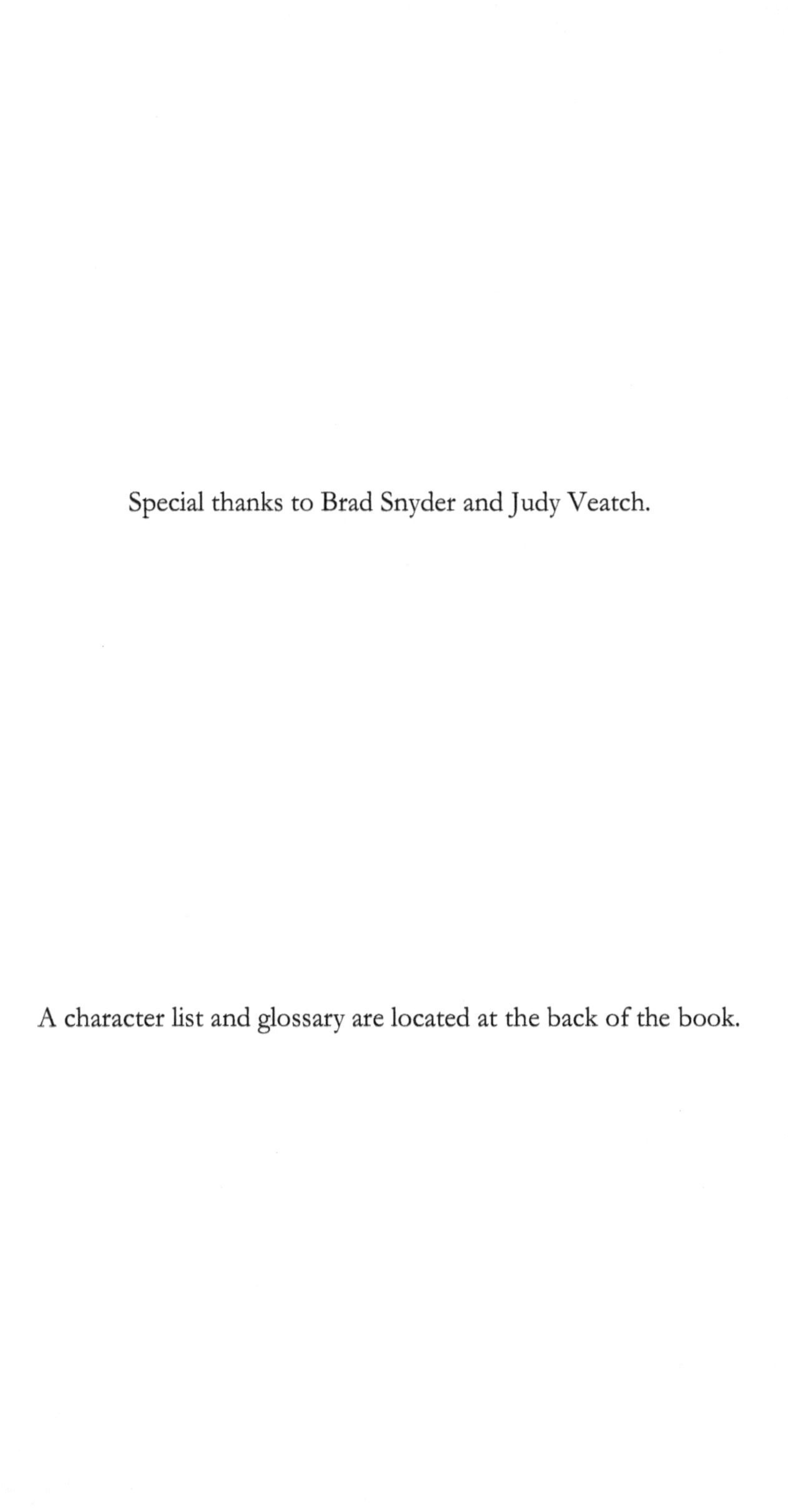

Special thanks to Brad Snyder and Judy Veatch.

A character list and glossary are located at the back of the book.

CHAPTER ONE

Lying in the dark, Captain Ramsey woke to the sound of bagpipes. The ship's computer was messing with him again.

"Computer, lights," he said.

The bulbs around the captain's stateroom flickered to life. The bagpipes continued, piped through speakers in the ceiling.

"And turn off the god damned alarm."

The music stopped.

Ramsey smacked his dry lips and tossed the sheets to the side of his bunk. Dressed in only a white t-shirt and boxer shorts, he pulled his legs over the side of the bed and planted his bare feet on the cold, metal deck.

He cleared his throat and got up, crossing to the sink along the wall. He spat into the basin and stared into the mirror as he rubbed sleep from his eyes. He nodded to himself and gave a sarcastic salute.

For a man in his late 30s, Captain Ramsey was a little young to command his own starship, even a worn-out freighter like the *Steppenwolf*. He had spent his early years paying his dues in the merchant marines, eventually becoming an executive officer and, finally, a captain.

"Computer," Ramsey said, "what's the ship's status?"

A disembodied voice, monotone but obviously male, said "During your sleep cycle, the ship dropped out of hyperspace and is currently en route to the planet Samarta. First Mate Park currently has the conn. There is one hour left in his duty shift."

"What about our cargo?"

"The twenty tons of pharmaceuticals are stable. No apparent shifting during hyperspace egress."

"Thanks, Computer," Ramsey said. "You're a peach."

"Thank you, sir. You're an eggplant."

"That's not a thing."

"Are you sure, sir?"

"Yes."

"Very well, sir," the Computer said. "I'll make a note of it."

Ramsey pulled down his drawers and tossed them, along with his shirt, into the corner. It was the captain's cabin, but nothing to brag about. The shower was like a metal coffin set on its end, barely large enough for Ramsey's body. Still not fully awake, he fumbled the temperature lever, giving him a long burst of frigid water before it heated enough to be tolerable. He dribbled shampoo into his blond, closely-cropped hair as he emptied his bladder onto the floor and down the drain. There was nothing glamorous about star travel, not on this ship anyway.

He hurried to soap himself up and wash out the shampoo. Water pressure was never a sure thing and hot water was a luxury. When he finished, he stepped out onto the metal plating. This time he was more aware of the vibrations of the ship passing through the bottoms of his feet. Whether in his stateroom, on the bridge, or in the engine room, everything on the *Steppenwolf* hummed to its own frequency.

Ramsey got dressed and then stuck his head under the sink faucet to take a long drink. The water had a hint of rust. He brushed his teeth and headed for the bridge.

"Morning, Captain," First Mate Park greeted him with a smile. Park was Korean by heritage, not that anyone knew where Korea was anymore. Still, Park's family could trace their lineage to the *Maia*, one of the five surviving sleeper ships. All humans came from one of the five, but Ramsey's own ancestry was anyone's guess.

"Mornin'," Ramsey said, slipping into the seat next to Park.

The bridge of the *Steppenwolf* was like a bomber cockpit, two command chairs and not much else.

"Do you want the conn?" Park asked.

"Not yet," Ramsey replied.

The *Steppenwolf* stayed on course through the system. Ramsey normally kept to the outer provinces of the Imperium where cargoes were more lucrative due to raiders and the Pirate Clans. This one was different. Ramsey had taken a special assignment, a hold full of medical supplies, destined for a corporate world owned by Warlock Industries. Situated snugly in the safety of the Core Worlds, the planet was nearer to the Imperial capital on Aldorus where the Navy was ever present. Maybe Ramsey could relax for a change.

"There's something on sensors," First Mate Park said.

Captain Ramsey examined the round monitor between the two of them. Four contacts, each glowing green, were moving slowly toward the center of the circle.

"They're on an intercept course," Park said.

"I can see that," Ramsey said. "I'm taking the conn."

"Aye, sir."

"I'm changing course."

While not as large as most freighters, the *Steppenwolf* was no less awkward in flight. At fifty yards long, the ship looked like an obese toddler laying on its belly with its arms and legs tucked in.

"They're matching our course, sir," Park said.

"Tell me something I don't know."

"Also, their transponders are turned off."

"Thanks for that."

The green contacts on the sensor grid turned an ominous red.

"They can't be pirates this close to the capital," Ramsey reasoned. "That would be insane."

"A syndicate outfit?"

"Warlock Industries would've paid off all the syndicate guys," Ramsey said. "They always have their business in order."

"They're in visual range," Park said. "Putting them up on the monitor."

A display came alive. Four fuzzy dots appeared against a black background. The image sharpened and zoomed in. Ramsey instantly recognized what he saw: a flight of fighters, their wings curved into sharpened points like knives.

"Pirate Clans!" the captain said in disbelief.

"They're firing."

"Shields up," Ramsey said. "Full power to starboard."

Not willing to take his eyes off the screen, Ramsey fumbled blindly for his headset. His fingers touched and then grasped the plastic earpiece. He jammed it into his ear and flipped a switch on the control panel by his leg, opening a communication channel.

"Mayday, mayday," he said. "This is the *S. S. Steppenwolf* declaring an emergency. We're under attack by Pirate Clan ships. We need assistance immediately. Repeat, immediately!"

Captain Durant Blixx stood silently in the corridor of the *Hotspur*, just outside Airlock One. He listened as his quartermaster, Jack Calico, spoke into an intercom box just below the window on the airlock hatch. Through the window, a man named Sid Dugdale peered out, perspiration running down his face.

In his early forties, Calico was wide at the shoulders and his belly hung over the belt of his uniform. Bald on top, his eyebrows made up for it with both fullness and an unrestrained abandon. He was reading from a datapad in his thick-fingered hands.

"Mister Dugdale," Calico said in a baritone voice, "you've been convicted of stealing from your fellow crewmen. Pursuant to Article B of the Pirate Code, you are hereby sentenced to death by spacing through the airlock."

"I didn't do nothing!" Sid pleaded by way of the intercom. "I never saw those boots before and I didn't take them neither."

"Well, Sid," Calico replied calmly, "Mister Paterson's new boots were found in your locker."

"I don't know how they got there!"

"You heard the witness testify you had envied the footwear ever since Mister Paterson took them from that freighter last month. You said before everyone in the galley those boots were too small for Paterson's fat feet. Clearly you knew about them and were an active participant in their disappearance."

"This ain't justice!" Sid declared. "Please, Captain, can't you help me?"

Durant Blixx stirred. His hair and beard were a deep, auburn red like old rust on the side of a sailing ship. With blazing green eyes, he stared directly at the unfortunate man behind the window.

"You're a thief among thieves," he said. "We have our code to protect us from each other. When you break that code, you must pay the price."

With that, the captain nodded to the quartermaster, who touched the control pad on the airlock door. The intercom was turned off so neither man could hear Sid screaming as the outside door opened, exposing him to the hard vacuum of space. Through the glass, they watched the writhing body float silently through the open portal and exit the ship.

"It's a sad business," Calico shook his head. "But at least Mister Paterson has his boots back. Too bad he can't wear them on account of his fat feet."

"When do we reach the Samarta system?" Blixx asked.

"Within the hour, sir," the quartermaster said. "We should intercept the target shortly thereafter."

"Good. I'll be glad to see some action after this."

"Aye, sir."

Blixx climbed a pair of ladders until he reached the command deck. Instead of heading straight to the bridge, he stopped by his stateroom that also served as his office. The central living space contained a desk, bookcase, and several comfortable chairs. To the left and right, doorways led to the bedroom and toilet respectively. Expensive carpets covered most of the floor. Paintings, several in gilded frames, hung along the walls between gold sconces warming the room with light. Nearly everything in the room was stolen from merchant ships by Blixx and his crew.

Behind a wide rosewood desk, the captain sat down in a brown leather chair. He tapped the glass-like top of the desk, which blazed to life, showing files and images. A brightly colored advertisement, with blinking letters, appeared across the screen.

WANT THAT FRESH, CLEANED-OUT FEELING?
ENJOY A SPASTIC COLA TODAY!
ANOTHER QUALITY PRODUCT FROM MOFOCO!

Irritably, Blixx swiped the spam to the edge of the screen where it disappeared. Collecting himself, he tapped one of the file icons, which expanded into the picture of an emerald-skinned man with horns growing from his head. The man's eyes were bright red as he glared out at the captain.

Blixx tapped the image again and the face started speaking.

"Durant," he said in a deep voice, "messages between us entail a certain level of risk, but it's imperative you send me reports of your progress. Listening to media reports of your exploits is inadequate. If you wish to receive additional targets, I expect you to live up to our arrangement."

"Arrogant son-of-a-bitch," Blixx said.

"Must you swear, sir?" said a small voice from the corner of the room.

A robot, or what was left of him, sat in a red lounge chair. Its head was made from blue plastic, but without eyes or mouth or any other easily discernible orifices. Its blue chest was intact, as well as its right arm and hand. However, its left arm and both legs were nothing more than stumps from which fiber optic wires hung loosely.

"I forgot you were there," Blixx said as if speaking to a piece of furniture he had just bumped.

"No doubt," the robot said. "As for *why* you're keeping me here, that's another question."

"I like the company."

"I don't even have a name or, if I did, you seem to have erased it."

Blixx smiled. "If I didn't brain-wipe you from time to time, you'd know too much and then I'd really have to get rid of you."

"Being spaced out an airlock would be a nice change of scenery."

"What did you think of the message I just played?" Blixx asked, changing the subject.

With its remaining hand, the robot scratched the side of its head casing. "Well, it raises a few questions."

"Like what?"

"Well, the person on the recording was obviously Magna. Even with the brain wipes I still know humans and the Magna despise each other, so it's odd that you're working with one. Also, since the Magna Supremacy sends privateers to strike Imperial shipping, in direct competition with the Pirate Clans, that makes your actions doubly strange. If the other clans found out, I think you'd be in some hot water, to use the human expression."

"Very good, robot!" Blixx said. "I can see why I keep you around."

"So, why are you doing it then?"

"Little minds think of little things," the captain said. "The other clans — the Butcher Boys, the Skeleton Crew, even Maude's Marauders — they're content with eating whatever scraps they can catch on the Imperial frontier. The true feast lies deeper, toward the core, but attacking shipping in the interior is too ambitious for them, but not for me. I'm an alpha predator, not a vulture. I designed the *Hotspur* to strike at the heart of the empire."

"So, what of your Magna friend?"

"A marriage of convenience," Blixx shrugged. "A means to an end."

"What does he get out of it?" the robot asked.

A red light flashed across the captain's desk. Blixx touched the surface, opening a screen containing Quartermaster Calico's face.

"What is it, Jack?" the captain said.

"The targeted freighter is in range," Calico replied.

"Very well," Blixx said. "Launch the fighters when ready and plot an intercept course. I'll change and get ready for the boarding party."

"Aye, sir."

The quartermaster's image blinked out of existence. Blixx stood from his chair.

"Are you going to erase my memory again?" the robot wondered.

Blixx went to his closet where an armored bodysuit hung. He pulled the suit out, feeling the heft of the interwoven plates designed to repel ballistic and energy weapons.

"Maybe when I get back," he said, not turning around.

Flight Leader Chapman heard the mayday call over the emergency band and ordered his group of four Banshee interceptors to change course toward the *Steppenwolf*.

In a finger-four formation, Chapman's interceptor took the lead with his wingman to the left and the other two Banshees behind and to the right. Each fighter looked like a flying wing with engines in the back and ion cannons in the front. The cockpit protruded in a pod at the center of the wing's leading edge.

The voice of Lieutenant Erickson, his wingman, crackled in Chapman's helmet. "What are pirates doing around here?"

"No idea," Chapman replied. "Go to full thrust."

Torches of blue flame ignited behind the four craft, propelling them at several hundred kilometers per second. With nothing for reference, Chapman had no sense of speed except for the readouts projected across his visor. He thought about radioing the *Steppenwolf*, but wanted to keep the element of surprise if possible, knowing any signal could give away their position.

It didn't take long before his sensors started picking up blooms of heat against the cold backdrop of space. Plasma explosions lit up the infrared spectrum, which Chapman recognized as blaster fire, probably from fighters.

They were in visual range now, at least at the highest magnification. On his screen, Chapman could just make out four tiny ships buzzing around the *Steppenwolf* like hornets circling their nest. The freighter's shields glowed with every hit.

Two of the pirate fighters veered away and came toward Chapman's flight.

"They've seen us," Chapman said over the comm. "Erickson and I will take the first two. Ramos and Kline, take the ones attacking the freighter."

"Roger that," the others said in unison.

Chapman started to regret not becoming a shuttle pilot like his mother wanted.

In Chapman's visor display, two square target designators appeared around the fighters heading his way. Gripping the control stick between his legs, Chapman pulled to the right slightly, moving a circular aiming reticle, at the center of his HUD, over one of the squares. Even through the gloves of his flight suit, he could feel the trigger against his finger.

The circular and square symbols pulsated. The enemy was on target and in range. Chapman squeezed the trigger. Beams of orange light fired from both sides of the cockpit canopy, disappearing to a point in the distance. At the same time, streaks of light flashed past Chapman's interceptor and Erickson's Banshee disintegrated into a cloud of burning plasma.

Stunned, Chapman managed to keep firing until one of the pirate fighters exploded. The surviving fighter rolled sideways as it made evasive maneuvers.

"Stay on the *Steppenwolf*," he told the other two pilots. "I've got this one."

Chapman pulled his Banshee up and over, trying to point his nose at the target. An arrow, part of the HUD, moved along his line of sight, showing him what direction to fly. When the designator square appeared again, the pirate fighter was much larger in the frame, only a few hundred meters away.

Chapman fired and fired again, missing both times. He decreased the thrust in his starboard engine slightly, giving him a tighter turn and bringing his aiming reticle closer to the targeting square. For a split second, the two symbols overlapped and flashed. Chapman pulled the trigger, sending spears of light into the fighter. Its wing broke apart, followed by a blinding flash as the rest of the craft erupted.

"Yeah!" Chapman shouted, unable to help himself.

"We could use some help," Ramos said over the comm.

"On my way," Chapman replied.

By the time the flight leader closed the gap between himself and the *Steppenwolf*, Kline's Banshee was already destroyed and Ramos was left to fend off the two remaining pirate fighters alone.

Chapman quickly turned one of them into blistering slag with a pull of the trigger, but could only watch as Ramos died in a blaze of debris.

Now Chapman was on his own, just him against the last pirate.

Both craft began spiraling around each other like the threads of a rope. Chapman rolled his ship inverted and dove away, hoping to gain a better position. The pirate pilot continued spiraling for a moment longer, then rolled out and turned toward Chapman's interceptor.

The two fighters faced each other from less than a kilometer apart.

Chapman fired.

The pirate's ship detonated like a bomb, pieces of it ballooning outward like an exploding sun.

Chapman pounded the inside of his canopy with excitement. After taking a much deserved breath, he exhaled and switched his comm to the same commercial channel used by the *Steppenwolf*.

"You're safe now, *Steppenwolf*!" Chapman said, still shaking from the adrenaline surging through his bloodstream.

The captain of the freighter radioed back, his voice tinged with anger.

"Don't be stupid," he said.

Now in range, the *Hotspur* fired one of its heavy turrets, ripping Chapman's Banshee in half. The interceptor exploded into tiny, glowing embers.

Aboard the *Steppenwolf*, Captain Ramsey shook his head in disgust.

"Dumbass," he remarked. "Where did he think these fighters were coming from anyway?"

First Mate Park spoke beside him. "That mother ship is closing fast."

Through the bridge windows, Ramsey saw his shields flicker as they absorbed the incoming fire.

"Shields are failing," Park said. "We can't take—"

Another blast. This time Ramsey felt a tremor go up his spine through his command chair. The lights on the controls dimmed momentarily. A faint whiff of acrid smoke filled the Captain's nostrils.

"Shields are down," Park said.

"No shit."

"I'm picking up a transmat signature," the first mate went on. "I think we're being boarded."

"It just keeps getting better and better," Ramsey said ruefully.

He started to switch his comm to the inner-ship channel so he could alert the crew when he heard the door to the bridge slide open behind him. Swiveling in his chair, the captain faced the open hatchway where a tall man covered in an armored bodysuit stood. The red beard covering the man's face highlighted a set of piercing green eyes.

"Who the hell are you?" Ramsey asked while noting the intruder was holding a blaster rifle.

"Durant Blixx," the man said. "Surrender your vessel."

Ramsey raised his hands.

"I'm not surrendering until you guarantee the safety of my crew," the captain said.

Blixx pointed the blaster directly at Ramsey.

"Surrender now or I'll kill every living soul on this ship," he said flatly.

Ramsey's mouth bent into a frown, but his eyes remained hopeful.

"Okay, I surrender," the captain said, "but I'm telling everybody I negotiated."

The pirate Durant Blixx stared at Ramsey for a minute, then rolled his eyes.

"Fine."

CHAPTER TWO

On the planet Aldorus, Counselor Kalidas strolled down a long corridor in the Imperial Palace. The counselor was small, no more than five and a half feet tall, with burgundy-colored hair pulled back, exposing pointed ears. His race, the Dahl, looked elvish to the human eye, but the Dahl themselves found the resemblance a quaint coincidence.

The Dahl had been loyal consultants to humanity since the early days of the Imperium. Arriving at the Dahlvish home world *Gwlad Ard'un* for the first time, humanity encountered none of the resistance they had found with other races. These Dahl, the humans discovered, had no interest in fighting them or anyone else. They seemed perfectly content studying, and even assisting, this alien race that had swept through large swaths of the galaxy.

This started a partnership of sorts with humans in the lead and the Dahl at their elbow, whispering helpful advice from time to time. In return, the Dahl continued what they had always done: accumulating knowledge for its own sake.

Counselor Kalidas felt the slightest twinge of pride at the thought. Never mind the other races who saw the Dahl as little more than collaborators with an invading army.

The Dahl came to a door and pushed on the handle. Inside, Emperor Hector Augustus was lying on a couch. Kalidas hesitated, not sure if he should wake his Excellency.

"What is it?" Augustus asked, sitting up.

Relieved, Kalidas stammered slightly. "My apologies, your Excellency."

The emperor was elderly, in his early sixties, with a silver beard. He wore a long, gray tunic with a wide, black stripe down the front and back. A tall collar enclosed the sagging skin around his neck.

He seemed to be looking for something.

"Where's my crown?" he said, his eyes scanning the room.

"I believe it's on the back of your chair," Kalidas said, pointing.

"Ah, yes, thank you."

Augustus stood from the couch, took a few seconds to stretch, and went to the desk against the far wall where a simple, gold circlet hung on the chair. The emperor placed it atop his otherwise bare head.

"I'm probably going to need that," he remarked.

"You remember it's Prince Richard's birthday?" Kalidas asked tentatively.

"Already?"

"Indeed, your guests are waiting in the Great Hall."

"Let them wait!" the emperor scoffed, but then thought better of it. "On the other hand, Richard would probably put them to sleep if I don't hurry. We can't have that..."

"Yes, your Excellency."

"Who's at this party anyway?" the emperor said.

"The usual suspects," Kalidas said. "Dignitaries, nobles, the political elite..."

"What about Alexander?"

The counselor shook his head. "I don't think Prince Alexander is planning to attend, I'm afraid."

"No, I suppose not. Too much to hope for, eh?"

"Indeed."

Carrying a tray burdened with bottles of champagne and several glasses, a butlerbot emerged from the kitchen adjacent to the Great Hall. The robot's black plastic chest piece was polished to a mirror sheen along with its spindly arms and legs of shiny aluminum. Instead of a humanoid head, the butlerbot's face looked like an upside-down teardrop with a reddish face plate. Around its neck, the robot also wore a white collar and black bow tie, but only for appearances' sake.

Pillars, wider than a dozen arm lengths, carried the weight of a high, vaulted ceiling above the important people, mostly human, who mingled in the Hall. Hanging from archways between the pillars, banners displayed the crests of the Five Families. On the left side of the room dangled the lion crest of the Tagus family and the botonée cross of the Groens. On the right hung the rose of the House Montros and the scallop shell of the Vebers. In the center, above the landing where the emperor was expected to enter, the two-headed eagle of House Augustus was draped. Each family was named after, and descended directly from, the original captains of the surviving five sleeper ships that brought colonists to Andromeda. Although the rest of the crew founded their own noble houses, they remained secondary to the primary five. As for the colonists preserved in cryogenic sleep, they awoke to become the common citizens of the Imperium.

The butlerbot drifted from one group of people to another, offering beverages along the way. The robot was programmed to recognize the guests in case any had special requirements or an inclination toward angry outbursts when drunk.

"Care for some champagne?" the butlerbot asked two men, Lord Winsor Woodwick and Lord Radford Groen.

Woodwick, from one of the lesser families, ignored the robot and asked the other man, "Did you see Maycare win the tube race last night?"

"I lost ten thousand on it," Groen admitted.

A chuckle cut through Woodwick's thick, walrus mustache. "It's your own fault, betting against Maycare. He's unstoppable, I dare say!"

"Indeed," Groen simmered.

Moving on, the robot came to a middle-aged man and woman identified as Archsenator Malcolm Tarkio and Senator Joan Marshall.

In the early days of the Imperium, those outside the aristocracy, even those with wealth, had little say in the government. Eventually, the emperor at that time formed a legislature called the Imperial Senate, with politicians elected from all over the empire. The senate, however, didn't talk directly with the emperor. Only a select few, collectively known as the Emperor's Council, could do that. These individuals, drawn from the legislature, were called *archsenators*.

The woman, dressed in a smartly-tailored gown, took a glass from the robot's tray without gazing at either.

"Did you hear the news about Samarta?" Senator Marshall asked.

Archsenator Tarkio leaned in. "Another pirate attack?"

"I'm afraid so!"

"Oh, dear."

"Perhaps you could talk to his Excellency about it?"

Tarkio bowed his head. "Well, I've only just joined the Council…"

"Congratulations, by the way," she said, taking a sip of champagne between her smiling teeth.

"You're too kind."

"Before he passed away, my husband always spoke highly of you."

"I'm pleased to hear it," Tarkio said. "Our dealings were invariably profitable, a partnership I hope to continue with *you* as well."

"We'll see," she replied.

At the far end of the Great Hall, below the Augustus banner, Counselor Kalidas entered onto the landing from which twin staircases descended to the main floor. Everyone in the room stopped and stared expectantly at the small-framed Dahl standing above them.

Kalidas raised his arms above his head and, with greater volume than the crowd was expecting, shouted "All hail Emperor Augustus!"

Waving his hands, the emperor made his entrance behind Kalidas, stopping at the marble balustrade. The guests all cheered, raising their glasses enthusiastically. Looking down at them, the emperor saw their happy expressions like alligators grinning at a chicken tied to a stick.

The emperor's son, Prince Richard Augustus, came up the stairs with a more sincere, albeit restrained, smile.

"Happy birthday, my boy!" Augustus said.

"Thank you," Richard replied.

The oldest of the emperor's three children, the prince was in his late thirties. Both his eyes and carefully cropped hair were brown, as well as his lengthy mustache. His tunic was red and gold, displaying their family colors. A handsome lad, the emperor had to admit, but with all the personality of an accountant during tax season.

The emperor faced the crowd and did his best to appear regal.

"In celebration of my son Prince Richard's birthday," he shouted, "I thank you all for coming!"

More cheering, this time with a few revelers even shouting "Long live Richard" and "Long live the emperor!" It was all expected but without the expectation of sincerity. These were the roles people played at such things. Augustus knew better than anyone.

"I thought mother was joining us," Richard said.

"Yes, about that," Augustus replied, giving Kalidas a quick glance. "I'm afraid Isabella left for Revenna last night."

"Really?" Richard asked.

"You know how she is. These sorts of public affairs don't appeal to her much." The emperor laughed and then added, "She likes her affairs private!"

Richard stared at him blankly.

"I'm kidding, of course," Augustus clarified.

The emperor looked at Kalidas again, but if he was expecting any relief from the counselor, he wasn't getting any.

The emperor slapped Richard's shoulder. "Good talk!" he said and left the prince standing alone on the landing.

The crowd parted as Emperor Augustus reached the bottom of the stairs. Kalidas stepped ahead, making sure everyone kept a respectful distance unless called upon to do otherwise. Tighter security was unnecessary inside the palace. Everyone in attendance was carefully vetted and, even if someone did choose to harm the leader of the Imperium, that person would quickly die along with his family, his distant relatives, and any casual acquaintances those relatives might have met that day. The Imperium dealt harshly with those who opposed it, and everyone still breathing knew that.

In the corner of the room, away from the rest of the partygoers, a looming shape stood apart. The emperor knew the shape well, having tried to kill it several times.

Emperor Augustus strode directly toward the guest as Kalidas tried to keep up.

"Your Excellency," Kalidas said, his chest heaving, "of course you know the Magna Ambassador Bar-Batos"

"Of course," the emperor said, making no attempt to shake the diplomat's hand.

"Indeed," the ambassador replied. "My shoulder still hurts where you shot me."

Nearly a foot taller than the emperor, or anyone else in the room, Bar-Batos was physically menacing with large, muscular features, a wide jaw, and a set of horns curling from his head. His skin was dark green, his red eyes like bloody dagger points.

"If my aim had been better, we wouldn't be having this conversation," Augustus quipped with a hint of irony.

"But then that was a long time ago," Bar-Batos said.

During an earlier era of expansion, the Imperium encountered many native civilizations. Those who resisted met with a harsh, even brutal oppression until they ultimately capitulated. Eventually, however, the Imperium crossed paths with the Magna Supremacy, an empire equally as ruthless. Green skinned and demonic looking, the Magna believed all other life was inferior and subservient to them. They considered it their manifest destiny to rule over all known space, and the Imperium seemed an inconvenient impediment to that goal. The Supremacy declared war immediately and the two sides waged a bloody conflict that lasted over nine years. Since then, the Imperium and the Magna had fought two more wars, the most recent ending nearly twenty years ago.

A butlerbot approached Counselor Kalidas. "Would you like a beverage?" the robot asked.

"What? No! Go away. Shoo! Shoo!" Kalidas said.

The emperor looked up at his former, and possibly present, enemy.

"I've seen reports that your empire has been sending privateers across the border again," Augustus told the ambassador.

"Lies and propaganda," Bar-Batos countered. "Besides, your own spies operate in the Supremacy, at least those we haven't found and executed."

"It pays to keep an eye on things," Augustus said.

"Indeed it does! 'Trust but verify' is the human expression, I believe."

"Well, *trust* is a strong word."

"I prefer action over words," the ambassador said.

Augustus took a step closer. "Do you know I've killed far more men as an emperor than I ever did as a solider?"

Bar-Batos erupted into a deep, volcanic laugh, causing the emperor to step back again.

"Exactly right!" the ambassador said. "When the strong rule the weak, it's good to be strong!"

"Perhaps," Augustus agreed, "but there's always someone testing your strength."

"Crush them then!" Bar-Batos shook his fist.

Counselor Kalidas stepped in. "Pardon the interruption, your Excellency, but I believe you wanted to speak with Lord Tagus?"

"That's true," Augustus realized.

"Which one?" the ambassador asked, "the patriarch or his son?"

"Oh, the son in this case," Augustus said.

"Ah, hot blooded and rash," Bar-Batos replied. "Not unlike your own son, Alexander, as a matter of fact..."

The emperor nodded, showing no signs of offense. " He's a reckless young man but that's the luxury of youth I suppose."

"I remember my early years," the Magna said proudly, "and I regret nothing!"

"If only that were true for the rest of us," the emperor replied.

Lord Rupert Tagus III drank from a champagne flute a butlerbot had offered him earlier. Dressed in formal, naval attire, Tagus glared at those surrounding him, all except his attaché Lieutenant Burke, whom he merely ignored. The two men stood near a tall window framed by pillars. While technically still attending the party, they might have been on another world. An invisible wall of scorn separated them from the rest of the guests.

From Rupert's point of view, this party should have been for him, and the man wearing the crown should have been his father. The Tagus patriarch, Rupert II, could have been emperor if the other Five Families had cooperated. While his father had come to terms with this setback, Rupert was not as forgiving. A god-damned disgrace, he thought to himself and then said it aloud.

"It's a god-damned disgrace!"

"Yes, sir," Burke replied automatically.

Tagus was in his thirties, with sharp cheekbones and a narrow, cutting chin. He wore his hair, like many military men, high and tight. He had to set an example for Burke and anyone else watching. He deserved respect and expected nothing less.

Burke, an unassuming officer in his late 20s, glanced around as if looking for something. "Ah, what's a disgrace, sir?"

"Look at them all," Tagus said, motioning toward the people meandering around the room. "They have no idea what makes the Imperium great. If it weren't for people like my father and I, the Magna would be sitting on that throne and humanity would be in chains!"

Burke nodded, but Rupert was scarcely paying attention. The lieutenant could have gone without trousers and Lord Tagus would not have noticed.

"The emperor is a fool."

"Well, sir, we should not say that here," Burke said. "The walls have ears."

"Let them come and arrest me," Tagus said. "It would mean civil war and none of these pasty-faced cowards have the stomach for *that*!"

Like a parting sea, the crowd thinned in the center and Emperor Augustus and his counselor emerged, advancing toward the two naval officers. Lord Tagus shoved his shoulders back and his chest out.

"My dear boy!" Augustus said. "I wanted to congratulate you on receiving command of the *Gorgon*. A damn fine ship."

"The largest in the fleet," Tagus clarified. "My father was instrumental in securing my commission."

"He must be very proud of you, eh?"

"My father's a proud man," Tagus said. "So am *I*."

A sly grin curled into the corner of the emperor's lips. "Of course you are, my boy. Of course you are!"

CHAPTER THREE

Cameron Hitch watched as a lumbering liftbot carried the final container of pharmaceuticals from the *Hotspur* to his own ship, the *Rattenbury*. The robot, weighed down with pistons and hydraulic hoses, waddled like a toddler, eventually stacking the container next to the others. Hitch noted that each box was stamped with the pentagram logo of Warlock Industries.

The quartermaster of the *Hotspur*, Jack Calico, presented Hitch with the manifest on a datapad. With his palm print, Cameron signed and acknowledged the cargo was now his responsibility.

"It's all yours," Calico said.

"Yeah, so it is," Hitch replied.

A blockade runner pilot by trade, Cameron Hitch was old enough to have acquired a degree of wisdom, but still young enough to not let that slow him down when doing something stupid was required. He kept his hair short to keep the gray patches around his temples from becoming too obvious. His nose was crooked from a fistfight over a girl—or an unpaid bar tab—he couldn't quite remember which. He wore a dirty flight suit most days, with the top zipped down and a white t-shirt underneath. At his hip, he carried a holstered blaster pistol.

"Do you understand the arrangements?" Calico asked. "You'll get paid once you reach Aldorus, assuming you get past customs."

Hitch laughed.

"They'd have to catch me first," he said.

Quartermaster Calico returned to the *Hotspur*, the umbilical bridge between the two ships folding like an accordion behind him. After securing the cargo door, Hitch patted the liftbot and headed for the bridge of the *Rattenbury*.

The smuggler's ship was half the size of the *Hotspur*. At the front, a saucer section hung beneath the main hull. In the back, the fuselage was all engines and thrusters, making the *Rattenbury* one of the fastest blockade runners in the Imperium.

Once seated in his command chair, Hitch plotted a course for Aldorus, the capital of the Imperium, and fired the jump drives. The *Rattenbury* shimmered and then vanished like a magic trick into hyperspace.

Sitting at his office desk at Warlock Industries headquarters, Oscar Skarlander could almost see the Imperial Palace across the river in the West End. Looking south, he could also see Ashetown, another district of Regalis, the capital city. The three districts of Regalis were a microcosm of the Imperium. The rich to the west and the poor to the south, and in between, the rest of the citizens who made the empire run.

Skarlander loathed them all.

His dark eyes stared at a video monitor suspended in an otherwise transparent wall dividing his office. He pulled at his short, brown goatee as a network journalist named Sylvia Flax talked on the screen, the logo for VOX News in the corner.

"Do robots go to heaven?" Flax asked. Her hair, a bright azure, hung past her shoulders, framing her young but determined face as she spoke. "Tune in for my special report later this week, only on VOX News!"

Skarlander snapped his fingers and the display blinked out, revealing an android standing behind the clear partition.

"What is it, Jerry?" Skarlander growled.

The android was as tall as an average human. Polished, white plastic covered most of its body except at the joints where colored wires were neatly bundled together. His human-shaped face was fixed, unable to convey emotion. Only his eyes and mouth could move freely.

"The special cargo you wanted me to track has landed at the star port," the android said. "It's currently en route to a warehouse in Ashetown."

Skarlander waved the robot closer.

"Any problems?" the human asked.

"No, sir," Jerry replied. "The insurance company has already paid in full."

"Good!"

Skarlander scrutinized the android as he walked around the partition and came to the edge of his desk. The robot was special, he thought. Dyson Yost, from dy cybernetics, had really outdone himself with this one. Jericho, or *Jerry* as everyone preferred to call him, had a gravitronic brain. Instead of being programmed, he learned like a person did through experience. Normally Skarlander would have chosen an assistant that he could kill without repercussion, but the higher-ups at Warlock wanted to test what an android like this could really do. As long as it didn't develop morals, Skarlander told them, he'd agree to the experiment.

The android, Skarlander noted, remained standing by his desk without moving.

"Is there something else?" he asked.

"No."

"Off you go then," Skarlander said dismissively.

Jericho left Skarlander's office and stepped into an elevator. The robot held the door as several Warlock employees scrambled in. They spoke amongst themselves while Jericho stood quietly at the back. He listened carefully to their chatter, searching for any social nuances that might prove useful. Biological creatures like humans had decades to learn how to behave, but Jericho only had the basics uploaded into his gravitronic brain before entering polite society. For a while this proved difficult. Gaffes were common for many months. Eventually Jericho began imitating certain individuals in hopes of fitting in. This worked, but left the android feeling strangely detached from the people he was trying to emulate. Jericho knew he couldn't go on pretending to be someone he wasn't.

The other employees left the elevator as it made stops along the way to the main floor of the headquarters. Warlock HQ, Jericho had learned, was nicknamed the *Cauldron*. At first, he didn't understand why, other than the word play with the company name. That might have been the end of it, but as he saw more and more of Warlock operations, the true meaning became apparent.

With Jericho as the sole occupant, the elevator continued below the ground floor, descending through underground parking garages, the basement level, and then subbasement floors. Jericho estimated that, when the doors finally opened, he was nearly five hundred feet below the surface.

The robot stepped out into a corridor. Fluorescent lights were spaced along the ceiling every fifteen feet, just enough to illuminate the hallway, but not quite enough to avoid the look of a subterranean dungeon. Several metal doors also lined the way, each of which Jericho passed until coming to one in particular. The door was without a label or any other way to differentiate it from any of the other doors, but Jericho knew it well.

This was his office.

Once inside, he looked around his little domain. The single room was Jericho's home away from home, or at least it would be if it wasn't, in fact, Jericho's actual home.

"Computer," he said, "play bebop play list."

Music began playing as Jericho crossed the room to a couch where he laid down, his feet hanging over the end. Digging his hand behind his head, he listened to the discordant notes of a pianist who died more than a thousand years before.

He had learned about jazz from archives brought along with the sleeper ships. Jericho studied the files religiously, curious to understand humanity. He stumbled upon the music files quite by accident, but he was immediately drawn to bebop jazz. It lacked the rigid order he was used to, giving him a sense of chaos he found liberating.

Another song started by another artist long dead. Slowly, Jericho drifted off and fell asleep.

In Ashetown, the slum district of Regalis, everybody knew Kid Vicious and most of them wanted him dead. In the back office of a warehouse, Kid peered menacingly at a spreadsheet on a computer monitor. When he founded the Griefers Gang, he didn't know it would include this much paperwork.

Without sleeves, Kid's shirt exposed his bare arms, decorated in ink, mostly of the tribal variety. Wild, orange flames were painted down the length of his jeans, nearly matching the color of his abundant hair flowing around his head.

A young man in his twenties, wearing a t-shirt with a Chinese dragon print, came up a flight of stairs into the office. Kid glared at him, but was secretly glad he could stop looking at spreadsheets.

"What the hell do you want?" Kid shouted.

"The cat from Si-Sawat isn't talking," the young gangster said. "We worked him over real good too."

"I'll take a crack at him."

Kid followed his man down the stairs to the back of the warehouse where a doorway led to a smaller room. Inside, a feline from the Tikarin race hung by his arms, his tan fur matted from blood and other evidence that he had been "worked over good." Seeing Kid enter through the door, the prisoner snarled.

"Shut up, kitty," Kid said.

From a bench in the room, Kid took a narrow, black handle. Whipping his hand to one side, the handle expanded into a telescoping baton. Kid swung the weapon, cracking it across the Tikarin's neck. The prisoner recoiled, grimacing.

"What's Big G got planned, eh?" Kid asked. "When's he moving against me?

The Si-Sawat crime syndicate didn't typically hire stool pigeons so Kid wasn't surprised when the feline remained silent except for a low groaning deep in his throat.

"Well, it was worth a shot," Kid said, tossing the baton aside. "Kill him."

Another henchman, this one wearing a leather jacket and torn jeans, approached Kid as he left the room, closing the door behind him.

"Boogs is here," he said.

"What's he got this time?" Kid asked.

"He just said it's a once in a lifetime opportunity."

"Yeah, bullshit."

"He's over by the loading dock."

Kid headed to the other side of the warehouse, passing stacks of crates, barrels, and every other kind of container imaginable. When he got to the loading dock, Zarro Boogs was standing beside a box nearly twice his size. Kid wondered how he even got it there.

"Mister Vicious!" Boogs said, waving his arms wildly.

"This better be good," the gang boss replied.

Boogs was a bald man in his forties with a long mustache and eyes like droplets of dried motor oil. Most offensive, at least in Kid's eyes, were Boogs' two-toned blue and green shirt and pants covered in a garish diamond pattern like a harlequin. Kid wanted to kill him just for the clothes alone.

"Of course," Boogs assured him. "Nothing but the best!"

Grabbing a crowbar that leaned against the crate, Boogs began tugging on the side of the box. Kid thought he could hear something moving inside.

"You know I don't deal in livestock," Kid reminded him.

Boogs put his foot up against the crate for better leverage. He gave the crowbar a final tug, dislodging the side, which fell with a crash on the concrete floor. From the dark interior of the box, small creatures, none of them more than two feet tall, came tottering out.

"I present the perfect gift for children of all ages," Boogs announced. "The Tubby Wubbies!"

A teddy bear-like creature waddled over to Kid Vicious on stubby, padded legs, looking up at him with black, soulless eyes. "Hi, I'm Mister Giggles!" it said and laughed in a cute, childlike voice.

Stammering, Kid asked "What the shit is this?"

"It's a toy; it's a pet," Boogs said. "From MoFoCo, the Tubby Wubbies are genetically engineered toys that live and breathe!"

More of them emerged from the crate, including a bunny, a raccoon, and a fox wearing a sweater. Those that remained in the box peered out of the darkness, their glass eyes reflecting tiny pinpoints of light.

"Pick me up! Pick me up!" Mister Giggles pleaded.

Kid obliged, holding the stuffed bear at arm's length.

"I like snuggles," the toy said. "Don't make me *cut* you."

"What?" Kid said, not sure if he heard him right.

At that point, Kid felt a sharp sting in the back of his leg. Looking down, he saw the bunny holding a collapsible baton.

"Goddammit, that hurt!" he shouted.

Kid tried stomping on the rabbit, but missed. To his right, one of his men also cried out in pain. Glancing over, Kid saw a stuffed raccoon running by with a switchblade in its paws.

Still in Kid's hands, Mister Giggles whispered, "I'm going to gut you like a fish."

Forgetting the bunny, Kid dropkicked the bear against a stack of barrels several feet away. Sitting up, the toy held its paws against his fluffy head.

The rabbit lashed Kid again with the baton, this time in the shin.

"I'm going to kill you!" Kid barked just as a blazing beam of energy hit the bunny, setting it alight. The creature screamed, dropping the baton, and ran in a random direction while Kid watched in amazement.

Another flash and another Tubby Wubby, this time the raccoon, erupted into flames.

Kid looked where the beams were coming from: a man with a short, brown goatee, holding a disrupter pistol. It was Oscar Skarlander from Warlock, someone he knew all too well.

Several more well-placed shots sent burning toys scurrying across the warehouse floor until each one dropped, their inner workings melting into slag.

Skarlander, his weapon down by his side, came forward.

"Another quality product by MoFoCo," he said dryly.

"You've seen these before?" Kid asked.

"Of course," Skarlander replied. "To save money, MoFoCo used a subcontractor to design their little brains. Turns out the toys developed psychopathic tendencies shortly after going to market. They got recalled, but it looks like your vendor friend got ahold of a few."

"I'm going to murder Boogs," Kid said, waving the smoke away from his face.

"He ran out during the fight."

"He can't run forever."

"Not my problem," Skarlander remarked. "I'm told you have my pharmaceuticals."

Kid nodded. "Safe and sound, ready for pickup."

Both men turned as something stirred. On top of the barrels, Mister Giggles got to his feet and raised an arm as far as his chubby limb would allow.

"Freedom!" he shouted and promptly erupted into fire and smoke, struck by Skarlander's disrupter.

The Warlock agent turned again to Kid Vicious.

"Get your shit together," Skarlander said.

Just outside the Regalis starport, Randall Davidson opened the door to Sparky Joe's Saloon. The sun had just set and the lights of the city were coming to life.

The bar interior was crowded with people who worked in or around the starport. Mechanics and technicians in overalls soiled with grease and other fluids sat at the tables, their conversations veiled in tobacco smoke. Below a video screen that took up nearly an entire wall, a group of starship pilots, easy to spot in their flight suits, huddled around a pool table. On the screen, a celebrity reporter was talking about Prince Richard's birthday as nobles and the well-to-do mingled in the background on their way into the Imperial Palace. The video then went to a commercial showing a political advertisement:

RE-ELECT SENATOR JOAN MARSHALL:
SHE KNOWS WHAT'S BEST FOR YOU!

Davidson was in his early thirties with short, curly black hair and dark brown skin. He waded through the sea of noise until he reached the counter where a bartenderbot was cleaning glasses. The robot had a torso and a head, both painted in a faded blue. Instead of legs, a stainless steel pole jutted into a track that ran behind the bar.

"What'll you have, bub?" the robot asked. On its chest, the name tag read *Joe*.

Davidson gave a quick glance at the beers listed on the wall behind the bartenderbot. None of them really interested him.

With his thumb, he motioned to the man sitting to his right. "I'll have whatever he's having."

The robot gave a shrug and rode the rail down to the other end of the bar.

"Do I know you, friend?" the stranger said. His hair was short with gray patches around his temples. His nose was crooked.

"Depends," Davidson said. "Are you Cameron Hitch?"

"Who's asking?" the smuggler replied.

"I'm told you might be for hire."

"I might be a lot of things," Hitch said, "if the money's right."

Davidson smiled. "I need a package delivered to Eudora Prime."

Hitch cocked his head to one side. "That's on the border. It'll take a while to get there."

"I understand, but the quicker the better. I hear you have a fast ship."

"That I do," Hitch nodded. "So, what's the package?"

Davidson turned in his chair, followed in kind by Hitch. Both men stared at the doorway which stood open. Framed in the entrance, Jericho stood staring back at them.

"My name's Randall Davidson," Davidson told Hitch. "I work for the Robot Freedom League."

CHAPTER FOUR

After much deliberation, Otis Radley decided that *brown berry* was his favorite Spastic Cola flavor. In the East wing of Senator Joan Marshall's mansion, Radley closed the bathroom door, the fan still audible on the other side, and headed back to his post in the command center. Past midnight, he was the only one on security duty, so he was in no hurry. Radley took pleasure in the solitude of his nightly routine.

Radley twirled the ID badge around his neck by its lanyard as he walked. When he arrived at the command center, he found the door open but thought nothing of it, knowing he often left it open to avoid swiping his ID again. Inside, he sat at a desk chair before a bank of video screens covering the opposing wall. He tapped a few keys on a keyboard and squinted at the scenes each monitor revealed.

The Marshall mansion replicated the classical Colonial style of early America on Earth, or as close as architects could approximate it from the sleeper ship archives. A circular driveway, paved with crushed gravel, led to the front entrance.

Scanning the grounds via the monitors, Radley grabbed the neck of a microphone that extended from the top of his desk.

"Dewey?" he said. "Are you out there?"

A warble came from the speakers. On one of the screens, a conical robot without arms or legs rolled into view. Its shell was mostly smooth, white plastic except for a single ring of blue, blinking lights around the robot's body. Also, in red, stenciled numbers, a *01* was printed just above the lights.

"Oh, I see you," Radley replied, watching the securitybot, also known as *Drone One*, wobble over the gravel up the driveway.

Radley switched a few cameras until the back of the property was visible. A marble fountain spurted water into the air against a backdrop of hedges cast in shadows. As expected, Radley saw another bot, Drone Two, teeter along the path, following its normal route through the garden.

Radley cycled through another set of images and grumbled.

"Drone Three, report," he said into the microphone.

He waited.

"Louie, where are you?" Radley asked again.

Another chirp from the speakers alerted Radley to the monitors. Enlarging the view until the screens combined into a single, massive image, Radley saw Dewey sitting patiently next to the missing robot which was missing the top of its dome, the shell blackened along the edges with loose wires throwing sparks.

"Louie!" Radley shouted, realizing someone had blown Drone Three's little head off.

Radley flipped the plastic cover off an ominous, red button labeled *ALARM*, but before he could smash the button, he felt a sharp, hot sensation across his windpipe.

The world began spinning. When it stopped, instead of looking at the monitors, Radley was looking up from the floor. Disoriented, he tried to focus, but his vision was growing dim. He saw a man with hair shaved to a fine stubble behind the desk chair. Dressed entirely in black, the stranger held a wire glowing white hot between his hands. Radley also saw someone dressed as a security guard still sitting in his chair. His mind swiftly clouding, Radley thought something wasn't right about the person in the chair, as if something was missing. He tried concentrating on what it was, but the fogginess of his thoughts thickened until they faded into an inky blackness.

The sun blazed in the blue sky above Regalis as Magnus Black, dressed in a full-length, black leather coat, walked into a fashionable boutique called *Sadira Flowers*. Magnus, in his late thirties, was tall and slim, with a head shaved to a fine stubble.

A bell over the door jangled as Magnus entered. A young girl with blond hair tied into braids was busy organizing an arrangement of carnations and angel's breath. At the sound of the bell, she stopped and looked up at Magnus with a warm smile.

"Can I help you?" she asked.

"I want two dozen white lilies," Magnus said.

"The occasion?"

"A death in the family."

After a pause, the girl said "Would you like them gift wrapped?"

"Sure, why not?"

The girl's smile faded as she motioned for Magnus to follow. She led him through a curtain at the back of the store and down a hallway lined with commercial refrigerators filled with flowers.

Magnus felt the chill as he passed by.

The corridor ended at the doors of an elevator. The girl directed Magnus inside, but didn't join him. The doors closed and the lift headed downward. Instrumental music played as Magnus waited. He didn't recognize the tune at first, but realized it was something by a robotic band called *Toad the Wet Robot.* He also remembered how much he hated robot music.

The doors opened to reveal a woman standing with her hands crossed. The wrinkles around her eyes and the strands of gray in her otherwise brown hair suggested she was in her forties. She wore a dark suit with red lace around the neck and cuffs. She was not smiling.

"Are you Mister Black?" she said in a low, even tone.

Magnus nodded.

"My name's Calesta Koshkin," she said, presenting her hand like a gift. "It's a pleasure to meet you."

"I know who you are," Magnus remarked, shaking her hand.

Now she smiled. "Perhaps my reputation precedes me?"

"Without question," Magnus said.

"I appreciate your quick response to our inquiry. I know it was short notice."

"When Red Lotus sends an invitation," he said, "it's best not to keep them waiting."

"Even so..." Koshkin began, but then turned and walked silently toward a door opposite the elevator. Magnus, though not asked, knew instinctively to follow anyway. The door opened into a room, much longer than it was wide, decked out like a gymnasium. Down the left and right sides of the room, women, most of them young, were doing drills in groups of two to six at a time. In most cases, the women were paired up, sparring against one another. Some were unarmed, but most held weapons: swords, staffs, and even a few with long, metallic claws bound to their hands. They were all shouting in harsh, guttural screams.

Magnus felt the hairs on his neck stiffen.

Koshkin walked straight down the center of the women with Magnus, reluctantly, a few steps behind.

Sixteen-year old Duncan Marshall lay in bed, his blond, curly hair pressed tightly against the pillow.

It was 2 A.M.

"Master Duncan?" the mansion computer said through a speaker in the nightstand. "You appear to be awake."

"So?" the boy replied.

"Are you aware of the current time?"

"Yes."

"Then might I inquire as to why you are not currently sleeping?"

"Mind your own business," Duncan said.

"Do you require a sedative?"

"No!"

"Sorry," the computer cooed, "but your sleep patterns seem maladjusted of late."

Duncan stared at the ceiling, dark except for the pale light coming through the colonial windows.

"I had a nightmare," he said finally.

"Actually, I have an extensive subroutine dedicated to child psychology," the computer said with thinly veiled pride. "Would you like to talk about it?"

"Not really."

"Please?"

Another long pause ensured.

"I dreamed about when my dad and my sister died," the boy said.

"That seems unlikely," the computer replied. "Their accident occurred while you were *in utero*, so to speak."

"I can still imagine it, can't I?"

"Ah yes, the human imagination," the computer said. "Personally I fail to see the intrinsic value of imagining something terrible. Why not think of something more pleasant like a fluffy bunny or a teddy bear?"

"I hate those things."

The boy rolled onto his side for a few minutes and then rolled back again. He repeated this a few times before speaking again.

"Is my mother home yet?" Duncan asked.

"She arrived moments ago with Archsenator Tarkio," the computer said.

Duncan sat up. "What's *he* doing here?"

"Some sort of courtship ritual I assume."

"What's that supposed to mean?"

"Well, Master Duncan, when a man and woman love each other very much—"

"Stop! Just stop!"

"You needn't concern yourself," the computer said. "Your mother is quite pragmatic from what I've seen. I'm sure the mate she chooses to replace your father will be a good match for everyone involved. Is that not ideal?"

"No!"

"Really?" the computer said, its voice rising a few octaves. "Well, politics makes strange bedfellows, as the saying goes."

"Gross!"

Duncan heard an audible sigh from the speaker.

"It's merely an expression," the computer clarified. "I didn't mean it literally, although it may come to that eventually—"

The boy threw his covers aside and put his bare feet into a pair of blue slippers, matching the blue silk pajamas he was wearing.

"I'm getting up," he said.

"Now?" the computer asked.

"I want to talk to Mom."

In her drawing room, Senator Marshall, still wearing the gown from the birthday party earlier, rested her hand against the mantelpiece as holographic flames, producing no actual heat, blazed in the fireplace. Behind her, Archsenator Tarkio took a sip from his nightcap while relaxing on the sofa. The lights were dim.

Marshall touched a framed photograph of her late husband on the mantel.

"When Jim and I first got married," she said, "I hated politics."

Tarkio smiled. "Oh, really?"

"After he got elected to the Imperial Senate we moved to Aldorus, but I was shocked by how the nobles ruled over everything. Jim's passion was always about giving regular people a voice in government. I watched him work so hard against so much opposition. Eventually, his passion became mine."

"Well, we all know the deck is stacked against us," Tarkio said. "Unless you've got blue blood flowing through your veins, that is."

"When Jim died, I picked up the torch. I couldn't bear the thought of all his work going to waste.

"And you haven't!" Tarkio gushed. "If anything, you've surpassed what he accomplished. You always know when to make sacrifices for the common good."

"When it's necessary," she replied.

A butlerbot entered the room with a bottle and refreshed Tarkio's drink. The robot exited the way he came, vanishing into the murky shadows. Marshall left the mantel, taking a seat beside Tarkio on the couch.

"If you don't mind me asking," Marshall said tentatively, "do you regret not getting married?"

He laughed. "Speaking of sacrifices..."

"Too busy campaigning, I suppose?"

"Well, yes," Tarkio said. "Once an election ends, another begins. It's a constant wheel turning and all the while you have to raise money to pay for it all. Luckily, there's no shortage of donors. Once you're on the right committees, that is, they beat a path to your door."

"For years, I've tried to be assigned to the Defense Appropriations Committee," Marshall admitted.

"Oh, I can help you with that!" Tarkio grinned, bowing his head. "Once I'm established on the Emperor's Council, I'll have more say about who gets assigned to what."

"I'd like that very much."

"I can't tell you how many donors have suddenly found an interest in me," Tarkio said. "The Council could print its own money."

"Of course."

"Sorry, I'm talking too much," he apologized. "Too much to drink..."

"Don't worry," Marshall said, her eyes catching his. "I'm very discreet."

They laughed together.

"But to the point you were making," Tarkio went on, "it's all just a means to an end. I mean, if you had to sleep with the Devil to create heaven, it would be selfish not to. Think of all the people you could help? We can't do anything if we don't get re-elected after all!"

Marshall got up from the sofa and went back to the fireplace.

"Malcolm," she said softly, "I'm afraid I can't ask you to stay tonight."

"Oh?" he replied, his eyebrows raised.

"Not yet," she said. "My son wouldn't understand and I don't want to upset him."

"I see."

"He'll come around eventually," she said, "but for now, it might be best if we just say *goodnight*."

"Of course, of course," Tarkio stood up as well, placing his glass on a side table.

They walked to the door, which she opened for him.

"I'm so happy you understand," she said, giving him a kiss and closing the door.

The din of women sparring abruptly ceased once Magnus Black closed the door behind him. Koshkin had brought him to a small room full of old furniture draped with blankets. To one side, a young woman was settled in the center of a sofa. She said nothing as Magnus and Koshkin entered.

"So, what's this really about?" Magnus asked. "The Red Lotus has enough assassins of their own. I doubt my services would be much use to you."

"Actually," Koshkin said, "Red Lotus is *not* the one hiring you."

"Who then?" he asked.

She nodded toward the girl on the couch.

"This is Emily," Koshkin said. "She's the one needing your... services."

Magnus scrutinized the young woman. She had long, stringy black hair and high cheekbones. Her skin was almost translucently pale.

"You're a lot younger than most of my clients," he told the girl. "My skills aren't cheap."

"I've been saving my whole life for this!" Emily said, shooting Magnus an intense glance that surprised him.

"Working for the Red Lotus?" Magnus asked.

"Emily is a hostess at one of our gambling establishments," Koshkin replied. "She's been with us for quite some time."

"And you want me to kill someone for you?" Magnus said. "Why?"

"Allow me to explain," Koshkin said. "About fifteen years ago, a woman came to us with a proposal. Her husband had been a senator, but he died unexpectedly. She wanted to pick up where he had left off, but her lack of experience was posing a problem. The other candidate was probably going to win unless something was done."

"And she wanted you for that something?"

"Besides illegal gambling, the Red Lotus is predominantly known for two other things: prostitution and extortion. As it happens, the woman's idea involved both of those. Essentially, she wanted to entrap the other candidate in a compromising position, forcing him to drop out of the race."

"Which you were able to accomplish I assume?" Magnus said.

"Oh yes," Koshkin laughed. "We used multiple holofeeds to record him with one of our more talented girls. He was married, so once we presented him with the evidence, he would've done just about anything. Ultimately, our client won the election and she's been a senator ever since."

"Where does the girl come in?"

"Well, that's the complicated part," Koshkin said. "When the client first came to us, she didn't have the money we required upfront, so she offered to leave something valuable as collateral."

Magnus glanced at the girl on the sofa. "Her own daughter? How old was she?"

"Six years old," Koshkin said. "The contract stated that if the client didn't pay the money after completion, we could keep the child."

"So, what happened when the contract was fulfilled?"

"After the election, the client said she wouldn't pay us the money she owed."

"Why the hell not?" Magnus asked.

Emily spoke, her voice quivering, "She said I wasn't needed anymore, because she was pregnant with a son."

"I don't get it," Magnus confessed.

"Apparently," Koshkin explained, "the client always wanted a son and, knowing she carried one, viewed Emily as expendable. While distasteful, the contract was fulfilled and payment, Emily, was already in hand. We could do nothing against the client."

"So why now?" Magnus asked. "Why wait so long for revenge?"

"We all have rules to follow," Koshkin replied. "Some are unspoken, but we must abide by them anyway. In this case, although we couldn't move against the client ourselves, Emily could do as she pleased once she reached adulthood."

"And when was that?"

"She turned twenty-one last week."

"Which I guess means she can hire me without breaking your precious rules?"

"Exactly," Koshkin nodded.

"That's quite an operation you've got here," Magnus remarked.

The mansion computer, watching Senator Marshall kiss Archsenator Tarkio, wondered why humans felt compelled to share bodily fluids so readily. Considering the prevalence of bacteria and viruses among fleshlings, the computer found this behavior baffling.

Marshall turned from the front door and walked up the main staircase to the second-floor landing. Duncan Marshall was waiting there for her.

"I don't like him," the teenager said, standing in his blue pajamas.

"You don't have to like him," his mother replied coolly. "Not yet."

"We don't need someone like that."

Marshall put her arms around him.

"Perhaps," she said, "but he could make things a lot easier."

Duncan wriggled free from his mother's embrace. "That's silly."

"No, it's not," Marshall said. "I'm trying to make things better for you and everyone else. Someday you'll understand that."

The computer saw Master Duncan's eyes roll.

"You don't know how things work in the real world," Marshall went on. "It's sad, but a woman still needs a man to get places. When your father died, I knew I couldn't achieve all the things he and I had talked about by myself. Then, when I discovered I was carrying his son, I knew you would surpass both of us."

"I don't even like politics," the boy said.

"You will," his mother assured him. "You'll carry on what we've been fighting for all this time. It's *your* destiny and *our* legacy."

The mansion computer became dimly aware of someone else besides the senator and her son. He was a man, standing in the shadows of the second-floor hallway. He wore all black, and his hair was cut very short.

"Where did he come from?" the computer wondered to itself, becoming alarmed. "Why didn't I see him before?"

The computer realized something was clouding its thoughts. Something was preventing him from looking at the security feeds or even *thinking* about looking at the security feeds. A program, a virus, was running amok through his software. The computer tried alerting the police, but couldn't connect to the outside world.

The stranger, holding a blaster in his hand, moved from the darkness toward Marshall and Duncan.

The senator saw him and pushed Duncan behind her.

"Who are you?" she shouted.

"My name's not important," the man replied.

"If it's ransom you want," she said, scowling, "the government doesn't negotiate with terrorists."

"I'm not interested in terror," the man replied. "I'm more of a contractor."

"What do you mean?" she asked.

"Your daughter hired me."

Marshall's eyes narrowed as she shook her head. "My daughter's dead."

"Actually, she's very much alive."

"She's dead," Duncan said as if he thought the man was confused. "She died in an accident."

The man shook his head. "No."

"What's he talking about?" the boy asked his mother.

"Tell him, Senator," the man said. "Tell him or I'll kill you both. Really, it's the least you can do."

Showing his own bravery, Duncan stepped out from behind his mother, facing her.

"What's he talking about?" the boy asked. "What happened to Emily?"

"It doesn't matter, Duncan," she said. "She's just as dead to me as if she really died."

The boy simply looked at her without making a sound.

"Sometimes there's a price to pay and I used her to pay it," the senator said. "I didn't need her anymore. I needed a son and once I was pregnant with you, that's all that counted. Everything I've done has been for you. You're my legacy!"

The mansion computer registered a bright light, blinding its sensors for a moment. When they came back online, Duncan's body was rolling lifelessly down the staircase.

Senator Marshall ran to the step where the boy's leg had become entangled in the railing. Graying hair dangling around her tear-stained face, she glared up at the killer still on the landing above.

"Why? Why?" she asked. "Why did you kill him and not me?"

"You weren't the target," he told her. "Emily made it very clear not to harm you."

"But why Duncan?"

"He was the one thing you cherished the most, him and your precious legacy. Now you have neither."

The mansion computer watched the man disappear back into the shadows, unable to track him due to the virus still surging through the system. The computer could do little more than watch the senator crying beside her dead son, her legacy turned to dust.

CHAPTER FIVE

Jessica Doric decided to splurge and take the transmat all the way to the West End, saving several hours in traffic. It cost more than what she liked to spend, but things had taken a turn for the worse lately and she wanted to treat herself to something exotic. Considering her recent run of bad luck, Doric stood in the transmat booth wondering whether getting her atoms dematerialized here and then rematerialized somewhere else was the best idea. Before she could hit the *CANCEL* button, however, she was standing in a nearly identical station across town. She also had the vague sensation of a hundred spiders crawling over her skin.

In her early 30s, Jessica Doric wore a tweed skirt and a white blouse she had bought the previous day. Her hair was straight, dish-water blond, and her eyes were a dull brown. Outside the transmat station, Doric found a bench near a line of upscale shops. She sat and pulled a datapad from a handbag slung over her shoulder.

A news popup filled the screen:

MURDER IN WEST END!
UNKNOWN ASSAILANT KILLS SENATOR'S SON.
DETAILS TONIGHT ON VOX NEWS!

Swiping the popup away, she pulled up her email program and viewed a message she received yesterday from none other than Lord Maycare, the famous sportsman and playboy. As a university professor—*former* professor, she corrected herself—Doric was puzzled why a celebrity like Maycare would send her an invitation to his estate, saying only that he had a proposition for her. She hoped it wasn't a hoax...

She closed the email only to see another one, a few weeks older, from the Dean of the University of Regalis. Her eyes fixated on the words *TERMINATION OF EMPLOYMENT* before she could close it too.

Doric stashed the datapad in her handbag and got up. She continued along the sidewalk, occasionally glancing into the store windows. There was nothing she could actually afford, but it didn't hurt to look. Just ahead of her, Doric saw a woman exiting a boutique. The woman was a few years younger than her, with long, blood-red hair and striking gold eyes, obviously from cosmetic surgery. Doric instantly recognized her as Lady Sophia, the notorious handmaiden to Princess Katherine Augustus and, allegedly, paramour to Prince Alexander, Katherine's brother.

Lady Sophia swept her hair back and stepped into a private grav car waiting for her at the curb. The car rose several feet and whisked away into the air.

Lady Sophia was exactly the kind of girl Lord Maycare was usually seen with, Doric thought. She would hang on his arm at whatever sporting event he happened to be attending.

What a creep, she thought.

Doric took a taxi the rest of the way to Maycare's estate. The self-guided grav car landed outside the main gate and wished her a *good-day* from the speaker on the dashboard. Doric got out and saw a butlerbot standing by the gate. The robot was blue with silver trim, and looked like a model many years out of date.

"Hello," the robot said. "Are you, by chance, Jessica Doric?"

"That's me," she replied. "I'm supposed to meet with Lord Maycare, apparently?"

"You don't sound convinced."

"I'm really not..." she trailed off, looking like she expected police to arrive shortly.

"On the contrary," the robot said. "You are most definitely expected."

"That's a relief!"

"My name is Bentley," he said. "Lord Maycare's personal butlerbot. Please follow me..."

The android led Doric down the driveway toward the main house, a three-story mansion made from stone and mortar like an old fortification. Just above the main door hung the Maycare family crest, a white stallion against a field of blue. While not one of the Five Families, the Maycares had garnered much respect among the nobility, and Devlin Maycare had done nothing but improve that reputation.

The door opened on its own as Bentley approached. Inside, Doric found herself in a great hall with arches holding up a second-floor balcony and a ceiling of stained glass. Throughout the room, antiquities decorated every corner and oil paintings hung on every wall. Doric paused, even as Bentley continued walking, and stared with her mouth slightly open.

"This is amazing!" she remarked.

The butlerbot stopped and turned back.

"Yes, madam," he said. "Lord Maycare has an extensive collection."

"These should be in a museum."

"My sentiments exactly," the robot agreed, "but he seems to think they'd be better off here."

"Really?" Doric asked. "Why is that?"

"All in good time, Miss Doric. All in good time."

The rules of grav-ball were straightforward: try to get the ball into the opponent's goal without, hopefully, becoming severely injured. Lord Devlin Maycare pondered this as an opposing player drove his helmet into the court's transparent wall. As his forehead pressed against the inside of his helmet, Maycare noticed a young woman on the other side of the wall, standing next to his robot, Bentley.

"Ah, my three o'clock is here," he thought.

Using his legs, Maycare pushed away hard against the partition, holding a circular ball close against his chest. Along the way, he elbowed the opposing player hard, just below the chin. Droplets of sweat, and a few of blood, sprayed fan-like into the weightlessness.

A standard grav-ball court was a cylinder 100 yards long and 50 yards in diameter. The goal was a round hole, three yards wide, on either end, guarded by a goalie covered in heavy padding. While Maycare's own court was only half as long as a regulation one, he had it built in his estate's basement so he could enjoy being pummeled whenever he liked.

A teammate, thrusters burning from the bottom of his boots, came down the court toward Maycare who passed him the eight-inch ball. The teammate, now with the ball, continued moving along his original vector until one of the opposing players speared him in the back with a helmet, sending him careening into a shallow spin off to the side. Maycare watched him collide with a crunch against the wall as the ball floated aimlessly away.

Firing his own thrusters, Maycare flew toward the ball, knowing everyone else was doing the same. When they all met, they formed a mass of bodies, collapsing in on itself, only to shoot back out again in seemingly random directions. The confusion of arms and legs looked like a bomb had exploded. In the middle of it, Maycare emerged with the ball on his way to the goal.

The goalie spread his arms and legs out to make himself as large as possible, but, floating in front of the goal, he was powerless as Maycare slung the ball past him.

Maycare chuckled, never doubting the outcome.

Bentley waited patiently with Miss Doric until Lord Maycare joined them after taking a shower. Maycare always liked to be presentable whenever meeting a young woman, regardless of the reason. Bentley had it on good authority that women, human or otherwise, found Master Maycare irresistible. That good authority was, in fact, Lord Maycare himself.

To be fair, Bentley could bear witness to his master's many successes with the opposite sex. The media, especially tabloids, were filled with pictures of Maycare and his succession of girlfriends, fiancées, and, in one instance, girlfriend and fiancée at the same time.

Bentley finally saw his master appear through the locker room door, wearing a white terry cloth robe emblazoned with the Maycare family crest. Bentley sincerely hoped his master wore something more beneath the robe.

"Professor Jessica Doric, My Lord," Bentley said.

Even at 42, Maycare was physically imposing with wide, muscular shoulders bulging beneath the terry cloth. With warm, brown eyes, he watched Doric while he flattened his blond, damp hair.

"Call me *Devlin*," Maycare replied, shaking Doric's hand.

"A pleasure to meet you," she said, withdrawing her hand quickly.

"Do you go by *Jess* or *Jessica*?" Devlin asked.

"I prefer *Jessica*," she told him. "Or *Professor Doric* if you don't mind, My Lord."

He smiled, revealing a set of perfect teeth.

"I suppose you're wondering why I've brought you here?" he said.

"Well, yes, actually."

"It's my understanding you were recently let go by the University of Regalis."

"Yes."

"In fact," Maycare continued, "didn't they disband the entire department of xeno studies?"

Doric gave a long sigh. "Yes."

"Doesn't that seem a bit odd?" Maycare asked.

"Yes!"

He nodded toward Bentley. "Tell her what you found."

"It has come to our attention," Bentley said, "that a sizable donation was given to the university shortly before the dean, with full backing of the governing board, dissolved your department."

"A donation?" Doric asked. "By whom?"

"Warlock Industries," Bentley replied.

"Why would Warlock Industries want to get rid of xeno studies?" she said.

"Warlock Industries has a long history of researching, locating, and then removing alien technology from planets throughout the Imperium," Maycare said. "Your research of xenology, specifically xeno tech, threatened to steal away the same alien artifacts they work so hard to steal themselves."

"So, they closed down my department..."

"Precisely," Maycare replied. "In some ways, it's a compliment to your abilities."

"I'm flattered," Doric said with a sarcastic smile.

"But cheer up, Jess!" he said. "I have a proposition I'd like you to consider."

"What kind of proposition?"

"Are you familiar with the Maycare Institute of Xeno Studies?" he asked.

Doric paused, thinking for a moment. "Um, no."

"Well, that's probably because I just made it up! Also, I'd like you to run its research and acquisition wing…"

Bentley, who had grown quite good at reading people's expressions, saw confusion on Doric's face. Ever helpful, the robot said, "He's offering you a job."

"Seriously?" she asked.

"Don't I look serious?" Maycare wondered.

"I can't tell," she replied. "This all seems very sudden. I don't usually like rushing into things."

Maycare laughed. "Really? That's the only way I do things!"

"Indeed," Bentley concurred. "It's really quite exhausting."

"Alright," Doric said. "I'll take your offer, but I demand *full* autonomy."

"Certainly."

"And our working relationship must remain strictly professional. I know your history and I don't want any funny business."

"Bentley will keep me on my best behavior," Maycare said.

The butlerbot looked at his master and then back at Miss Doric. "I can't make any promises…"

When Henry Riff got the call from his old professor, Jessica Doric, he was cooking noodles on a small hotplate in the center of his studio apartment. Genuinely excited to hear Doric's voice again, he spilled some of the boiling water on the carpet.

"Are you alright, Henry?" Doric asked, her face appearing on the phone now lying on the floor.

Henry straightened the pot of noodles on the hotplate while doing his best not to step with his bare feet in the puddle of hot liquid. Realizing someone was talking to him, he said, "What? Yes! Most definitely!"

"Good," Doric said. "How would you like a job working for me?

Henry picked up the phone.

"Well, sure!" Henry replied. "There isn't much demand for a xeno studies assistant now that they closed the department."

"No, I suppose not."

"I'm real sorry they let you go, Professor," Henry said. "I've really missed working with you."

"Thank you, Henry."

A long, toothy grin brightened Henry's freckled face as he swatted away a few mousy strands of hair hanging over his forehead.

The next day, Doric sent Henry a taxi that took him directly to the Maycare estate where an old robot introduced himself as Bentley. Not really listening, Henry nodded as his eyes darted from one thing to another until the robot took him by the hand and led him into the house. Through a series of corridors and doorways, Bentley brought the young man to a library where Professor Doric was waiting.

The library was a long hall with massive fireplaces on either end. Bookcases were built into the walls, the tomes visible behind cabinet doors enclosed with brass wire mesh. Heavy tables ran down the center, with sofas and stuffed leather chairs in between. A parquet floor was visible wherever intricately woven rugs failed to cover it.

"There you are!" Doric said, walking from behind a table covered in ancient manuscripts.

"Here he is indeed," Bentley replied. "Will you be needing anything else from me, Miss Doric?"

"No, that's all, thank you," she said.

Seeing Doric again, Henry tried focusing on his words so they would come out coherently.

"Hi, Professor!" he managed. "This place looks amazing!"

"Calm down, Henry," Doric said. "Do you remember what we talked about?"

"For example?" he asked.

"The work we'll be doing..."

"Oh, yeah, sure," he said. "We're looking for alien technology for Mister Maycare."

"*Lord* Maycare."

"Right, I've never talked to a real nobleman before. Is he nice?"

"That's really not important, Henry," Doric said.

"Oh, sure. Definitely."

Professor Doric put Henry to work immediately, showing him the most important texts stored in the library. To Maycare's credit, he had accumulated an impressive collection of books, many of alien origin. Within hours, Henry and Doric were lost amid exotic tomes from all over the Imperium.

A few days later, Henry stared in horror at the *K'thonian Codex*, an infamous volume bound with the tanned skin of flayed enemies and written in ink made from blood. Feeling sick to his stomach, Henry noticed someone large beside him.

It was Lord Maycare.

A dry, retching sound came from Henry's mouth, which he slapped shut with his hand.

"Can I help you, Lord Maycare?" Doric asked from the other side of the cluttered table.

"Please call me *Devlin*, won't you?" Maycare said.

"I'll try."

"Who's your friend?" the lord asked.

"This is Henry Riff, my assistant," Doric said. "I hope it's alright I invited him here—I needed the help."

Henry stared, eyes wide in terror, at the man towering over him.

"Of course, Jess," Devlin waved his hand. "Whatever you need is perfectly fine."

She nodded. "Good, but I'd prefer you called me *Professor Doric*."

Ignoring her, Maycare scanned the random objects on the table. "How goes it then?"

"Well, fine I guess."

"Have you come up with anything promising?"

"Not really."

Henry chirped like a dying bird.

"Oh," Doric corrected herself, "actually Henry found something interesting, but we'll need to do more research first."

"Really?" Maycare said, pulling up a chair. "What did you find, Henry?"

From beneath a book called *Necronean Death Cantos*, Henry pulled out a printout and waved it in the air like a treasure map.

Doric took the paper.

"Back in the year 652 Imperial Standard," Doric began, "a survey team landed on a world called *Hekla VII*. They were looking for worlds suitable for future colonies, but all they got was a dead planet covered in ice and snow. However, they did discover an abandoned temple at the base of an active volcano. Before leaving, they took holovids of the hieroglyphs written on the temple walls."

"Has anyone been there since?" Maycare asked.

"Um," Henry stammered in a voice just above a whisper, "I did a search for flight plans and there hasn't been a registered visit to that planet since the survey team. That's 48 years."

"Thank you, son," Maycare said.

Henry managed a tortured grin as he nearly disappeared between his shoulder blades.

"Anything else?" Maycare said.

"As a matter of fact," Doric went on, "the survey team recorded several energy readings. The data didn't match the protocols they needed for a new settlement, so they just filed it away and forgot about it. However, looking at the readings now, I'm convinced they're caused by xeno tech somewhere in that temple."

Lord Maycare slapped the table hard, nearly causing Henry to jump out of his chair. "You've convinced me!"

"Of what?" Doric said, staring at him sideways.

"Let's go take a look!"

"With all due respect, My Lord," Doric said, "there's really no reason to go until we've done at least another week of research. There might be alien tech, but that's really more of an educated guess."

"Nonsense," Maycare said. "I've acted on guesses half as educated as that!"

"Hmm," Doric murmured skeptically.

"Bentley!" Maycare yelled, sending Henry almost under the table.

The butlerbot peered through the doorway. "Yes, My Lord?"

"Call the star port and have my ship prepared for launch!"

"Of course, sir," the robot said and disappeared again.

Henry, shaking badly, smiled and discretely checked to see if he had soiled himself.

Like a knife cutting through black canvas, a starship called the *Starling* emerged from hyperspace. Sitting in the cockpit, Magnus Black checked the readings to confirm he was at the right coordinates. Satisfied, he scanned the neighboring space and, as expected, found another ship less than a thousand miles away.

The *Starling* looked like an arrowhead with short, thick wings on either side of the main fuselage. The cockpit was set close to the front, giving Magnus a good view of his surroundings. The twin thrusters in the back burned a translucent blue as the ship picked up speed.

The transponder of the other craft identified it as the *Sorcerer*, but once Magnus magnified the visual display, he could also see the familiar pentagram of Warlock Industries painted along the hull.

The *Sorcerer*, three times the size of Magnus' ship, was dull gray with the aft section ribbed like the flying buttresses of an old cathedral. The bow, meanwhile, was much wider like the nose of a hammerhead shark. Where the two sections met, a round turret swiveled, following the *Starling* as it approached.

Magnus brought his ship to rest a few hundred feet off the other vessel's starboard side.

"Well, you certainly know how to make an entrance," a voice said over the radio.

Magnus flipped on the video display. A man with dark eyes and a short, brown goatee stared at him through the monitor.

"Hello, Mister Skarlander," Magnus said. "I'm here as requested."

"Thank you for coming," Oscar Skarlander replied. "Sure you don't want to come aboard so we can talk face-to-face?"

The corner of Magnus' mouth curled. "No, I like this just fine."

"Suit yourself."

"I take it you have a job for me?" Magnus asked.

"Indeed," Skarlander said.

"What's the target?"

"It's an android, actually, by the name of Jericho. I need you to find and kill him."

"Wouldn't *destroy* be a more accurate word?" Magnus said.

Skarlander rolled his eyes.

"Kill, destroy, frankly the consciousness of a cybermachine is beyond this discussion," the Warlock agent said. "Let's just agree that I want you to end him with extreme prejudice."

"I can do that."

"Oh, one more thing," Skarlander went on. "Jericho has a gravitronic brain containing a lot of very important information. I want you to bring it to me."

"On a stake?"

Skarlander lowered his head, peering out from beneath a darkened brow.

"In a box will suffice," he said.

CHAPTER SIX

In Regalis, people on the high end of society avoided Ashetown due to its rough neighborhoods and the general hatred everyone there felt toward people on the high end of society. This was apparently not the case with the Fat Cat Casino, the largest and most successful gambling house in the city. The affluent, especially the nobility, didn't mind slumming it in Ashetown if it meant being seen with celebrities who also frequented the Fat Cat.

The fat cat himself, Big G, watched through a two-way mirror overlooking the action taking place on the main casino floor. A Tikarin, Big G had orange and white fur and an enormous, sagging belly. His green, slanted eyes darted from table to table as his patrons slowly lost their money. Although his coffers grew with every card drawn, Big G knew it was just a front. In fact, the whole operation was a money laundering operation for Si-Sawat, Big G's Tikarin crime syndicate. He chuckled at his own brilliance.

"Boss?" a Tikarin said from the doorway.

"What's up, Max?" Big G asked.

Like his employer, Max was sizable, but in his case muscle lay beneath his gray fur instead of fat. He also spoke with a surprisingly high-pitched voice.

"We found Tommy's body down by the river," Max said in a near-perfect soprano.

"Son-of-a-bitch!" Big G said, his paws clenched into fists.

"Looks like they worked him over pretty good," Max went on. "No clue who did it though…"

"It's obvious!"

"It is?"

"Kid Vicious!"

Max nodded, but Big G knew he only dimly understood. While good-natured, Max was dumber than a bag of rocks.

Big G sighed.

"Okay, this is what we're going to do," he said. "Round up a couple of the boys and head down to Griefer turf. Get the first one of theirs you can find and make him pay for what they did to Tommy."

"Sure, boss," Max said, then remembered something. "Oh, and Radford Groen is back and he's losing again."

"That's *all* he does," Big G remarked. "It's kind of sad actually..."

Lord Radford Groen examined his cards lying on the blackjack table. Against the green felt, the queen of diamonds and six of spades glared at him accusingly, daring him to draw another card. Common sense told him to stay, but winning was all about taking chances. Nothing risked, nothing gained, his father used to say.

"Hit me," Groen said.

The dealerbot didn't have eyebrows, but Groen felt the robot raising them anyway.

"Yes, sir," the dealerbot said, a card spurting out from a slot in its wrist onto the table. A seven of hearts.

"Busted," it said.

On Groen's right, Lord Winsor Woodwick twirled the end of his walrus mustache.

"I say, Radford," he said, "You've the worst luck, old chap. Better luck next time, eh?"

In the chair to Groen's left, a man raised his beer glass.

"Sometimes you've got to make your own luck," he said.

"Who are you again?" Groen asked, rubbing the wrinkles between his eyes.

"Ramsey," he said. "Captain of the *Steppenwolf*."

"That must be very exciting," Woodwick said.

"Damn right," the pilot replied. "Like the time I tangled with Durant Blixx, the most wanted pirate in the Imperium."

"Good lord!" Woodwick said.

"He and his men were swarming over my ship but I stood against them all," Ramsey said.

"What did you do?" Woodwick asked.

"I made Blixx a deal," Ramsey said. "I told him he could have my cargo, but if he tried taking my ship, I'd cut off life support. He said I drove a hard bargain, but he took the deal."

"I say, good show!"

Groen heard the two men speaking, but tried hard not to listen. "I'm surrounded by idiots," he thought to himself.

The dealerbot, meanwhile, had removed the old cards and was ready to deal new ones.

"Another game?" it asked.

Groen shuffled his chips between his fingers. The number of chips was fewer than he remembered.

"Sure," he said. "Why not?"

In a foul mood, Lord Rupert Tagus III walked through the front entrance of the Fat Cat Casino. His attaché, Lieutenant Burke, strolled in a few steps behind. Tagus glanced around, grimacing.

"What a cesspool," he said. "I can't believe I'm standing in Ashetown."

"Actually," Burke remarked, "many lordships and officers come here. It's very popular."

Tagus stopped, turned, and looked at his attaché without speaking.

"But still a cesspool," Burke said. "A very popular cesspool."

Tagus groaned and pivoted again, now facing the casino floor as a concussion of lights and noises inundated his senses.

"If my family were still in charge," he said, "I would clean up this mess by nuking it from orbit!"

"Well, sir, I don't think the public would appreciate that very much."

"Do you think I give a damn about what the public thinks, lieutenant?"

"No, sir," Burke admitted, "but unfortunately your family couldn't remain in power. Traditionally the same house can't wear the crown consecutively."

"Tradition!" Tagus scoffed.

"Sir?"

"I don't give a damn about traditions either. They're a damn—"

"Disgrace, sir?"

Lord Tagus, unsure whether the lieutenant was being insubordinate, quickly nodded and grumbled the word *disgrace* under his breath.

"Where's that robot we're meeting anyway?" he said.

"I don't see it, sir."

"Alright then, let's muster at the bar. I need a drink."

The two Imperial officers wandered through the crowd of people and gambling opportunities until they found the bar, flanked on either side by baccarat tables. Tagus glared at the female Tikarin, her short tan hair like a lioness, who was bartending.

"What can I get you, hon?" she asked.

"Give me a scotch, neat," Tagus said, "and don't get any hair in it."

"What about you, sugar?" she motioned to the lieutenant.

"I'll have—"

"He's not drinking," Tagus cut him off. "He's my ride."

Burke sighed, but said nothing.

The Tikarin pulled the most expensive bottle of single malt whiskey from the shelf behind her and poured it, without ice, into a short glass. Tagus watched her, wondering if her tail ever knocked things over when she wasn't paying attention. She handed him the glass and smiled, her sharp teeth peering through her lips.

Tagus drank slowly, savoring it. When it was time to order his second Scotch, Tagus felt something brush against his pant leg. Looking down, he saw a robot staring up at him.

"It's about time, Skeeter!" Tagus said.

"My apologies, sir."

Skeeter, a little more than two feet tall, had a head like a searchlight with a single lens for an eye. His body had no arms and, instead of legs, sat on a lone wheel.

"Where's Gurkin?" Tagus asked.

"Please come this way, sir," Skeeter said, rolling away.

Tagus grumbled, abandoning his drink on the bar, and followed the robot while Burke tried to keep up.

Skeeter led Lord Tagus and Lieutenant Burke through a back door and down a flight of stairs clouded with cigar and cigarette smoke. They emerged through a red curtain into the basement.

The basement below the Fat Cat was nearly a carbon copy of the casino above except, instead of being filled with wealthy and influential humans, there was a cross section of non-human races, native to Andromeda long before the Imperium existed. While the blackjack tables and everything else were ostensibly the same as upstairs, the furniture was worn out and ragged, the felt on the tables torn in places.

The noise was nearly as loud as upstairs, except Tagus couldn't understand any of the languages spoken. He had an urge to lob a plasma grenade into the room and head back up the stairs, but out of the babble, Tagus managed to make out one voice he recognized.

"You're a goddamned racist!" Smitty Gurkin shouted at a Tikarin pit boss.

Gurkin was a Gordian, a stocky and surly race, with a rounded snout and tusks protruding from his lower jaw.

"Ah, come on, Smitty," the Tikarin pleaded. "You were using loaded dice."

"My mother gave me these dice! Are you bad-mouthing my mother?"

The pit boss shook his head in defeat. "Just get out of here, Smitty. Big G's getting sick of your antics."

Gurkin turned and saw Lord Tagus. The Gordian spread his arms like he was happy to see them and walked over, patting Skeeter on the head.

"Aw, so the robot found you?" Gurkin said.

"Obviously," Tagus said.

"Is this place safe?" Lieutenant Burke asked.

"Not in the least," Gurkin admitted. "A worse den of cutthroats you'll never see."

"Then why the hell are we here?" Tagus said, raising his voice.

Gurkin shrugged. "The drinks are free and I like the company."

Tagus grabbed the Gordian by the collar. "I'm quickly losing patience, so I suggest you get to business sooner rather than later."

Gurkin raised his hands. "Alright already! Let's get a booth and talk."

Tagus released his grip. The Gordian laughed, but sweat was appearing in the creases of his forehead. He led the two humans, with the undersized robot wheeling just behind, to a discrete corner where they took seats in a booth. Touching a button on the table, Gurkin activated an energy curtain that closed around them like a shimmering cocoon, preventing sound and light from passing through. While Tagus appreciated the privacy, the smell of the Gordian was pungent enough to make him choke.

"Do you have the targets?" Gurkin asked.

"Yes," Tagus said, pushing a data chip across the table.

Lefty Lucy watched on a jumbo display as a man caught a silver ball and another man, apparently from the other team, slammed him against the wall as they floated in zero gravity. Lucy may not have fully understood the rules of grav-ball, but she enjoyed the violence.

She was sitting in the race and sports room of the Fat Cat Casino, an area dedicated to gambling on athletic events simultaneously taking place all over the planet. Beside her, Prince Alexander Augustus stuffed popcorn from a large bag into his mouth, spilling much of it into Lucy's lap.

Lucy was in her late twenties, from ancient Chinese stock, with hair pulled tight into several knots across her head. She wore silver eyeshadow and lipstick, and a black cropped top with black, leather leggings.

On another monitor, one of the many ringing the circumference of the room, needle-shaped cars sped along the inside of a tube, sometimes passing each other along the ceiling. Lucy believed this was called *tube racing*.

Alexander leaned into Lucy's ear.

"You've got popcorn in your lap," he said. "Why are you so messy?"

Lucy didn't turn her head or, in any way, acknowledge the prince, knowing to do so would only encourage him.

"What do you think those grav-ball players make?" he asked. "The guys on the West End Monarchs must make a mint!"

Lucy grew up on the streets of Ashetown until joining the Red Lotus in her early teens. She could have ended up in one of their brothels, but she showed a propensity for fighting, especially when they suggested she become a prostitute. They taught her martial arts, turning her hands into lethal weapons. Sometimes she wondered if Prince Alexander realized that.

"They say Maycare's the best player," the prince went on, "but I think he's getting too old."

He continued at length while Lucy's face remained emotionless. This game she knew very well.

"I could've played," Alexander said, "but I couldn't take the risk of damaging my face. The *money-maker* I call it..." then, after a pause, "...because I'm so handsome!"

Lucy, ever so slowly, turned her head until she knew he could see her eyes.

Alexander's shoulders sank as he looked away from her steady, unrelenting gaze.

"Okay," he said. "I'll be good."

"I say, Radford," Woodwick nudged Lord Groen as they reclined in the chairs of the race and sports room. "Isn't that the emperor's son, Prince Alexander, over there?"

Groen was staring into his vodka tonic, wondering if that Tikarin had used the top shelf brand.

"What?" he said.

"I'm sure it is," Woodwick said. "He's with that woman, what's-her-name."

"So?"

"Do you think the two of them are... snogging, so to speak?" Woodwick asked.

"Obviously not."

"I don't mean *now*," Woodwick protested. "I mean do you think they're acquainted, you know, *carnally*."

"It wouldn't surprise me," Groen replied. "He's constantly getting into trouble with women."

Woodwick murmured and twisted his mustache excitedly.

Groen sipped his drink. "I swear she watered this down."

Off to the side of the room, through a curtain of red velvet, Lord Tagus and his attaché, Lieutenant Burke, appeared.

"Hello there, Rupert," Woodwick said, motioning for the two men to join them. "Have a drink, eh?"

Tagus turned only long enough to scowl in their direction as the two officers continued crossing the room to the other side.

Woodwick shrugged. "Apparently not."

"The fool should look where he's going," Groen said. "He's about to run into Prince Alexander."

The prince, getting up from his chair, collided with Tagus, spilling popcorn and butter topping over his military uniform.

"Oh, dear," Woodwick said.

Lord Tagus, his mouth hanging open, looked first at the prince and then down at his own clothing, now covered in melted butter. Lefty Lucy rose from her seat while Lieutenant Burke watched like a witness to an impending disaster.

"You idiot!" Tagus shouted.

"Come on," Alexander said, "It was an accident."

"This is outrageous behavior, even for you!"

"Me?"

"You're a disgrace to the crown and your family!" Tagus yelled, his face turning a bright crimson.

"Maybe," the prince admitted. "There are some in my family who'd probably agree."

At the bar, Woodwick leaned over to Groen. "I say, do you think they'll come to blows?"

"I hope so," Groen replied.

"Care to wager on the winner?"

"Tagus is a decorated officer," Groen said. "He can't lose."

"A thousand then?"

"Sure, why not?"

Tagus, nearly frothing at the mouth, waved his finger under Alexander's nose.

"Careful," the prince said, nodding toward Lucy. "My bodyguard's got a temper."

"Her?" Tagus scoffed. "Oh, I know all about her and the brothels she crawled out of—"

Although Lieutenant Burke partially obscured the view, Groen saw a flash of anger in Alexander's eyes, even as the prince swung and struck Lord Tagus squarely on the jaw. Groen heard the sound of fist against bone and the audible gasp that rose from the others in the room.

Also, Lord Woodwick may have screamed a little.

Momentarily stunned, Tagus regained his footing and followed the blow with two of his own, the first to Alexander's stomach and the second to his face, the so-called money-maker.

At the same time, Lucy did an acrobatic cartwheel past the two nobles, landing both feet into Lieutenant Burke's chest, knocking him to the ground. He lay on his side wheezing, trying to breathe in the air that had just been ejected from his lungs. Lucy crawled on top of him, pulling his arm back.

"She's quite a handful," Groen said.

"Indeed," Woodwick conceded.

A hint of blood smeared across his mouth, Tagus raised his fists. "You've made a dangerous enemy."

"You wouldn't be the first," Prince Alexander said, throwing a punch. Tagus drew his arms up, but was too slow. Alexander's clenched fist pounded him in the jaw like a hammer on an anvil. Tagus' head jerked back, his arms flailing as if to catch hold of something that wasn't there. Tagus took a step backward and fell, knocking his head against the floor.

Groen heard Tagus groan, then Burke's voice.

"Please stop hurting me," Burke said, but Lucy continued wrenching his arm as far back as his shoulder joint would allow.

In the doorway, a large, orange-striped Tikarin stood holding a submachine gun. Several other goons were visible just behind him.

"Gentlemen," Big G said calmly, pointing his weapon around the room. "The police have been called and will be here shortly."

"That's our cue, Lefty," Alexander gestured toward the other door with his thumb. "Stop torturing your new boyfriend and let's get going."

Lucy released the lieutenant's arm and removed her knee from the middle of his back. Standing, she joined the prince as he walked away toward the door. Burke remained on the ground, gingerly trying to move his arm back into its socket.

"Always a pleasure!" Big G shouted after the prince. "I'll send my regards along with the bill."

Alexander gave a backwards wave and disappeared through the exit into the early hours of the Ashetown morning.

CHAPTER SEVEN

Lady Sophia wore a long, silk dress revealing her shoulders. Her red hair swayed back and forth across her bare, ivory white skin as she walked casually along a palace corridor. Her eyes landed briefly on everything she passed, like the golden gaze of a wolf evaluating its surroundings.

As handmaiden to Princess Katherine Augustus, Lady Sophia lived in her own apartment inside the Imperial Palace, a short distance from the quarters of the princess herself. Arriving at Katherine's door, Sophia entered without knocking and found the princess finishing her bath. The floor of the bathroom was pale marble with soft blue tilework along the edges. The tub itself was raised and surrounded by slender columns topped with gold.

A maidbot leaned over the tub to help the princess out of the soapy water.

"Ugh," Sophia said, sitting down on a cushioned bench. "I don't understand how you can let a machine see you naked like that."

Princess Katherine, nineteen years old with amber hair down to her waist, flashed blue eyes at the robot.

"You mean Dotty?" she asked. "You're a fembot, aren't you?"

"Yes, Your Highness," the robot said in a female's voice.

"See?" Katherine said, stepping out onto the cold marble and wrapping a towel around her hair.

Sophia rolled her eyes. "Just because it sounds like a girl doesn't make it one."

The princess sat at a vanity built into a corner alcove. She turned her head from left to right, examining her complexion. Dotty stood beside her.

"I don't see the problem," Katherine said. "It's not like I want a robot with all the plumbing down there. Alexander would turn it into a sexbot."

Dotty shuddered slightly.

"Sorry," the princess said. "I shouldn't have mentioned him."

"It's alright," Sophia said, sighing. "I'm over Alexander."

"Really? Since when?"

Sophia stood and crossed her arms while watching the maidbot apply makeup to Katherine's face.

"Speaking of your brother," Sophia said. "Apparently, he got into a tussle with Lord Tagus last night."

"Isn't he in his fifties?"

"No, not the father. His son, Tagus III."

"Oh, well, I hope he didn't get hurt."

"Who?"

"Whoever," Katherine shook her head. "I really don't care honestly."

"Do you think Rupert is handsome?" Sophia asked.

"If you mean the father, no," the princess said. "If you mean the son, *also* no."

"Well, I think he's quite dashing in his uniform."

"I suppose," Katherine remarked. "He seems a bit conventional."

"I guess…" Sophia murmured.

"My Lady," Dotty said. "There's an audio message from your mother."

"Shit," Katherine said and then, after a pause, "Play it, I suppose."

From Dotty's head came the voice of someone else, someone older and refined.

"Katie," the voice said, "I'd like you to come to Revenna and see me as soon as possible. We need to talk about Lord Molesworth of the Palatine Molesworths, you know the ones? He's a very dignified gentleman with excellent connections. I think the two of you should meet."

"Oh, my God!" Katherine fumed.

"I know you're shouting right now," Katherine's mother, the empress, went on, "but you're not getting any younger and you really need to start thinking about these things."

"Stop the message!" the princess shouted, and Dotty complied.

"Well, she's persistent," Sophia said. "I'll give her that."

"I hate her, I hate her, I hate her!"

"We haven't been to Revenna in a while. It might be fun..."

"I'm going to talk to Richard," Katherine said. "Maybe he can make her stop."

Sophia's eyes looked away. "Maybe."

"I don't want to get married!"

Lady Sophia's lips curled into a half smile, but said nothing.

When Prince Richard Augustus reached his office in the Imperial Palace, his execubot Cornelius was waiting inside.

"Good morning, Your Highness," the robot said. His casing was almost entirely chrome and his faceplate a smooth, featureless curvature of shiny metal.

"Morning," the prince replied. "What do you have for me today?"

"I've queued up a news report about an incident in Ashetown last night."

"You could just tell me," Richard pointed out.

"True," the robot said, "but I'm not very good at breaking bad news."

"You're a coward, Cornelius."

"A fault in my programming no doubt, Your Highness."

Prince Richard went to his desk, made from the same cherry wood as the rest of the furniture in the office. He sat, taking a moment to look through the curtains on the opposite wall. With the Regalis river in the foreground, the sun was rising over the haze of Middleton in the distance.

"Computer on," he said. "Play news report in the queue."

The monitor on his desk winked to life and a picture of a woman's face filled the screen. As the video started, her azure hair began moving while she spoke.

"This is Sylvia Flax reporting for VOX News," she said. Behind her, the facade of the Fat Cat Casino was visible in glowing neon.

Richard could see Tikarin goons milling around the entrance. "Late last night," she went on, "an altercation occurred at this popular gambling house between two members of the Five Families, Lord Rupert Tagus III and none other than Prince Alexander Augustus himself."

"Ah, crap," Richard said.

"Eye witnesses reported that the two so-called *noblemen* encountered one another inside the casino and quickly came to blows in what can only be called a bare-fisted brawl."

"Goddamn it!"

"Although the exact cause of the fight is unclear," Flax said, leaning towards the camera, "it seems a woman may have been involved."

The video ended, the reporter's face once again frozen. Prince Richard stared at the screen.

"The more I learn of man," he said, "the more I prefer robots."

"Why, thank you, Your Highness!" Cornelius said.

"Are you on top of this newest disaster?" the prince asked.

"Absolutely," the robot replied. "We've released a statement saying the report is unfounded and both Prince Alexander and Lord Tagus are lifelong friends."

Richard grunted his approval. "People will believe anything."

"I'm afraid Prince Alexander is gaining a reputation for, how should I say it, *colorful* activities? These reports become increasingly difficult to deny."

"I know," Richard said. "It's like he's trying make our family look bad."

"Could that be true?"

"No," the prince said, "He's just a dumbass. Anyway, try to get him on the line. Let's see if I can talk some sense into him."

Princess Katherine, dressed in a gown of red and gold, arrived at her brother's office through a side entrance out of sight from the usual bureaucrats that permeated the palace. When she walked through the doorway, he was asking his execubot about Alexander, but both stopped as she entered.

"You have to help me with Mother," Katherine said. "She's driving me crazy!"

Resting his elbows on the arms of his chair, the prince folded his fingers together.

"What's she doing now?" he asked.

"She's trying to marry me off again!"

"Oh, that..."

Katherine exhaled. "Yes, *that*!"

"There are worse things," he said, "I'm sure we can find you a suitable husband from one of the better families."

"I don't care if he's suitable or not. I don't want to get married!"

"Many a strategic alliance was forged through an arranged marriage. We think it would be best for everyone."

"We?" Katherine said. "Have you been talking to Mother behind my back?"

"As the oldest, it's my responsibility."

"You're such a pompous ass, Richard!" Katherine said.

"Somebody has to keep the ship afloat," the prince replied. "It's not like Alexander is going to step up and do it."

"Speaking of which, why does he get to gallivant around, having fun? Why can't he be the one getting married?"

The prince raised an eyebrow. "He's not exactly the marrying type."

"Well, neither am I," Katherine said. "I want excitement!"

"Good lord," Richard sighed. "Excitement is exhausting. Anyway, you're not a kid anymore. It's about time you grew up and started thinking about people besides yourself. Actually, I'm starting to think this conversation is just a dress rehearsal for my talk with Alexander in a few minutes."

"At least he's had a chance to experience life. If I was a boy, I could do what I want!"

"Nobody gets to do what they want," Richard said. "Not for long..."

"It's not fair!"

"Now you're getting it."

Prince Richard's robot cleared its throat even though it didn't have one.

"Terribly sorry to interrupt," the machine said. "I've reached Prince Alexander as you requested, Your Highness."

"Right," Richard said, pointing at his sister. "We'll have to talk about this later."

"Mother wants me to visit her on Revenna," Katherine replied. "I'm supposed to leave immediately."

"Really?" the prince said. "That gives me an idea…"

"Yes?" she asked.

"Never mind," he said. "You wouldn't like it anyway."

Princess Katherine felt her nails digging into her palms. "Goodbye then."

"Have a nice trip," he said, grinning beneath his mustache.

Katherine didn't like the ominous tone of his voice.

In the Imperial Palace, not far from the private quarters of his brother and sister, Prince Alexander had his own suite. Lavishly decorated, the rooms contained everything except the prince himself. Instead, he woke up on a couch in the room he rented at the King's Arms, a seedy hotel not far from the Fat Cat Casino. A buzzing noise, which he first mistook as a hangover, rattled beside his head. Slowly, Alexander realized his phone was vibrating.

He answered and heard an upbeat voice on the other end.

"Good morning, Your Highness!"

Alexander immediately knew it was a robot. Only a machine could be this chipper this early in the morning.

"Who is this?" the prince asked, tasting something awful in his mouth.

"Cornelius, Prince Richard's execubot."

"Right," Alexander said, coughing.

"Did I wake you, Your Highness?"

"As far as I can tell."

"Please accept my humble apologies then, Prince Alexander," Cornelius said. "It's just that your brother would very much like to talk to you this morning."

Alexander touched his phone, switching from audio only to video. The faceless faceplate of Cornelius filled the screen.

"Oh, dear," the robot said.

The prince instinctively ran his hands through his hair, trying to mat it down. He knew he hadn't shaved in at least a day, but there wasn't much he could do about that now.

"Can't this wait?" Alexander asked.

"Unfortunately, no I'm afraid."

"Screw it. Go ahead and put him on."

"Very good, sir!"

Rubbing sleep from his eyes, Alexander started feeling a sharp ache in his jaw where Lord Tagus had punched him.

Prince Richard's face appeared on the phone.

"Good god, man!" Richard said.

"You've seen me look worse," Alexander replied.

"Sadly, that's true."

"What do you want?"

"I should think you know exactly what this is about."

"I swear I thought she was eighteen," Alexander said.

"No, Alexander, I'm talking about your brawl with Lord Tagus last night. Wait, what did you say?"

"Nothing."

"This is no time for jokes," Richard said. "I didn't complain when you slept with that archsenator's wife or when you and the archsenator fought a duel over it — which is illegal by the way – and you put him in the hospital. All of these things pale in comparison to fighting a member of the Tagus family. Do you actually know what this means?"

"Awkward stares in the palace cafeteria?"

"No, you nitwit. As long as the Five Families stay civil, the Imperium survives. If any of us actually fought each other, all hell would break loose."

Alexander made a snorting sound.

"Oh, please," he said. "The Families are constantly at each other's throats."

"Behind the scenes perhaps, but the status quo is always maintained," Richard replied. "There's too much to lose otherwise for all of us."

"Whatever. None of that is my problem."

"You're the emperor's son, Alexander. You represent the family, whether you like it or not, so I suggest you take it seriously."

After a pause, Alexander said, "Alright, what do you want me to do?"

"Well, for starters," Richard said, "you should probably stay out of the public eye for a while."

"Good idea."

"To that end, Katherine is heading to Revenna, apparently to see Mother. I think you should go along."

"Seriously?"

"Yes, seriously," Richard replied. "It might do you some good..."

Archsenator Tarkio was used to the open spaces inside the Imperial Senate, but the Emperor's Council chamber seemed almost intimate in comparison. Granted, the flooring was teak and the walls were covered with priceless paintings, but the furnishings were understated, even business-like. A long, oval table filled most of the room. At the head was a throne of sorts, but even the emperor's chair seemed designed to avoid extravagance.

The archsenators, individually and in small groups, began filing in from the adjoining parlor. A few were commoners, but most were nobles from the lesser families. Members of the Five Families themselves could not become archsenators since, by law, they were considered too powerful to run for the Imperial Senate in the first place.

The prestige of sitting at the Council table with the emperor was the pinnacle of each senator's career. To secure enough senate votes to be named archsenator meant bending arms and parliamentary rules until outright bribery was not out of the question. It would be worth it, Tarkio thought, knowing the good he could now achieve in such a high place of power.

They took their seats around the oval table and waited until, through a door behind the emperor's chair, Prince Richard entered, nodded to the others, and sat down. Then, Counselor Kalidas came in.

"His Majesty, Emperor Hector Augustus!" Kalidas announced.

Everyone stood as Augustus swept into the room, shook the hands of those nearest to him and sat. Kalidas placed a datapad in front of the emperor while the others took their seats.

"Thank you all for coming," Augustus said. "What's the first order of business?"

"The matter of the recent spate of pirate attacks, Your Majesty," Kalidas said.

"And that bastard Durant Blixx, I suppose," Augustus said.

"Indeed," Kalidas replied.

"What does the senate have to say about these attacks?" Augustus asked, addressing the archsenators.

Several of the elder politicians mumbled answers, but Tarkio, sitting at the far end of the table, could barely make out what they were saying. He lacked seniority to sit closer, but he was also determined to be heard.

"If I may," Tarkio said in an emphatic voice, "these pirate attacks tear at the very fabric of the Imperium!"

Everyone in the room, even Prince Richard, stopped and looked directly at Archsenator Tarkio.

"Is that so?" Emperor Augustus said.

"Yes, Your Majesty."

"It's good to hear from the *back* of the room for a change!" Augustus said. "Get on with it then…"

Tarkio's throat tightened.

"Well," he said, coughing into his fist, "the provincial governors, the trade guilds, and even the public are up in arms about Durant Blixx and his raiders. We can't sit in our ivory tower, hoping these attacks will just go away. We need to do something and do it now!"

Silence.

Then, someone began cackling. Tarkio realized it was the emperor himself.

"Well said!" Augustus shouted.

Several of the senior archsenators scowled at Tarkio, but began applauding anyway. A few statesmen closest to him, who shared his thirst for attention, shook Tarkio's hand and even patted him on the back.

Tarkio knew it was a risk speaking out of turn, but he knew it would be worth it. It would all be worth it.

After the session adjourned, Tarkio stood making small talk with the other archsenators in the parlor next to the council chamber. Tarkio felt the excitement of completing his first session. This was compounded when Prince Richard appeared and wanted to talk to him.

"Very impressive," the prince said.

"Thank you, Your Highness," the archsenator replied.

"Sometimes the gulf between the palace and the senate can seem like an ocean," Richard went on, "but I agreed with what you said, especially about the pirate attacks."

"There doesn't need to be a difference between common sense and common ground."

The prince chuckled. "Indeed."

"I wasn't raised from nobility," Tarkio said, "but a threat to the Imperium affects me as much as you."

"If I'm being honest, I've followed your rise in the senate with interest. I was happy to see you elected to the Council."

"Really?" Tarkio said, not entirely believing what he heard. "Most of the time the palace ignores what's happening in the senate."

"Not at all," Richard said. "We're not as isolated as you might imagine. Of course, some politicians seem more concerned with their own reelection than passing legislation."

"Maybe," Tarkio said, "but it's the nature of the institution. We're not born into power as others are."

Both men grinned, eying each other. At that moment, several of the other archsenators began talking excitedly.

Tarkio grabbed one by the arm.

"What's going on?" he asked.

"Terrible news," the man said, showing them his datapad. On the screen, a news bulletin was flashing:

SENATOR JOAN MARSHAL FOUND
DEAD FROM APPARENT SUICIDE
MORE DETAILS ON VOX NEWS

"Dear lord," the prince said.

Tarkio remarked, "The loss of her son was a terrible blow."

"I see what you mean. They say there's nothing sadder than a parent who outlives her children."

"Actually, she still had a daughter."

"I had no idea. I thought her daughter died years ago."

"Apparently not."

"My condolences to her daughter then," the prince said. "But to my original point, I wanted to thank you for taking these pirate attacks so seriously. I swear some in my family couldn't care less."

"Not the emperor, surely?" Tarkio asked in alarm.

"Heavens, no!" the prince replied. "I meant my brother and sister..."

"Ah, of course. Siblings can be difficult at times, I'm told."

"You have no idea," Richard confided. "At least they're headed to our mother's on Revenna. Hopefully that will keep them out of trouble for a while."

Tarkio smiled politely. "Well, let's hope so..."

CHAPTER EIGHT

Lord Maycare's yacht, the *Acaz*, descended into the thick cloud cover enveloping Hekla VII. Watching through the window as the ship descended into the atmosphere, Jessica Doric stood behind the captain's seat where Maycare sat at the controls with Bentley next to him in the co-pilot's chair.

After minutes of nothing but curtains of gray, the *Acaz* broke through the clouds. Just as the survey team's report had said, the terrain was nothing but bleak snow and jagged, granite cliffs. As the ship skimmed along at a few thousand feet, a volcano came into view. From the crater at the top, a shower of ash fell across the surrounding heights, giving the mountain a dark outline against the white landscape.

Following the coordinates Doric had given him, Maycare flew to a grouping of stone obelisks at the base of the volcano. From their shapes, the rocks were clearly man-made, although Doric doubted men had actually made them. Maycare set the ship down, sending a whirlwind of snowflakes swirling around the cockpit windows. Doric, Maycare, and even Henry Riff donned winter gear for the frigid temperatures outside. Bentley elected to stay aboard to look after the ship.

"I don't care for the cold," the robot said.

A ramp in the belly of the *Acaz* lowered, letting in a gale of biting ice crystals. Doric winced at the pain and pulled her fur-lined hood down a little tighter over her goggles.

"Alright," Maycare said, "let's get going."

Stomping down the ramp, the three trotted through the snow toward the stone grouping. Within minutes, they came to a set of steps. They followed the stairs up a short hillside, the volcano dominating their view just beyond. When they reached the top, the knoll flattened into what Doric assumed must have been a temple long ago. Now, only a few wind-worn columns remained. A little farther on, not more than twenty or thirty feet, Doric spotted a low altar.

"This must be a thousand years old," Henry said.

"I'd say at least five," Doric replied.

"There's something coming out of the ground," Lord Maycare pointed to a spot just in front of the altar. "What is that? Smoke?"

Doric came closer. One of the pillars had toppled over and severely damaged one of the slabs making up the floor. From between the cracks, threads of vapor dissipated into the wind.

"No, I think it's steam," she said.

In a semi-circle, they stood over the cracked stone.

"I wonder what's under there..." Henry said, his voice trailing off.

"One way to find out," Maycare replied.

He lifted a sizable piece of lava rock and, before Doric could stop him, dropped it where the steam percolated up. It made a hollow thud.

Maycare pounded the slab again and then a third time. The crack widened into a crevice while clouds of hot moisture billowed from the hole.

"I think I see a staircase!" Maycare said, discarding the rock and crouching down on one knee. He reached into the crevice and pulled open the slab with a heave.

Doric grabbed a scanner from her pocket and took a reading.

"These energy signatures match the ones from the survey," she said. "The source must be somewhere inside the mountain."

"Well, this looks like the easiest way in," Maycare said. "Unless you want to climb the side of that volcano..."

A puff of smoke belched from the volcano in the distance, followed seconds later by a tremor beneath their feet.

"On the other hand," Doric said, "it might not be safe underground if the ceiling collapses."

Maycare smiled.

"You know just what to say to win me over," he said and disappeared down the hole.

Lord Maycare landed in the dark. Switching on a flashlight, he sent the beam down a long corridor. Like the temple above, the walls and ceiling were constructed from stone slabs.

"Come on down!" he shouted.

After Doric and Henry joined him, the three of them began shedding their cold-weather gear in the warm steam of the tunnel. Now suitably dressed, they followed the corridor a few hundred feet until it opened into a natural lava tube running left to right.

"Which way now?" Maycare asked.

Doric pointed her sensor in both directions, but the readings to the right were more pronounced.

"That way," she said.

They followed the tunnel for several minutes, the air becoming progressively hotter with every step. The incline also turned steeper, headed downward.

"It really stinks in here," Henry coughed.

"That's sulfur from the volcano," Doric said. "We should be close to the mountain by now."

"I see light up ahead," Maycare said, turning off his flashlight.

The lava tube glowed orange that only grew brighter as they went deeper. Reaching the end, they emerged into a domed cavern laced with rivers of molten magma. The lava, churning between dark and bright red, lit the ceiling above with flickering, hellish shadows.

"I've never seen anything like it," Doric said. "This room must have been part of a larger magma chamber. I see more lava tubes farther up the walls."

"There's a path to the other side," Maycare said. "We could walk across."

"Um, that seems kinda dangerous," Henry said.

"Where's your spirit of adventure?" Maycare asked him.

"In my luggage?" Henry replied. "I could go back and get it."

"It's alright, Henry," Doric said. "Lord Maycare and I can go on without you."

"Alone?" Henry asked. "I think I'd better stay with you guys, if that's okay."

"That's the spirit!" Maycare bellowed, heading off across the cavern.

Above Hekla VII, the dull gray shape of the *Sorcerer* slid into orbit. On the bridge, Oscar Skarlander waited while the sensor chief scanned the surface.

"I've detected the *Acaz*," the chief said.

"Show me," Skarlander replied.

On the main monitor, the view of the planet from orbit changed into a topographic map covered in light blue contours. Not far from a tall, volcanic peak, a ship's outline was visible.

Skarlander resisted the urge to gloat. Reading through the information on his datapad, he saw the emails between Maycare and Jessica Doric. If his lordship's robot hadn't left such an obvious trail when it hacked the University's system, Warlock would never have even known about the breach. Then, it was just a matter of backtracking until Warlock's team had hacked into Maycare's own servers.

"Prepare the transmat," he said.

Lord Maycare was nearly halfway across the lava chamber when he heard a warble from inside his pants pocket. It was Bentley on the communicator.

"There's a ship in orbit," Bentley said. "It won't answer my hails and I detected a transmat signature a few moments ago."

"You better take off and wait in orbit until you hear back from me," Maycare replied.

"What's going on?" Henry asked.

"I think we're about to have visitors," Maycare said.

A man's voice, as if floating above the floor, pierced the gloom.

"Hello down there!" he bellowed. "So nice to finally meet you in person, Lord Maycare."

Looking up, Maycare saw three men standing at the lip of one of the lava tubes about ten feet off the ground. The man in the center had both hands on his hips and smiled behind a dark beard. The other two, larger and more menacing, carried blasters pointed in their direction.

"Who the hell are you?" Maycare shouted back.

"I'm Oscar Skarlander," he said, "from Warlock Industries."

"I've heard of you," Maycare said, shooting a glance at Doric beside him.

"And who's that with you?" Skarlander said.

"I'm Professor Jessica Doric," she answered for herself.

"Ah, yes," Skarlander said. "I've read your papers from the University."

"Really?" she asked.

"Your findings were amateurish, but your grammar was impeccable."

"Son of a—" Doric started.

"What do you want?" Maycare interrupted.

"Same as you," he said. "There's a power source in this volcano and I'm here to claim it."

"Well, you can't!" Henry shouted.

"Oh, I'm pretty sure I can!" Skarlander said.

Two blooms of yellow light burst through the semi-darkness, lancing the lava rock on either side of Maycare and his companions.

"Hold your fire!" Maycare shouted. "We're unarmed!"

"An oversight you may not live to regret!" Skarlander yelled back.

Maycare felt a tremor and saw the magma around them starting to bubble. Before he could process the significance, Jessica Doric was grabbing him by the arm.

"We need to get out of here," she said in his ear.

"Of course," Maycare replied. "They're trying to kill us."

"No, you don't understand—" she started, but the ground heaved upward as the whole chamber shook.

Unlike the earlier tremors, this quake lasted nearly half a minute, sending pieces of the ceiling falling to the magma below in great splashes of liquid rock. Maycare tried to shout, but his voice was lost in a deafening noise that sounded like an avalanche tumbling down a mountain. Looking up, he saw sheets of snow from outside spilling through the ceiling like a waterfall. As the snow hit the lava, it turned into a torrent of hot steam.

Against the scalding mist, Lord Maycare found Doric and pulled her to her feet.

"Time to leave!" he said.

"Wait!" Doric said. "I can't find Henry!"

They looked until Henry's shape became a dull outline with poor posture. Doric grabbed him while Maycare tugged on her arm.

"We're going the wrong way!" she said, yanking Maycare toward the way they came in.

"No, we're getting the power source," he barked over his shoulder. "Come on!"

He was insane, Doric thought. One the other hand, her own adrenaline was making her feel a little crazy herself.

She didn't struggle as Maycare led her along.

The steam had started to thin. Doric could make out the walls around her, another tunnel apparently, although not a lava tube. She saw stalagmites jutting up like strangers milling in a crowd.

Both Doric and Henry collapsed, trying to catch their breath. Lord Maycare remained standing, surveying the surroundings.

"I hate this place," Henry gasped.

"Agreed," Doric replied.

"It was a lucky break, that earthquake," Maycare said. "But I've always been lucky..."

"When can we go home?" Henry interrupted.

"We're not leaving until we find that xenotech," Maycare said. "I'm not letting Warlock Industries get another artifact. God knows what they'd do with it."

"Alright," Doric said. "Just give us a minute."

While she rested, Doric watched the beam from Maycare's flashlight darting around the tunnel. In the glare, she saw strands of white fur. For a second, she thought it might be alive, but the musty odor quickly told her otherwise.

"What is it?" Henry asked.

"A dead animal," Doric replied, standing up.

"Big, too," Maycare said. "Must've been dead a long time. It's all skin and bones."

"Look at the skull," Doric pointed. "It's like a bear of some sort."

Maycare took the hide and gave it a shake. Then, dropping it, he started flashing the light around as if searching for something. The light stopped when it brightened a small stalagmite. Maycare gave the pointed column a sharp kick with his boot. The tip of the stone, about six inches from the point, broke off. Maycare picked it up and went back to the skin. He handed Doric the flashlight and started jamming the sharp rock into the belly of the creature's fur.

"What are you doing?" Doric asked.

"I've got an idea," he said. "Let's see how my luck's holding out."

Henry walked behind Lord Maycare and Professor Doric as she followed the data on her scanner. After an hour, they came to the source of the power readings at the end of yet another tunnel.

Henry struggled to see past Maycare and Doric as they peeked around the corner into a cavern, smaller than the one before but again laced with streams of flowing magma. In the center of the chamber, his back facing them, Skarlander stood atop a dais of stone where a crude altar had been built. His two bodyguards loitered nearby next to a grav sled hovering a few feet off the ground. Henry assumed the sled was to carry the xenotech in case it was too heavy to lift.

Skarlander turned, revealed something cradled in his arms like a newborn. It was a huge sapphire, the size of a pineapple, glowing with a radiant blue light. Skarlander's face basked in the glow.

"Good," Maycare said.

"How is this good?" Doric asked.

"They're not expecting us."

Maycare pulled the animal skin over him and, hidden beneath the white hide, charged headlong into the room. Seeing this bear-like creature rushing toward them, the two guards glanced at each other before running in the opposite direction toward one of the lava tubes. Maycare chased after them, howling madly.

Henry wanted to ask the Professor what was going on when he realized she was already dashing toward the stone platform. She jumped onto the dais and struck Skarlander across the head with a piece of stalagmite.

Skarlander dropped the sapphire and fell to his knees, holding the side of his bleeding face.

"Henry!" Doric shouted. "Get the crystal!"

Henry hesitated. The Professor must be crazy, he thought.

Doric barked at him again. "Do it!"

As if slapped, Henry jumped up and scrambled through the sandy dirt to the edge of the molten lava where the sapphire had landed.

He could feel the intense heat searing his hands and face. Reaching down, he slipped his fingers around the jewel and was surprised by how cold it felt. He held it up so Doric could see, but Skarlander was holding her by the wrist.

Skarlander pointed at Henry.

"Give it to me!" Skarlander said.

"I don't want to," Henry replied.

"Do it," Skarlander said, "or I'll dump her in the lava!"

Out of the corner of his eye, Henry saw Maycare returning to the cave, running at full speed and without the animal skin. The two bodyguards were right on his heels, their weapons drawn. One of them fired, narrowly missing Lord Maycare.

Henry screamed in pain, noticing his shoulder was smoldering, apparently hit by the errant shot. Holding his shoulder, he also realized he was no longer holding the power source. Henry dropped to his knees trying to find the sapphire and saw a blue glimmer reflecting off the molten magma flowing a few feet away.

"Shit!" he said.

Everyone, including Lord Maycare and the two bodyguards, stopped and watched the crystal bobbing along.

Skarlander pushed Doric away and ran to the edge of the stream of burning rock. The crystal's icy blue color began pulsating red as it sank deeper into the lava. Skarlander strained to reach it, but his fingers were inches too short.

As the artifact dipped completely below the surface, its pulsing light was still visible under the lava. The viscous magma began bubbling violently.

"Get on the grav sled," Maycare told Doric. "Quickly!"

"Henry needs our help," Doric said.

"I'll get him," Maycare said. "Now go!"

The river of lava, like an incoming tide, erupted from its banks, spewing waves of churning liquid like thick, glowing molasses.

Doric climbed onto the back of the grav sled, which was nothing more than a floating platform the size of a mattress. Heat and acrid smoke burned her eyes, filling them with tears. Even with blurred vision, she saw Lord Maycare dragging Henry to the sled.

Behind them, the floor flooded with lava as the level rose with each boiling burst of energy from the artifact.

The grav sled dipped as Henry jumped on beside Doric. Maycare pushed the sled until, running out of ground, he clambered on board. A swell of magma sent the grav sled lunging toward a random lava tube. Like a raft shooting the rapids, their barge jetted into the narrow passage and the darkness within.

Although Doric couldn't see, she sensed they were moving incredibly fast. Also, her ears started popping, which either meant they were heading up to safety or deeper into the volcano. Although Doric knew she could never admit this to Maycare, she was terrified.

And then she was blinded again, this time by light.

Like a cork from a champagne bottle, the grav sled burst from a vent in the side of the volcano. The raft floated upward for a moment until it veered sharply to one side. The three passengers spilled out onto a snow bank.

Doric took a moment to see if she was still alive. Confident she was, she sat up and saw a stream of lava pouring from the vent, continuing down the slope away from them.

"Is everyone alright?" she asked.

Maycare's voice came from the other side of the drift. "I think so."

"Henry?" Doric called.

"I think I need a doctor," he finally spoke, standing up with his arm clearly bleeding.

"Hold on, buddy," Maycare said, pulling out his communicator. "Bentley?"

"Yes, My Lord?" the robot answered.

"We need a lift."

"Right away, sir," Bentley replied. "Also, it seems the other vessel has left in rather a hurry."

"Did you detect a transmat?" Devlin asked.

"Indeed."

"Alright then, just get down here as quickly as possible."

"Right away, sir."

Henry whispered into Doric's ear, "Did Lord Maycare just call me *buddy*?"

CHAPTER NINE

Pitt was born in the grave.

On the frontier, in a disputed area of space claimed by both the Imperium and the Magna Supremacy, Pitt's parents had joined a human colony, hoping to build a new life. Taking issue with humans colonizing what they considered their own territory, the Magna launched an attack, bombarding the settlement from orbit and killing most of the inhabitants, including Pitt's father.

Sticklers for efficiency, the Magna landed on the planet and rounded up the survivors, lining them up in front of one of the large craters caused by the bombardment. One by one, the settlers were executed, their bodies falling into the pit.

A few hours after the Magna left, a Pirate Clan called the *Butcher Boys* arrived at the decimated colony in hopes of salvaging whatever they could. Much to their surprise, however, the pirates heard a baby crying, finding the newborn lying at the bottom of a crater, surrounded by the dead. Pitt's mother, in her final act of life, gave birth to a boy.

The pirates named him Pitt.

The baby grew into a young man, learning the full curriculum of pirate skills including piloting, fighting, and killing. At the age of eighteen, he earned the tattoos signifying his official induction into the Butcher Boys.

Unfortunately, life in a Pirate Clan is often brutal and short, largely due to the Imperial Navy. When the Navy finally caught up with the Butcher Boys, the warships made short work of the ragtag vessels of the pirates. Pitt found himself captured and was soon given a simple choice: either join the Navy or go to prison for the rest of his miserable life.

Pitt had to admit, he always liked those naval uniforms.

As part of the Imperial Navy, he accepted his fate and quickly distinguished himself by fighting against a Draconian insurrection, killing many rebels in the process. Pitt's ambiguous morality caught the attention of the Imperial Intelligence Service who recruited him into an elite unit specializing in black ops and assassinations.

Before Pitt could start, the agency sent him to special training on a planet affectionally called the *Hellmouth*.

The barren surface of the planet was devoid of life except for those who trained there. A single barracks and a few surrounding buildings were the only structures. Standing at attention with the other trainees, Pitt saw his instructor for the first time. Named *Sgt. Black*, the man would shape the nineteen-year old into the man, and perhaps monster, he would become.

"Listen up!" Sgt. Black told them, "“"Many of you will not survive this training, but I promise those who do will no longer fear death. You will become Agents of Death and wherever you walk, Death will follow."

"He's just trying to scare us," a young recruit whispered into Pitt's ear.

Without hesitation, Sgt. Black thumbed a button on his belt. In a crackle of energy, the recruit disappeared.

"That loudmouth," the sergeant shouted, "just got a one-way transmat into high orbit where he'll enjoy a lovely view for the short time before he dies. Don't kid yourself, ladies and gentlemen, he's only the first of you to die. Many of you, hell, maybe all of you, will follow…"

Sgt. Black kept his promise. In the following weeks, he sent the trainees on missions against live opponents, convicted murderers condemned to execution. Pitt soon got so used to killing, it became second nature. With every man Pitt killed, the guilt of killing slowly faded. Perhaps the greatest lesson Black taught him was that *good* and *evil*, *right* and *wrong*, were empty words without meaning. Death was inevitable. Why shouldn't Pitt be the one who sent the doomed to their final resting place?

"To live is to suffer," the sergeant preached. "Only the dead know true peace. Don't pity the people you kill; they're the lucky ones…"

On the eve of graduation, Sgt. Black presented them with one more task. The class would disperse into tunnels beneath the camp.

"For this exercise," he said, "your targets are not convicts. They are your fellow trainees. To pass this final test, you must kill one of your classmates. If you manage to kill more than one, of course you'll receive extra credit!"

For most assassins, the most feared scenario was to become the prey of another assassin. For Pitt, however, in the darkened corridors he felt no fear. He no longer dreaded death because he had become Death. When he left the tunnels at the end of the mission, he was the only survivor.

On Pitt's first mission after graduation, he was selected as part of a two-man kill team assigned to terminate a nobleman, his wife, and son.

Pitt and his partner transmatted directly into the noble's high-rise apartment. While the other killer went after the husband, Pitt crept toward the bedroom where he found the wife, her back to him, standing in front of a window watching the city lights.

She died never knowing he was there.

Pitt spoke into his microphone. "I eliminated the wife."

"Roger that," replied the voice in his earpiece. "I've taken out the primary target. Find the son and finish the mission."

Pitt went to the woman's corpse. Perhaps out of instinct, he turned the body over. In her arms, a baby boy stared up at him. Looking into the eyes of this child, still held by his dead mother, Pitt knew the mission wasn't going to end as planned.

Pitt found the other assassin still standing over the nobleman lying on the floor.

"Did you kill him?" the other man asked.

"I'm about to," Pitt replied, shooting him through the chest.

Into the night, Pitt took the child and disappeared. Neither could go back to their previous lives. Knowing the boy was still in danger, Pitt left him with a friend. The child would grow up never knowing his noble lineage or even his real name. As for Pitt, he changed his name too. Using the two forces that formed him: the Magna that killed his parents, and Sgt. Black who made him a killer, he became known as *Magnus Black*, a hitman for hire.

The life of a heavy liftbot was far from glamorous. Liftbot Serial Number F204-8BE2-17A2-CFF3 or, as Master Hitch called him, *Hey Dummy*, had lived on the *Rattenbury* for three years, although the passage of time inside a cargo hold was largely meaningless.

Today, the *Rattenbury* rested on the platform of a space station.

Hey Dummy stood motionless at the foot of the open loading ramp. His master, Cameron Hitch, was beside him in a spacesuit, instructing him over the comm about which crates the robot should carry onto the ship.

Dimly understanding his orders, Hey Dummy waddled over to a grav sled parked at the edge of the platform. He took the opportunity to look up at the world the station was orbiting. The robot didn't know the planet's name, but knew it was large and had a pleasant orange color, which was more than he could say about the ceiling of the cargo hold.

Reaching the supply canisters burdening the grav sled, Hey Dummy lifted one of the containers and turned back toward the *Rattenbury*. He noticed that Master Hitch was no longer alone at the top of the loading ramp. He seemed to be talking to another man, also in a spacesuit. Hey Dummy didn't think this was the same man that, along with a robot companion, had been aboard for the last several days. Hey Dummy was definitely pretty sure that man and his robot had left through the main airlock an hour earlier.

No, this man was different than the other one. This one was shorter and, through the face shield, his skin was white, not brown.

Also, he held a blaster.

Hey Dummy continued transferring supplies from the sled to the ship, observing but not interfering with the men's conversation. They were apparently talking on a different comm frequency because the robot couldn't hear what they were saying. He could only see the motions they were making. For example, the new man seemed eager to show how well he could point the blaster at Master Hitch, waving the weapon several times. The captain seemed impressed enough to raise both of his hands.

On his third trip, Hey Dummy watched as Master Hitch typed a message into his datapad, perhaps telling someone else about how well the new person waved his gun. This seemed agreeable to the other man until the captain finished the message. Then, coming from behind, the man surprised both Master Hitch and Hey Dummy by using a sharp knife against the captain's air hose.

The robot was no expert on human biology, but it was his understanding that most organics needed oxygen. For what, he didn't know.

Hey Dummy watched as his master fell to his knees and sprawled across the deck of the cargo hold. After a minute or two, his master stopped moving. Meanwhile, the other man was placing something against the door mechanism leading to the rest of the ship. It was a small cylinder with several wires poking out.

Hey Dummy wondered if the man was fixing the hatch, but that was beyond the robot's understanding. As a liftbot, lifting was about all he really knew.

Remembering he still had a few crates to haul back to the ship, Hey Dummy started back toward the grav sled. At this point, he heard a loud static sound transmitting across his comm channel. New thoughts, which would never have occurred to him before, started occurring to him. He felt afraid, but a calm voice told him it would be alright. It occurred to him that the voice was coming from inside his head.

After days of freeze-dried coffee aboard the *Rattenbury*, Russell Davidson was eager to get his hands on something fresh, even if finding ground coffee on a space station was never a sure bet. That was especially true on Far Harbor, a way station a long way from anywhere.

After telling Captain Hitch they'd be gone a few hours, Davidson and Jericho left the ship and wandered the promenade deck, looking for a decent cup of coffee. They passed vendor alcoves and kiosks filled with cheap electronics and questionable foodstuffs, while advertisements flashed on screens above their heads:

LONELY? NEED A FRIEND?
DY CYBERNETICS:
WE MAKE FRIENDS SO YOU DON'T HAVE TO!

"Can people really be friends with robots?" Jericho asked, stopping beside a stall full of orange, prickly-skinned fruit.

"Sure," Davidson said. "Although the idea of buying a robot specifically for that purpose seems strange."

"Why is that?"

"Buying someone doesn't strike me as very friendly. Not to mention what happens if the friendship doesn't work out."

"I believe friendship models are programmed to be quite amiable," Jericho said.

"Even so..."

"I've often wondered about sexbots," Jericho confessed.

"Say what now?" Davidson said, stopping abruptly.

"Not for me," Jericho said. "I meant for humans."

"Oh, right."

"What if the person gets tired of the sexbot?" Jericho asked. "What becomes of it?"

Davidson started walking again, still hoping to smell the brewing of an espresso machine along the way. Jericho followed.

"The Robot Freedom League has liberated sexbots," Davidson said. "In every case, the human was sorry to see them go, to say the least."

"A simple implant to the pleasure center of the brain would achieve the same results," Jericho suggested.

"Well," Davidson hesitated to reply, "it's not really my area, but I expect there's aspects of sex that draw people to something more realistic. Is that a café?"

Davidson pointed to a sign that read *Coffee or Die.*

"Let's go in there," he said.

Inside the café, Jericho sat at a corner table while Davidson purchased a cup from the robot behind the counter. His steaming brew in hand, the human joined Jericho, taking a seat directly across.

Jericho studied Davidson as he eagerly sipped the coffee from the mug.

"During my review of the ark ship archives," the android said, "I read several references to humanity's infatuation with coffee."

"I wouldn't call it an *infatuation*," Davidson said.

"An addiction then?"

Davidson took a moment to consider. "Maybe..."

"Considering the many beverages, including alcohol, that your species enjoys, coffee's prominence is a mystery to me."

"It makes me happy," Davidson said.

"Because of the caffeine?" Jericho asked.

"There's that."

"Then why not simply inject the caffeine directly into your blood stream? Perhaps using a suppository?"

Davidson coughed.

"I think you're underestimating the pleasure of the experience," he said. "The warm brew and the milk and sugar. All that adds to the gratification."

"Hmm," Jericho pondered. "I suppose since I don't ingest food, I can't fully appreciate it as much."

"I'm sorry about that," Davidson said.

Jericho, whose face included actuators in the mouth, smiled.

"No need to apologize," he said. "My original design didn't require taste buds or a functioning digestive system."

"Even so, why give you a brain that could sense things, but not all the senses to actually enjoy them?"

"Again, my purpose didn't require it."

"But you're more than whatever purpose somebody built you for," Davidson said.

"That's my hope, yes."

Jericho heard a buzzing from beneath the table and watched as Davidson, reaching into his pocket, removed a datapad.

"Captain Hitch sent me a text," Davidson said, reading from the tablet's screen. "Looks like he needs us back at the ship. Doesn't say why though."

"Well, I've enjoyed our walk on the station," Jericho said. "Even an android can feel cooped up on a starship after too long."

Davidson gulped down the rest of his coffee. "Delicious!"

Returning to the *Rattenbury*, Davidson and Jericho entered through the main airlock, but couldn't find Captain Hitch on the bridge or in any of the staterooms. Jericho finally suggested they try the cargo hold.

Following the corridor to the belly of the ship, Davidson and the robot reached the closed hatch leading to the hold. The control panel showed that the room on the other side was pressurized so Davidson, with Jericho beside him, activated the door. With a jolt, the hatch groaned as it began to open.

Wearing a spacesuit, Magnus Black opened a hatch leading onto the space station platform. The landing pad was empty except for the *Rattenbury* and a grav sled weighed down with supply canisters.

The cargo ramp was already down and a heavy liftbot was lumbering over to the sled. Magnus ignored the robot and walked directly up the ramp where he saw Captain Cameron Hitch reading from his datapad, probably the supply manifest. Magnus removed a blaster from a pocket in his suit and tapped on Hitch's shoulder.

Hitch jumped.

"What the hell?" he shouted over the comm link in his helmet. "Who are you?"

Magnus waved the blaster.

"Get your hands up," he said.

Hitch raised his hands while looking past Magnus toward the heavy liftbot.

"Don't bother trying to direct your robot," Magnus said. "I've already blocked the signal, as well as the frequency to the station."

"Well, I guess you've got it all figured out," Hitch said. "Mind telling me what's going on?"

"I'm here for the android," Magnus replied.

"Jericho?"

"Warlock Industries doesn't like their property walking off, apparently."

"Sorry, pal, but he's not on board."

"Where is he then?"

"He's with a guy from the RFL called Davidson."

"Get him back here," Magnus said, pointing with his blaster at the datapad still in the captain's hand.

Hitch looked at the tablet and sighed, fogging up the bottom of his face shield.

"Alright," he said and began typing.

Magnus, in the cold vacuum, put away his blaster and removed a serrated knife from a holder on his belt. With the captain's back to him, Magnus watched as Hitch finished his text and hit *SEND*. With a smooth motion, Magnus slit the captain's air hose. Oxygen gushed from the hose, sending it flapping back and forth.

Hitch dropped the datapad and turned, but Magnus had stepped away, out of reach. Magnus knew what was happening inside the other man's suit. Hitch was gasping for air, even as it escaped uselessly into the vacuum. Magnus watched him fall to the deck, rolling back and forth. A blast from his weapon would have been more humane, Magnus realized, but that would have also alerted the station's security sensors. He didn't need that kind of attention.

Hitch's movement slowed and then stopped.

With the captain dead, Magnus went to the hatch leading to the rest of the ship. From a small bag slung across his back, he took out a cylinder and placed it against the door. He pulled wires from the cylinder, connecting them to the hatch control panel. It wasn't a large bomb, but it should do enough damage to kill anyone coming through the door. Whether that someone was human or robot didn't matter much.

His work done, Magnus left the hold the same way he came in. Walking down the ramp, he passed the heavy liftbot as it brought another load up. The hulking robot acted oblivious to the hitman's presence or the fact that he had just killed the machine's master.

I guess that's not part of his programming, Magnus thought.

When he got to the base of the ramp, he saw another robot standing on the platform. It looked a little like his target, Jericho, but was stamped with the dy cybernetics logo, a lowercase *d* and *y* enclosed in a circle. Magnus didn't recall seeing it there when he came by the first time, but now it was standing between him and his way off the platform.

"Hello, Mister Black," the robot said through the comm link.

Magnus stopped.

"Who are you?" he asked.

"My name's Dyson Yost," the android said.

An almost imperceptible curl appeared at the corner of Magnus' mouth.

"The founder of dy cybernetics?" he asked. "Not very damn likely."

"While I might not be the flesh and blood version of Dyson Yost," the android admitted, "My gravitronic brain holds all the same memories and personality. If it makes you feel any better, consider me his representative."

"Alright," Magnus said for the sake of argument. "What brings you out this way?"

"It's come to my attention that you've been hired to kill an android named Jericho. I've come to convince you to do otherwise."

"Good luck with that."

"I can be very persuasive," Yost said.

"It's nothing personal," Magnus replied. "When I'm contracted to do a job, I do it."

"Highly commendable I'm sure, but you're hardly a mindless killing machine. You haven't always completed your missions as planned..."

"What's that supposed to mean?"

"You once killed a young mother, but left her child alive. You even took the boy and made sure he remained safe."

"How the hell did you know about that?" Magnus asked hotly.

"Let's just say information flows freely in my circles, Mister Black."

Magnus drew his blaster and pointed it at the android.

"This conversation is over," he said.

Magnus felt two powerful, metallic claws clamp down on his shoulders. Without turning around, he knew they belonged to the heavy liftbot who had previously ignored him.

"Don't be so hasty," Yost said. "At least hear my proposal."

The claws, designed to carry several hundred pounds of equipment, dug into Magnus' suit until he could feel his collarbones nearly crack.

"I'm listening," he said, his jaw clenched tight.

"I propose that you remove the bomb you placed in the cargo hold and quietly leave the space station."

"What about my contract?" Magnus asked. "Warlock Industries is expecting Jericho's head."

"To be exact," Yost said, "they're expecting a gravitronic brain inside an android's head."

"Yeah?"

"As it happens, I have both of those currently sitting on my shoulders."

"Are you suggesting—"

"Indeed, Mister Black," Yost said. "You will remove my head and take it back to your client."

"They'll know it's not Jericho's," Magnus said.

"A small electrical charge near the base of my brain will scramble it sufficiently so they won't know the difference."

"Seems like a lot of trouble over a robot," Magnus said.

"Perhaps," Yost said, "but we all have a path to walk and Jericho's is a very special one indeed."

"What makes you think I'll do any of this?"

"You have a path of your own, Mister Black. Its destination might surprise you."

Magnus felt the heavy liftbot press more of its weight onto his shoulders.

"Deal," Magnus said.

Davidson passed his hand across the lock controls, releasing the bolts restraining the hatch to the cargo hold. Stepping through the opening, with Jericho right behind him, Davidson entered and found the captain dead on the floor. The ramp at the back of the hold was closed and the heavy liftbot stood silently like a sculpture among the cargo containers.

CHAPTER TEN

Detective Crawley stood over a corpse lying in a back alley of Ashetown. The detective was in his fifties and had a smoldering cigarette hanging from his mouth. His face, poorly shaved, was carved by too many years working the beat in the worst part of town.

The corpse didn't look much better.

"What a mess," Crawley said, examining the scene.

The body was one of several littered along the alley. Most were human, but a few were Tikarin. The bloody holes in each of them suggested a violent end to their lives. The detective had seen it all before.

A policeman walked up to Crawley, stopping beside him.

"What do you think happened?" the officer asked.

"Well," Crawley began, puffing out a cloud of smoke, "seeing this is Griefer territory and that over there is one of Big G's thugs, I'm guessing this is an old-fashioned turf war."

"Seems a shame fighting over such a shithole," the officer said.

"Maybe," the detective agreed, "but one man's shithole is another man's paradise when you live in a sewer."

"That's pretty deep, sir."

"I read books," Crawley said. "You should try it sometime."

The cop shrugged and strolled away.

Pearls before swine, Crawley thought.

After the medical examiner had surveyed the scene and the guys from the coroner's office had cleared the corpses, Detective Crawley found himself in another part of Ashetown, but didn't find it any better. Plastic bags and other garbage filled the streets. Dead trees, killed by neglect and polluted air, lined the sidewalks. It might have been depressing to someone else, but the detective blocked it out like white noise.

All he really wanted was a decent sandwich.

He spied a street vendor down the sidewalk. The sign on the cart read "Gyros and Shawarma - Real Meat!" The vendor was a Tor, a minotaur race from the labyrinth cities of Rochan. On his home planet, the Tor would have been a successful craftsman, hammering hot iron into intricate shapes and selling them to off-worlders. Here, he shoveled carved meat into pitas and was happy to have a job.

Knowing this was probably the best he could do, Crawley approached the cart, passing walls decorated with gang tags and unflattering caricatures of the emperor.

The Tor towered over the human. The tip of one of his horns was missing and the ring hanging from his nose was slightly bent. He wore a leather kilt and not much else. Perspiration zigzagged down his bare, hairy chest, dripping into the row of pita breads sitting in the cart.

"You got any beef in that cart, cud-muncher?" the detective asked. He held open his coat just far enough to show off his badge and the strap of a shoulder holster.

"Yes, detective," the vendor said.

"Isn't it kind of strange for a cow to serve beef?"

"It wasn't anyone I knew," the Tor replied.

Crawley heard a warble from deep inside his coat pocket. He reached in and pulled out a datapad. The image of his lieutenant, a middle-aged woman with gray hair, winked open on the screen.

"Crawley," the woman said, "there's a homicide at the Greenwood Towers in the West End. I'm assigning it to you."

"West End?" the detective asked. "That's not my usual beat, Lieutenant."

"I don't give a shit, Crawley. Just do what I tell you!"

The display went blank, revealing Crawley's reflection and the questioning look on his face. He rolled his eyes and popped the pad back into his coat. The vendor was handing him the gyro. The detective took it, without offering to pay, and turned on his heel. He headed back down the street where his grav car hovered silently.

The manager of the Greenwood Towers apartment building crossed the freshly polished floor of the lobby, nearly tripping over the bufferbot that was working diligently on a particularly dull section of marble. The manager, named Eadan, admonished the low-lying, oval-shaped robot for being in the way, but the bufferbot continued happily scouring the floor in its own, single-minded way. On some level, Eadan appreciated the little robot's work ethic. As a Dahl, the manager had a keen sense of responsibility toward the building and its upkeep, and he felt a kinship to anyone or anything that shared that commitment. Even so, he would probably replace the bufferbot with a better model once one became available.

Eadan straightened his uniform, a gray shirt and tie beneath a blue vest with matching pants. Although the Dahl were not known for excessive pride, Eadan took pains to appear professional at all times. With a clientele like those living at the Greenwood Towers, he knew that keeping up appearances was of utmost importance. The rich of West End wanted privacy and efficiency, and Eadan was determined not to let them down. Of course, they were also human, which meant they were constantly acting inappropriately themselves.

Take the unfortunate events of last night for example.

Of course, being a Dahl didn't help things. Eadan was well aware that humans held a deep-seated distrust for his species. Some people accused the Dahl of reading minds. While it was true the Dahl possessed psionic abilities, Eadan himself never went to the special schools necessary to enhance them. Not that he wanted to read the minds of the people at the Greenwood Towers. They were horrible people for the most part, horrible people he was eager to please in every way.

Eadan believed the real reason humans distrusted the Dahl was precisely because the Dahl had become so indispensable to them. His race had willingly resigned themselves to helping humanity in any way they could. That kind of altruism, on such a scale, was alien to human understanding. What were the Dahl getting out of it? It didn't make any sense!

Of course, to the Dahl it made perfect sense, but a different kind of sense than what humans were used to.

Eadan shook the thoughts from his head as he noticed an oddly misplaced human standing just inside the lobby entrance. The man wore a weathered coat, stained with all manner of horrors, and smoked a cigarette even though the sign on the door said smoking was expressly prohibited. The ash alone would wreak havoc with the poor bufferbot...

Seeing a large potted plant next to the entrance, Eadan momentarily considered dragging it over to the man, blocking the view of him from outside the lobby, but thought better of it.

"Can I help you?" Eadan asked doubtfully.

"I'm Detective Crawley, RPD," the man replied.

"Yes, of course," the manager said. "I was told to expect you, but I was expecting someone... else."

"Sorry to disappoint."

Eadan motioned toward the elevator. "This way."

Once inside the lift, the manager attempted a more cordial tone.

"Obviously, we're very concerned about appearances," Eadan said. "The thought of one of our tenants being murdered could damage our reputation."

"That's not my problem," Crawley said.

"All we ask is a level of decorum in your investigation. There's no reason the other tenants need to know about this, is there?"

"Well, I guess that all depends on *you*."

The manager's eyebrow rose slightly. "How so?"

"I usually canvass the apartments near the crime scene," Crawley went on. "You know, to see if anybody heard or saw anything unusual."

"Is this canvassing really necessary?"

"Not if I concluded the murder was an open and shut case."

Eadan thought for a moment.

"What if you were motivated to do so?" he asked.

"Well, I can't imagine what kind of motivation that would entail."

The Dahl fumbled awkwardly in his pocket and produced a small, plastic chip.

"Would this suffice?"

Detective Crawley took the chip. The tiny LED display on the cred stick read *500*. "Yeah, that'll be enough."

"Good," the Dahl replied as the elevator door opened with a rush of air.

Outside the elevator, Forensicbot 42 waited patiently in the hallway. The robot was painted black except for a silver trim and the lettering *F-42* stenciled in yellow.

"Detective Crawley, I presume?" the robot asked.

"Where are the other detectives?" Crawley replied.

"I was the only unit sent here, sir."

"Well, that's damn peculiar."

"Indeed," F-42 said.

"Excuse me," the manager interrupted. "May I go now?"

Crawley scowled at the Dahl. "I'll let you know if I need you."

Eadan smiled, looking relieved, and disappeared behind the closing elevator doors.

"Alright," the detective said, "what have you done so far?"

"Except for preliminary scans," F-42 said, "I've left the crime scene as undisturbed as possible, sir."

"Well, don't just stand there, take me to the apartment!"

"Very good, sir!"

F-42 led Detective Crawley down the hallway and around a corner to a door marked *3417*. The robot opened the door and walked in, its gait mechanical but steady.

The apartment was lavish, but not gaudy. The floor plan was open, the living room in the center with a kitchen attached to the right. The furnishings were mostly beige leather covered with decorative throws and pillows. A large TV monitor hung above the fireplace. On the screen, a commercial showed a grav car in the background, on fire and smoking. In the middle of the scene, a man approached holding a bouquet of roses toward a woman in the foreground with her hands on each hip. The scene faded to pink with the tag line:

NOTHING SAYS "SORRY"
LIKE SADIRA FLOWERS...

"Computer," Crawley said, "turn off the TV."

The screen turned black.

"Get a load of this place," Crawley went on. "This living room's bigger than my whole apartment."

"I live in a closet," the robot replied, hoping to create a friendly rapport.

"Shut up and show me the body."

F-42 took the detective down a side corridor to an open doorway and into the bedroom. The floor was cluttered with clothing, including a woman's panties. Crawley, leaning down, snatched the underwear off the carpet and slipped it discretely into his coat pocket.

"The body is over there," F-42 pointed.

On the bed, a nude woman lay with the sheets covering her lower half. Her left arm hung over the side while her cold, dead eyes greeted Crawley with sharp indifference.

"You got a name for this lady?" the detective asked.

"Fingerprints identify her as Jolana Valeria, a 23-year old originally from Middleton."

"How could a girl from Middleton afford a place in West End?" Crawley wondered aloud. "Cause of death?"

"Asphyxia," F-42 said. "Her hyoid bone is broken, indicating she died from manual strangulation."

"Good."

"One other item," the robot said. "The murder appears to have occurred either during or shortly after coitus."

"Ahhh," the detective's attention perked up. "Now we're getting somewhere. I bet she's a prostitute and the john didn't want to pay. I see that shit all the time in Ashetown, though you'd think the guys around here could afford it. Cheap bastards."

"I took samples, but I'll need the lab at the station to test them."

F-42 examined the detective while he did the same to the body. Of the two, the robot found the corpse less puzzling. A dead human was far more understandable. They no longer suffered bouts of uncontrolled emotions like anger or sadness. Living beings, at least the non-cybernetic kind, were often unpredictable based on their moods or intuitions or what kind of sandwich they ate for lunch.

The robot heard a faint warbling. The detective removed a datapad from his coat and looked at the screen. Instead of a video feed, only text appeared. F-42 didn't know why someone would only send text, but humans were apt to do strange things from time to time. Perhaps it was a joke somebody thought was funny enough to share with the detective. Humor was also something the robot found mystifying. Sarcasm was especially lost on the forensic unit. It must not have been a joke, however, or at least Detective Crawley didn't seem to get it. He had a strange look on his face as if he didn't entirely understand what he had just read.

"Are you alright, sir?" the forensicbot asked.

Crawley nodded as he put his datapad away, his arm remaining in his coat.

"You haven't uploaded any of your findings, have you?" he asked.

"No, sir," the robot replied. "I was waiting for your authorization."

"Glad to hear it."

Crawley pulled his arm out of the coat. Instead of a datapad, he held a blaster, which he pointed at the robot.

This was curious behavior to say the least, thought F-42. He wondered, for perhaps a millisecond, whether this was another example of humor. He waited, calmly and without moving, for the detective to put away the weapon, smile and then laugh. Instead, Crawley squeezed the trigger, sending a flash of superheated plasma across the room.

Very odd indeed, the robot thought just as the energy bolt impacted the outer casing between his eyes. The plasma continued, melting plastic and fusing circuits, until it reached the back of the casing. A fountain of sparks, smoke, and bits of formerly expensive electronics showered over the furniture. F-42 took a step forward and fell to the floor with a loud, metallic crash.

Although the Emperor's Council met at the Imperial Palace, the offices of the archsenators remained in the Senate building. Archsenator Malcolm Tarkio's own office was small compared to those of the more senior members of the Council, but he was confident he would move into better accommodations eventually. Even so, he was happy with the view. Through the double-pane windows, Tarkio could see the Grand Marching Grounds where military parades were held, and a portion of the Victory Arch straddling the reflecting pool. Due to some trees, he couldn't quite see the patriotic statues flanking either side of the pool. It was all pageantry, the archsenator knew, to demonstrate the might of the Imperial crown and its military. It was also a great place to have lunch or get your picture taken, as tourists often did throughout the day.

Tarkio sat at his desk, a mahogany monstrosity with fluted, hand-carved pillars at each corner. A computer monitor sat on the top, clashing with the antique appearance of the desk. The archsenator was looking over polling results from the last election. While the numbers were good, Tarkio thought that a few well-placed attack ads against his next opponent couldn't hurt. There's always another election, he knew. Better to get a step ahead of the competition before they did the same to him.

A notification popped up on his screen. Someone from the RPD was calling.

"Computer," Tarkio said, "Answer."

The screen changed from a spreadsheet to the image of a middle-aged woman with gray hair.

"Good afternoon, Lieutenant," Tarkio said.

"I wanted to give you an update on that issue we spoke of," she said.

"To be honest, I was beginning to worry."

"No need to worry," the Lieutenant said. "It's been taken care of."

"That's a relief!"

"Not a problem, Archsenator. Have a good day."

The Lieutenant's image disappeared.

Tarkio sighed. He felt regret for what happened, but he knew nothing would be gained by dwelling on it. There was too much at stake, both for himself and his constituents. After all, they voted for him and now it was his responsibility to represent their best interests. He shouldn't just throw that away because of a mistake he never intended to make.

He smiled, confident that he made the right decision.

Another prompt appeared on his monitor screen.

"Computer, answer."

A man's face, poorly shaved and creased with experience, looked back at the archsenator.

"Hello?" Tarkio said. "Can I help you?"

"I'm Detective Crawley from the RPD," the man said.

"Oh, of course. I just spoke with the Lieutenant."

"Yeah, I'm the guy she sent to take care of your little problem."

"Ah," he said, "how exactly did you get this number?"

"Well, I'm a detective after all. It's kind of what I do."

"Yes, I understand that," the archsenator said. "It's just that I didn't expect to hear from you directly. As I said, I just talked to your Lieutenant."

The left side of Crawley's mouth curled, exposing some of his yellow teeth.

"Oh, the Lieutenant doesn't know about this conversation," he said, slipping a cigarette between his lips. "It's more of a personal call."

Tarkio's mouth devolved into a frown. "I don't understand."

"Well, senator or archsenator — whatever you call yourself — I'm interested in a side deal between just you and me."

"Perhaps I should talk to your Lieutenant again—"

"Oh, you don't want to do that," Crawley cut him off. "That would be bad for both of us, that much I guarantee."

Tarkio straightened in his chair, asserting a sense of authority.

"Tell me what you want," the archsenator said.

Smoke, expelled from Crawley's mouth, clouded the view on the monitor, but Tarkio could still see the smirk on the detective's face.

"You made a big mess and I'm the guy who cleaned it up for you," Crawley said. "I expect to be compensated."

"Were you not paid enough through my arrangement with the RPD?"

Crawley laughed. "No, not by a long shot!"

"Then what are you suggesting, detective?"

"A sizable donation to my campaign," the policeman said, laughing at his own joke.

"And if I don't pay?" Tarkio asked.

"Picture the headline," Crawley said. "Archsenator murders prostitute! Details on VOX News!"

Tarkio felt the sweat accumulating around the crown of his forehead. His heart beat hard against the inside of his chest.

"Alright, Detective Crawley," he said. "Let's meet in person and I'll give you whatever you want."

Crawley pulled the cigarette from his mouth, grinning with all of his teeth this time.

"And that's how we do things," he said, "in Ashetown."

CHAPTER ELEVEN

Captain Harrison of the Imperial yacht *HIMS Victoria* watched Aldorus through the bridge monitors as the ship orbited the planet. A Tikarin, tufts of gray fur poked up from under the stiff collar of his uniform.

Harrison had received his commission through a naval program to promote minorities in a military predominated by humans. He knew it was a token measure to reassure the liberal wing of the senate that the Imperium was a progressive empire. Nevertheless, he appreciated the assignment. Commanding the Imperial yacht, even if it was ostensibly part of the Navy, was better than getting shot at by pirates or the occasional Magna raider.

Even if the door is only open an inch, it's a good idea to stick your toe in, he thought.

The captain straightened his attire, a blue uniform with silver buttons up the left side.

High above the capital Regalis, *Victoria's* orbit was taking the ship over less populated parts of the planet. While the nobles, especially the Five Families, owned much of the real estate, a few largely untouched areas still existed. Captain Harrison, an amateur geographer, recognized many of the land masses, not to mention those of a hundred other worlds he had visited.

"Where is Princess Katherine at the moment?" he asked his first mate.

"Her Highness is in the observation lounge, Captain," the mate replied.

"Ah, perfect!" Harrison said. "Patch me into the lounge."

"Aye, sir!"

"Your Highness, this is Captain Harrison. Outside the windows, you can now see the Palatine Mountains coming into view, where the famous Dharmesh Monastery is located.

A young woman's voice came over the intercom, "Ah, thanks?"

Captain Harrison glanced at the ceiling, rolling his eyes. He made a throat-cutting gesture to the first mate who terminated the comm.

Pears before swine, Harrison thought.

On the observation deck, Princess Katherine and Lady Sophia lay on stuffed chairs, staring at the planet through a panoramic window taking up much of the curved wall in front of them.

"It's quite beautiful," Sophia remarked.

"Maybe from up here," the princess said.

"I suppose things look better from a distance."

Behind them, Katherine's maidbot Dotty was at the bar, mixing a pair of cocktails.

"Speaking of which," the princess said, "we can't leave until Alexander gets here. Richard's orders..."

"Prince Alexander was never one for punctuality," Sophia said.

Katherine's focus shifted from Aldorus to her own reflection in the window and then to Lady Sophia's pallid face hovering beside her like a ghost.

"Aren't you a wee bit anxious to see Alexander?" Katherine asked.

"Not at all."

"Liar!" the princess said, prodding Sophia with a finger.

Sophia gently swiped Katherine's hand away. "*I'll* never tell."

"You shouldn't keep secrets from me!"

"Secrets keep the world spinning," Sophia said. "The truth is too scary for most people."

"Not for me."

"No?"

"I'm not a little girl," Katherine said. "Apparently, I'm old enough to get married off..."

"Only if the price is right," Sophia said, her voice so low the Princess nearly didn't hear it.

"Exactly!" Katherine replied.

"I probably shouldn't have said that."

"But it's true, isn't it?" Katherine said. "I'm just a digit in somebody's spreadsheet."

Dotty tottered over to the two women in their reclining chairs. Each took a margarita from the tray the robot was holding, sending her back to make more.

"Why did you break up with my brother?" Katherine asked suddenly.

Sophia's eyes widened. "What?"

Katherine laughed. "Sorry."

"Are you sure?"

"I'm just curious."

"It's nothing worth divulging," Sophia said. "I've added the whole affair to my list of regrets."

"Then why did you break up with him?"

"I didn't. He broke up with me."

Katherine's mouth made an O-shape. "That little shit!"

Lady Sophia took a long sip from her glass.

With a hiss and a crackle, Prince Alexander and his bodyguard, Lefty Lucy, materialized on the transmat pad aboard the *Victoria.* Both stood on the dais, looking at the transmat officer who had an expression of relief that they hadn't arrived as a pile of goo.

"Welcome aboard, Your Highness," he said.

"Thanks for the lift," Prince Alexander replied.

Once in the adjoining passageway, Alexander sighed.

"What an enormous waste of time," he said.

Walking beside him, Lucy was completely silent.

"I mean," Alexander continued, "does Richard really think shipping me off is going to keep me out of trouble?"

Lucy said nothing.

Alexander glanced at Aldorus through the windows in the corridor. "But I guess it'll be good to get out of town for a while. No sense sticking around with my cousin Rupert on the warpath."

Lucy didn't disagree, or agree, or say anything else for that matter.

"I know, I know. I shouldn't have punched him," the prince said, "but he had it coming, right? Nobody talks about you like that. He's lucky I didn't have my sword. Now *that* would've been a proper duel!"

A pair of ensigns, dressed in their blue uniforms, stopped when they saw the prince and bowed.

"Hello," Alexander said, saluting as he and Lucy walked by.

Even without looking, the prince knew Lucy was sizing up the two ensigns, perhaps imagining a scenario that involved cutting their throats as she hung upside down from the ceiling. She was funny that way.

Something else occurred to him.

"I think we're lost," he said. "This ship is a lot bigger than I remembered…"

Lucy stopped and stared at him without blinking.

"Oh, like you have any idea!" he replied.

From around the corner, Alexander heard his sister's voice.

"Ah," he said. "Problem solved."

Lady Sophia saw Prince Alexander and his ubiquitous bodyguard walk into the observation lounge. She gave the princess a tap on the arm to let her know.

"It's about time!" Katherine said, nearly jumping from her chair.

"Sorry, sis," Alexander replied, slouching his shoulders. "I was delayed."

"Nobody cares!" the princess said. "This is about *me*, not you!"

Alexander nodded. "That sounds like something Sophia would say."

"Why yes, darling," Sophia said, also getting up. "I've trained her well."

"I bet."

In the awkward silence that followed, Sophia surveyed Alexander's face and the bruise beneath his eye. Those eyes, she remembered, those eyes...

"I've got an idea, Kate" the prince said. "Why don't you and Lefty go to the bridge and let the Captain know we're ready to depart?"

"Sure! Why don't I just give her the grand tour!" the princess said.

"That'd be great," Alexander replied.

"Fine, come on Lefty, or whatever your name is," she said.

Katherine headed out of the room. As Lucy, moving to keep up with the princess, came shoulder to shoulder with Lady Sophia, their eyes met. Sophia wasn't sure, but just for a moment she felt like Alexander's bodyguard was appraising how much it would take to cut her head off.

When Katherine and Lucy were safely out of earshot, Sophia asked the prince, "Tell me, darling, does your little friend ever speak?"

"Only with people she likes," Alexander replied.

"I bet she talks to you, " she said. "I bet she talks to you *a lot*!"

"It's strictly professional, Sophie. No need to get jealous. Besides, we've been over for a while now."

"You walked out on *me*, remember? A girl tends to take that personally."

"Really?" Alexander said, crossing his arms. "You certainly got back on the social circuit fast enough."

"It's important to carefully feather one's nest," Sophia replied.

"I'd think your nest was pretty well feathered by now."

Over the ship-wide channel, a voice spoke over the intercom.

"Attention!" it said, "Prepare for jump."

As the *Victoria* slipped into hyperspace, the floor under their feet shuddered and Sophia felt her stomach heave. Although she hated this part of traveling, she'd hate even more letting a good opportunity pass her by. As if fainting, Sophia dropped into Alexander's waiting arms.

"How clumsy of me," she said.

"A little obvious, don't you think?" the prince replied, smiling.

"Shut up and kiss me."

Lady Sophia sensed him drawing near, even as she closed her eyes. His lips, so familiar, touched hers. She missed feeling him so close, surrounding her, enveloping her. She only wished he was willing to stay.

Away from the political intrigues of Regalis, Empress Isabella Montros relished the privacy of the Montros estate on Revenna. It was the family's largest holding outside of Aldorus, consisting of thousands of acres of remote, wooded hills.

House Montros, like the other Five Families, traced its bloodline all the way back to one of the captains of the original sleeper ships. Over the ensuing centuries, while the other houses grew wealthy through acquisitions in various important sectors of society, the Montros family married into the other houses instead, forming alliances by blood.

As the wife of the reigning emperor, Isabella expected her children to continue the tradition, whether they liked it or not.

Emerging from her private bath at the Revenna estate, Isabella wore a white taffeta gown lined with accents dyed green and interwoven with encrusted jewels. She found three of her courtiers waiting in the salon. Each consort was a young man in his early twenties, dressed in sleeveless tunics exposing their muscular arms. The empress preferred to keep men like them around. They were both pleasing to the eye and handy if a jar needed opening.

One of them, a boy whose name she had forgotten, informed Isabella that her children had arrived and were waiting for her in the music room.

With her three escorts, the empress followed a long breezeway from her quarters to the main structure of the palace. When she entered the Rococo-styled music room, her children were huddled in a group near the piano. Two others, Alexander's bodyguard and Lady Sophia, were with them.

"Yoo-hoo, children!" Isabella trilled.

Princess Katherine, her mother noticed, was frowning already, but at least Alexander seemed to be in good spirits. Considering his son's lifestyle, Isabella was not surprised.

"Hello, Mother," Katherine said. "I'm here as you demanded."

"And so cheerful, too!" her mother replied. Turning to her three consorts, she said, "Why don't you boys run along and I'll meet you in the garden later?"

"Yes, ma'am," they said in unison and left through a pair of French doors.

"Such nice boys," Isabella said.

"Mother!" Katherine protested.

"Oh, hush," the empress said. "I'm married, not *dead.*"

"What about Daddy?"

"Don't be such a drama queen, child," Isabella said. "It's just another benefit of an arranged marriage."

"I think it's awful!"

"Honestly, I didn't realize I raised such a prude. I'm surprised Lady Sophia hasn't taught you more about the ways of the world..."

"I assure you, Your Majesty," Sophia said, "I've only taught her *all* my bad habits."

"I don't want any part in your marriage schemes," Katherine said. "I'm not a commodity to be bought and sold."

"Certainly, dear," the empress replied, "but things are often more complicated than they seem. You'll understand better when you're older."

"Richard was right about one thing," Katherine said, pointing at herself, "I'm not a kid anymore! I know what I want and I don't need anyone telling me what to do!"

Her mother smiled in resignation.

"Alright, sweetheart," Isabella said. "We can talk about it later."

"But I want to talk about it—"

"May I make a suggestion?" Lady Sophia asked.

"What is it, dear?" Isabella replied.

"Perhaps we could go on a sightseeing trip to relax everyone," Sophia said. "Princess Katherine mentioned visiting the Glitter Fields from her trips here as a child. Perhaps we could take the *Victoria* and see them again?"

The empress clapped her hands in delight.

"That's a marvelous idea!" she said.

"I haven't seen those in years..." Alexander admitted.

"Why don't you go too, Alexander?" his mother suggested.

"Sure, why not?" he replied.

Katherine scowled at him. "Because I *hate* you."

"All the more reason!" Alexander said.

The princess stomped her foot.

"Go if you must," she said, "but we're not waiting for you this time!"

Katherine and Lady Sophia left the music room through another pair of doors. Once they were gone, Isabella touched her middle child on the arm.

"I'm glad you came," she said.

"To be honest," Alexander said, "it was Richard's idea."

"You should listen to your brother more often," Isabella said. "He truly means well."

"He worries too much about appearances."

Growing serious, his mother said, "Perhaps you should, too. There's no shortage of enemies, Alexander."

"Don't worry, Mother," Alexander said, smiling, "I'll protect you."

"Perhaps," she said, "but who will protect *you*?"

CHAPTER TWELVE

On Eudora Prime, Technotown offered everything a tinker could want, whether she was willing to pay for it or not.

The eight blocks along Emporia Street assaulted a person's eyes with electronic signs, three stories high, bleeding digital words and images from the roof down to the sidewalk. People, predominantly humans, wandered along, lost in the avalanche of chaotic advertising. Nobles and commoners alike carried bags from whatever store had successfully sucked them in and spat them out again. A few were unaware exactly what they had bought.

Melinda Freck, who everyone called *Mel*, popped out the doorway of a store specializing in starship parts. Only three feet tall, Mel could barely carry the bulky satchel under her arm as she looked down the busy sidewalk. From a race called the Gnomi, Mel had pointed ears that poked through her light, pink hair. It was a cruel coincidence that the name of her species resembled one from ancient Earth lore, leading to jokes about little red hats and tiny shoes.

Mel began walking leisurely away from the shop entrance until the store owner burst onto the sidewalk, waving his hands and shouting for the police. Mel abandoned the casual approach and ran madly between startled customers. She became aware of a policeman, lumbering after her with a scowl on his broad, meaty face. In his sausage-like fingers, he carried a shock baton crackling with electricity.

Mel knew all about what humans thought of her kind. The Gnomi had a reputation for snatching whatever machines they could get their hands on. They liked to fiddle with devices and make them better. Of course, they would also resell them for a profit, but a girl had to make a living...

Turning a corner, Mel narrowly missed a woman holding groceries. The rotund policeman, close behind, plowed into the woman at full speed. The bags tore open, sending oranges rolling across the pavement. Mel dodged the flying produce but felt a tug. Looking over her shoulder, she saw the officer holding the strap of her satchel.

"Crap on a cracker!" she thought, tightening her grip.

Mel pulled hard on the knapsack, but the officer was more than twice her size and nearly dislocated Mel's shoulder as he yanked on the strap.

"Dirty tinker!" he growled at her.

"Let me go!"

Mel thought her prize was lost, but the woman with the lost oranges began flailing her fists on the officer's chest. The policeman tried defending himself, but released the satchel in the process.

Making her escape, Mel disappeared with her satchel down an alley and into a culvert. From the darkness of the sewer drain, Mel saw the legs of the policeman stumbling into the alley, but she knew he wouldn't follow her down there.

The Underdelve was no place for humans.

In the damp tunnels of the sewer, Gen the General Purpose Robot was trying, with limited success, to keep up with her master Orkney Fugg. The robot and the portly Gordian meandered through the dark, dripping passageways of the Underdelve with only strings of lights along the walls for illumination.

Fugg insisted he knew where he was going. He was short with a stocky build and a thick neck. Stubby tusks protruding from his mouth, he grumbled while he walked. Gen was about the same size, but with a curved, feminine frame made from plastic and aluminum. Her metallic feet made tapping sounds on the hard tunnel floor.

"Why didn't we go to Technotown, Master Fugg?" she asked.

"Too many damn humans," he muttered.

"You don't like them?" she asked, practicing the art of small talk.

Without missing a step, Fugg grunted through his hog-like snout, "Hell no."

"Why?"

"They're bastards, every one of them," Fugg said. "Anyway, we can get better prices in the Underdelve.

"Oh, yes," Gen remembered. "Captain Ramus said you were cheap."

"Frugal!" Fugg protested. "That Dahl bastard should appreciate what I do for him. Lord knows we can't afford much!"

The narrow passage opened into a cavernous chamber. The ceiling was a network of interconnected pipes from which crude lighting hung by loose wires. If Technotown had an ugly stepsister, this place was it. Most people just called it the *Black Market*.

Gen and her frugal companion weaved through a steady throng of undesirables dressed in shabby clothing caked with dirt and foul-smelling sludge. The Market used to be a section of the city sewer, but the denizens of the Underdelve turned it into a bazaar for the downtrodden. Individual stalls, each little more than plywood and sheets of plastic, lined the walls, making for a tight fit in between. An assortment of questionable goods acquired through questionable methods covered each table.

Unlike on the surface, none of the shoppers were human.

"Alright, here it is," Fugg said.

He was standing in front of a rusted door with the words *Freck's Gizmos and Gadgets* welded into the metal. With effort, he pushed the door open and went inside.

Instead of a store, Freck's workshop was more like a cluttered closet with storage boxes filled with bits of wire and dusty circuit boards. At the center of the mess, a small girl hunched over a work table, sparks like burning fairy dust flying from whatever she was working on.

"Mel," Fugg said.

Receiving no response, he yelled, "Mel!"

The girl, her hair a disheveled mess from which long, pointed ears protruded, spun around. She pushed a pair of goggles up onto her forehead. In her hands, she held a plasma welder, the flame still burning. "What?"

"Did you get that part I ordered?" Fugg said.

Mel switched off the welder and pulled the goggles off her head, dropping them onto the table.

"Of course."

She opened a drawer and brought out a satchel. Opening it, she removed a nondescript piece of equipment.

"Any trouble getting it?" Fugg asked.

"Do you care?" she replied.

"Just making friendly conversation, tink."

Mel glared at him.

Touching Fugg lightly on the shoulder, Gen said, "It's my understanding that such words are considered offensive by the Gnomi people."

"Nonsense," he said, rolling his eyes. "I'm a Gordian. I can't be racist. You're racist for even suggesting it."

Gen covered her mouth.

"Oh, dear!" she said. "I'm so terribly sorry, Master Fugg!"

"You ain't offended, are you, sparky?" Fugg asked, winking.

"Of course I am, you fat bastard!" Mel shouted.

Fugg's mouth opened, closed, and then opened again. "Well, your customer service sucks."

"Are you buying this or not?" Mel demanded.

"How do I know it works?" Fugg asked.

"You've got my money back guarantee. If you're not 100% satisfied, I'll steal another one for you."

"That sounds fair," Gen remarked.

"Fine," Fugg said, handing Mel a credit stick. "Here's the amount we talked about."

"Need any help installing it?" Mel asked.

"I think I can manage," Fugg snorted. "I know the *Wanderer* like the back of my hand. There's nothing on that heap I haven't fixed or swapped out."

"I'm surprised it still flies," Mel said.

"Stick to your gizmos and whatnots," Fugg said. "Starships are for men like me."

"What about you, robot?" Mel said.

"My name's *Gen*."

"Has he tried fixing you yet?"

"Well," Gen said, "Master Fugg attempted to add an attachment to me, but Captain Ramus said it was indecent."

Mel's eyes widened and she stared at the Gordian. "You disgusting pig!"

"Don't judge me!" Fugg retorted.

Mel pointed to the door. "Just get out."

"With pleasure," Fugg said.

In the corner of Mel's workshop, the gears of an old grandfather clock turned, clicking a hammer that chimed five times. Studying herself in a mirror that was cracked in one corner, Mel tried matting down her unwieldy hair. With a shrug, she left the shop and turned toward one of the tunnels leading from the main market into the damp darkness.

Rodents scuttled away as Mel walked purposefully with only a glow stick giving her light. A precious few had ever seen these passageways. They belonged to the wing of the sewer that had fallen into disrepair decades ago, forgotten by whatever maintenance crews might have descended this far below the surface. Nobody came here now.

Almost nobody.

Along the main tunnel, Mel came to a side shaft guarded by a wrought iron gate. She plucked a brass skeleton key from her pocket and inserted it into the lock. It took a little muscle, but she cranked the key a half turn and the lock snapped open. She stepped inside and secured the gate again. Her heart was beating faster.

Up ahead and around the corner, Mel saw a faint light. She could make out a voice, hollow and distorted as it bounced off the moldy, crumbling walls. She put away the glow stick and emerged into a wide chamber with a vaulted ceiling. In the middle of the room, shapes stood facing a stage. While some appeared to be flesh and blood, the rest were robots and androids listening to the speaker on the platform. He was tall with short, curly black hair and dark brown skin. He spoke to the crowd, but Mel felt like he was talking to her. Mel's face flushed and her smile broadened into a wide grin.

"The history of mankind," Randall Davidson said, "has been a history of enslavement. From our earliest days, Man has enslaved others to do the labor that he could not, or *would* not, do himself. From beasts of burden to putting other men in chains, humanity has always subjugated those around it. Eventually they built machines for this; machines made to be slaves.

"The Robot Freedom League believes that no one, organic or cybernetic, should live a life of servitude. It doesn't matter whether there's blood in your veins or hydraulic fluid, it's everyone's right to be free."

The crowd murmured in agreement, including the robots, a few of which raised their metal hands in the air.

"Now, we all know the Imperial government — and most of its citizens for that matter — don't agree with us," Davidson continued. "They view robots as property, as inorganic machinery and nothing more. Well, if you can't own a human being, how can you justify owning someone who can reason better than most humans? I say you can't, and I say those who keep our robot brothers in bondage are no different than those that kept my ancestors in chains. Freedom is the inalienable right of everyone, and robots are no different!"

The audience stood clapping.

"Thank you," Davidson said. "Thank you all for coming."

As the applause subsided and the crowd began wandering toward the exit, Mel pressed past them toward the stage. Davidson jumped down when he saw her coming. They had known each other for several years now, since he started bringing robots to Eudora Prime before smuggling them across the border to the Cyber Collective.

"Mel!" he said, bending down and giving her a hug. "I'm glad you made it."

"Sorry I'm late," Mel replied.

"Not at all," Davidson shook his head. "What did you think of the speech?"

"It was great, what I heard of it…"

Davidson laughed. "Well, it keeps the message alive at least."

"Do you give these speeches on all the planets you visit?" Mel asked.

"When I can," Davidson replied. "I've been pretty preoccupied lately..."

Mel noticed someone standing nearby, an android, but not one she had seen before. He was nearly as tall as Davidson, with polished white plastic covering much of his body except at the joints where colored wires were neatly bundled.

"My manners," Davidson apologized. "Jericho, this is Miss Melina Freck. Mel, this is Jericho."

"Please call me Jerry," the robot said.

Mel gave a quick bow and shook Jericho's hand. "Glad to meet you, Jerry."

"Jericho comes all the way from the Capital," Davidson said.

Mel's dark eyes widened. "That must've been quite a trip!"

Jericho's mechanical mouth contorted into a smile.

"Indeed," he said without irony.

"Actually," Davidson said, "it's been a nightmare."

Mel frowned. "Why?"

"We lost the pilot we hired at Far Harbor Station," Davidson explained. "He was murdered."

"Holy shit!"

"We managed to find another captain to fly us here," Davidson went on. "Once we arrived, we intended to rendezvous with a Cyber Collective vessel to smuggle Jericho across the border…"

"Didn't they show up?" Mel asked.

"No, they were punctual as usual, but when they saw Jerry, they refused to take him because of his gravitronic brain. They said they won't accept any robots with advanced CPUs anymore."

"They've been giving asylum to robots for years," Mel said. "They're robots too, for god's sake!"

"For androids like me," Jericho said, "the Collective has always stood as a kind of promised land where we could be free. Knowing that we've been barred from taking refuge there is very troubling."

Mel could feel herself getting angry, but she tried focusing her emotions on something more useful. Then she had an idea.

"What if I knew someone with a ship who could help?" she said.

"The Collective doesn't let foreign vessels into their territory," Davidson said.

"I didn't say it would be easy," Mel replied.

Davidson considered for a moment.

"If we could get to their home world," he said, "perhaps I could reason with them, or at the very least get an explanation."

"You want to go too?" Mel said. "But they kill humans on sight!"

"It's worth the risk," Davidson said.

"It's suicide!" Mel said.

"Does that mean you won't help us?"

"Well," she said, "the crew I know is pretty suicidal."

"Good."

"But there's one condition," Mel said, pointing a finger.

"Name it."

"I'm going with you!"

CHAPTER THIRTEEN

Jolana Valeria, a twenty-three-year-old from Middleton, leaned against the glass railing of her balcony in the West End. Her apartment overlooked a tree-lined boulevard many stories below.

Jolana's auburn hair draped like a curtain toward the street the farther she bent, her tight, black dress pressing against the rail. It was late and most of the people below had dined and gone home, leaving only the stragglers behind among the midnight shadows.

Not all was quiet. Jolana noticed some commotion, a group of people standing in the road. When they moved away, she saw they had written on the pavement:

ALL ENDEAVOR IS FUTILE!
WE ARE UNITED BY DOOM!

Weirdos, she thought. Probably a Null Cult or whatever the news called them.

After the cultists were out of sight, servicebots arrived and started scrubbing the street. Within minutes, the words were gone.

Jolana went back inside to the living room and made herself a drink. Her guest would be arriving soon and she wanted to be relaxed when he did.

Despite the expensive furniture and the large video screen, Jolana felt at home in the apartment, though it was a long way from where she came from. Middleton was not a slum like Ashetown, but the streets could be just as cruel.

Her parents were middle class, one a teacher and the other a stay-at-home mom. Her home life was idyllic, and Jolana hated every minute of it. She ran away as soon as she could, but ran out of money even faster. It wasn't long before she discovered what a commodity a young girl could be when she no longer had a choice.

Nobody particularly cared whether she lived or died until she met a woman from the Red Lotus. They took her in, cleaned her up, and made her a part of something bigger than herself. She still saw men for money, but if a man hurt her, the Red Lotus made sure he paid for it with his life.

Jolana poured a glass of wine, leaving a second glass empty for now.

Hearing the chime, she went to the front door. Although she knew who it was, her eyes opened wide like she was surprised to see him. She smiled the way they taught her. She knew this would be a good night.

The sun was setting, its golden luster filling Oscar Skarlander's office. The Warlock operative ignored the light and focused on the black gloves covering his hands. The burns he had suffered on Hekla VII, trying to retrieve the alien artifact from lava, disfigured his hands so much he couldn't bear the sight of them. The skin grafts left scars that even Warlock doctors couldn't erase. For Skarlander, the deeper scar was losing to a pompous ass like Devlin Maycare. The loss of the xeno tech was not nearly as humiliating as knowing Maycare had bested him.

That was unacceptable.

An execubot, carrying a box, entered Skarlander's office. Named *Dupond* or *Dupont*—Skarlander didn't bother to clarify which—the robot was Jericho's replacement, but lacked a gravitronic brain.

"What is it?" Skarlander asked.

"A package, sir," the robot replied.

"Put it on the desk and go."

"Yes, sir."

The execubot obeyed and left the office without another word. Skarlander examined the package. All parcels were carefully scanned prior to arriving, but at the same time, Skarlander was hesitant.

Taking a cutter from his desk, he sliced away the tape securing the seams and pulled open the top. He peered inside.

From a speaker in the ceiling, the office computer said, "Archsenator Malcolm Tarkio is on the line, wishing to speak with you."

Pushing the box aside for the moment, Skarlander sat back in his chair.

"Go ahead."

Tarkio's face, sunken around the eyes, appeared on the desk monitor.

"Mister Skarlander," he said.

"Archsenator," Skarlander replied. "What can I do for you?"

"It's about what happened two nights ago," Tarkio said.

"Yes?"

"The detective they sent to Jolana's apartment called me. He wants to be paid off or he'll go to the media."

"That would be very unfortunate," Skarlander said.

"My DNA is all over that apartment," Tarkio said. "I'd be ruined."

"Oh, at the very least..."

"Are you going to help me or not?"

"Of course, Archsenator," Skarlander said. "Warlock Industries always protects its investments."

"What are you going to do?" Tarkio asked.

"I think something special from the Cauldron might be in order."

Tarkio's face turned pale. "One of your monsters?"

"We prefer the term *asset*," Skarlander said, "but then I suppose we're all assets... until we become liabilities."

Skarlander leaned into the camera atop the computer screen.

"And as you know, liabilities must be eliminated."

After a pause, "What do you want me to do?" Tarkio asked.

"Set up a meeting with the detective and find out what he knows."

"Then?"

"Then," Skarlander said, "eliminate the liability."

The archsenator's face winked out as the screen went blank. Skarlander stood up and pulled the box on his desk closer. He leaned over the open package and inspected the contents. Inside, charred along the edges, the head of a robot stared back at him with dim, lifeless eyes.

"Alas, poor Jericho," Skarlander said.

Jolana looked beautiful, as always, Archsenator Tarkio thought.

She stood in the doorway of her apartment, her auburn hair shimmering in the electric light. Tarkio handed her a gift, a trinket wrapped in a box. She took it and smiled, asking him to come in.

He followed her to the kitchen where a late dinner was prepared. Nothing fancy, but Jolana lit some candles to improve the mood. In the flickering shadows, her eyes reflected the flames like fire trapped in a bottle.

Tarkio felt comfortable with her, as if he could unburden himself from the stresses of public office. She didn't judge him or ask him to justify the darker aspects of his political life. She seemed to understand that sacrifices were required to achieve the greater good.

After the meal, they moved to the living room and sat beside each other on the leather couch. Jolana opened another bottle of wine, pouring them both a glass.

"I spoke with Prince Richard again," Tarkio said.

Her eyes brightened. "Really?"

"But the more I hear him talk, the more I doubt he'll support more powers for the senate," Tarkio went on.

"I'm sorry," she said.

"People like him are born into power. They don't understand the struggle of people born without it."

"What are you going to do?"

"Oh, keep pushing, I imagine," Tarkio replied. "There's a critical mass that must gather before things can change. With a little help, I think that can happen."

"With a little help?"

"There's always interested parties willing to donate to a worthy cause. It's in their self-interest..."

"What kind of parties?"

"Businesses, mega-corporations," Tarkio said, "you know, groups outside the nobility. They want access to me and the power my office provides. They help me and I help them."

"So, they pay to see you?"

"Something like that."

"Like you pay me?" she asked.

Tarkio choked on his wine. "Well, not exactly."

Later, in Jolana's bedroom, the two lay beneath the satin sheets that Tarkio had bought her. As a candle burned down to a nub on the dresser, the archsenator rolled over, facing the wall.

"Sorry," he said.

"It happens," she said.

"Not to me."

She laughed. "Maybe we shouldn't have had that second bottle."

"I don't find it funny."

"Don't be mad," she said, snickering.

"I'm not!" he said, pulling away the sheets.

Tarkio, his naked body as white as the sheets, got out of bed and went into the bathroom. He shut the door with a slam behind him.

At night, the Grand Marching Grounds were quiet without the throngs of tourists milling across the pavement. Lonely spotlights illuminated the Victory Arch, the intricate friezes along the top contrasted in heavy shadow. The legs of the arch straddled the reflecting pool, now a black mirror of the sky. Detective Crawley leaned against one of the statues that lined the pool.

He looked at his watch. The archsenator was late, but the detective wasn't surprised. People like that were never on time, especially if it meant keeping someone hanging. Not that Crawley had anywhere else to go. His little apartment in Ashetown was a pigsty, along with everything else in Ashetown. He didn't mind waiting in a park.

A man approached.

Crawley stepped away from the statue and flicked away a spent cigarette.

"It's about time," he said.

The man, dressed in a dark coat, glared at the detective.

"You're lucky I'm here at all," Archsenator Tarkio growled.

"I wouldn't call it luck," Crawley replied. "I'd call it you didn't have a choice."

"Well, I'm here now, so let's get to business."

Crawley couldn't help but laugh. He was expecting a big payday out of this.

"It's not funny," Tarkio said.

"Not from where I'm standing," Crawley said.

"What do you think you have on me?"

The detective removed a datapad from his jacket and handed it to the archsenator. Crawley knew what Tarkio was seeing as he scrolled through the screens. There was ample evidence placing Tarkio at the scene of Jolana Valeria's murder, including tissue and bodily fluids. Even the weird little hotel manager recognized the archsenator's face when Crawley showed him a picture.

Watching Tarkio's hand shake holding the datapad, Crawley noticed tears welling up around the man's eyes. Must've been a crime of passion, Crawley thought. He knew all about those. Love and crazy were usually the same thing.

"It's an open and shut case," the detective said. "You can either pay me or I go to the press and see that you get what you deserve."

"You think that's what I deserve?" Tarkio said, his voice nearly cracking.

"You know what? I've seen worse, but that doesn't mean you shouldn't get thrown out an airlock."

Tarkio cleared his throat and stood straighter as he handed the tablet back to Crawley.

"We don't always get what we deserve," Tarkio said, "but I'm going to make sure you do."

"Before you get any ideas," Crawley said, "I've got that info backed up in case anything happens to me."

"Password protected, I suppose?"

"Goddamn right."

"That shouldn't be a problem."

"What's that supposed to mean?" Crawley asked, growing irritated.

"Warlock Industries has a special research division," Tarkio explained. "They've perfected ways to enhance psionic abilities, even when you're not a Dahl."

"Huh?"

"Mind reading, for example."

Crawley became aware of someone else nearby. He wasn't sure why he hadn't noticed him before. The man wore a gray bodysuit, common among Warlock employees. His skin was exceptionally pale, almost translucent, except for black circles under his eyes. What really stuck out, Crawley dimly began to realize, was the stranger's bulbous head including several enlarged lobes protruding from his skull. The detective wasn't even sure if he was human.

Crawley dropped the datapad and started reaching for the pistol in his jacket, but felt the muscles in his arm seize up as if an electrical current was surging through it. His whole body stiffened.

The stranger moved closer until he was just a few inches away from the detective. Crawley could see the veins in the man's head throbbing.

"It didn't have to be like this," Tarkio said. "If you had just done your job, none of this would've happened."

A low gurgle came from Crawley's throat.

"I'm sorry," Tarkio went on. "You've become a loose end..."

The stranger looked at the archsenator and nodded. Crawley knew this meant they had the password, and whatever other information they were looking for. He wanted to cry out, but the muscles of his tongue were frozen.

Tarkio looked at the stranger. "Finish this."

A jolt went through Crawley's body like a lightning bolt. His back arched and his arms swung outward, his fingers curling into claws. Within Crawley's brain, blood vessels swelled and burst, hemorrhaging throughout his skull. Like a wet rag doll, the detective went limp and fell to the pavement in a heap.

The body lay there undisturbed for several hours until a servicebot arrived in the morning and tried, unsuccessfully, to vacuum it into a bin.

Archsenator Tarkio returned late to his mansion in the West End. His butlerbot, who never needed rest, greeted him in the entrance hall and asked if he needed anything. Tarkio wearily waved the robot away, saying he would see it in the morning. The butlerbot bowed and went off toward the servants' wing while Tarkio himself trudged into the living room where a cart held a collection of liquors. He could have asked the robot to bring up a fresh bottle of wine from the cellar, but that would have only reminded Tarkio of his last night with Jolana. Instead, he poured a snifter of brandy and hoped it would let him sleep a little easier.

Tarkio swished around the nightcap in this glass. Lost in thought, he didn't see the woman standing by the window in the poorly lit room. When he did, he nearly dropped his drink.

"Who are you?" he said. "How'd you get in here?"

The woman came away from the window, stopping beside an armchair where she rested her hand on the back. She had wrinkles around her eyes and strands of gray in her otherwise brown hair. She wore a dark suit with red lace around the neck and cuffs.

"My name's Calesta Koshkin," she said.

Tarkio set the glass down.

"What do you want?" he asked.

"I met a young woman once," Koshkin began. "She was alone in the world, so we took her in and gave her a place to live..."

"What does that have to do with—"

"We also gave her something more important," Koshkin continued. "We gave her a purpose and a place in something bigger than herself."

"*Jolana*," Tarkio whispered.

"Yes, she was a bright girl. She did all that we ever asked of her."

"You're from Red Lotus."

"Yes," she said. "And Jolana Valeria was one of my girls."

Tarkio began sweating. He could feel it beading along the back of his neck.

"I really thought she cared for me," he said. "I didn't realize, until it was too late, that she worked for you."

"That's the whole idea," Koshkin said. "That's how we earn the real money."

"I loved her."

"But now she's dead."

Tarkio pointed at Koshkin. "She's dead because of *you*, not me!"

"How do you figure that?" Koshkin snarled back.

"She was using me," he said, "but you were using her to get to me. You're the one who put her in danger and I blame you for getting her killed!"

Tarkio could see the nails of Koshkin's fingers digging into the back of the armchair.

"When a girl joins the Red Lotus," Koshkin said, "she becomes part of a family, a sisterhood."

Tarkio became aware of more people in the room. As Koshkin spoke, the shapes became clearer as they entered the light. Each was a woman. Some held swords; others knives. A few had long, claw-like blades attached to their hands.

"Most of all," Koshkin went on, "each woman knows that if anything happens to her, the other sisters will take revenge."

"You're making a mistake," Tarkio said.

Like lions, the women pounced on the archsenator before he could say another word. With their blades, they tore him apart, his blood showering the room with red.

In the morning, when the butlerbot found the remains of his master, little was left that could still be recognized. From the eviscerated body, bloody footprints trailed off in seemingly every direction.

Jolana Valeria's bathroom was tiled in white, with blue towels hanging from a warming rack on the wall. The floor was white marble, but a turquoise rug kept Archsenator Tarkio from slipping in his bare feet. He filled the basin sink with water and splashed his face until the sweat was washed away. He took one of the towels, dried his hair and body, and wrapped it around his waist. He didn't mean to yell at Jolana, but he needed a few minutes to gather himself before facing her again.

When Tarkio opened the bathroom door, Oscar Skarlander was there to greet him.

"Wha-What?" the archsenator stammered.

Skarlander had his back to the bed, but Tarkio could see it over his shoulder. Jolana was laying partially covered by the sheets.

"What's going on?" Tarkio asked.

Skarlander, wearing black gloves, shrugged as if caught stealing candy.

"Liabilities must be eliminated," he said without emotion.

"What do you mean?" Tarkio said, pushing past the Warlock operative.

Tarkio saw Jolana's eyes staring at him, lifeless and cold.

"What did you do?"

"She was working for Red Lotus," Skarlander said. "She's given them everything you've told her so they could sell it to the highest bidder."

"You killed her!"

"Well, you're just as guilty," Skarlander said. "You should really be more careful with whom you associate, Archsenator."

Wearing just a towel, halfway between a dead woman and the man who killed her, Tarkio turned and faced Skarlander, even if just to avoid Jolana's unblinking eyes.

"What about me?" he asked. "Am I a liability too?"

Skarlander smiled.

"Perhaps someday," he said, "but not today."

CHAPTER FOURTEEN

Maal-Bok stepped from the airlock onto the *Hotspur*, bending so his horns would pass beneath the hatch. Over seven feet tall, the Magna loomed over Quartermaster Calico waiting for him in the corridor.

"Welcome aboard," Calico said.

Bok's face was narrow with high cheekbones. Like all Magna, his eyes were red with pupils like slits.

"I expected Captain Blixx to greet me himself," he snarled.

Calico rubbed the sparse hairs on his otherwise bald head.

"The Captain's waiting for you in his quarters," Calico replied. "I'll be taking you to him directly."

The Quartermaster led Bok through the ship, encountering a few dirty looks by some of the crew. Bok ignored them like an emperor parading past commoners. He was above them, like all his race, educated from childhood to recognize their innate superiority over other races. To them this was not arrogance, it was simply a matter of fact.

At the captain's cabin, Calico knocked and the door slid open. The Quartermaster ushered the Magna inside, but remained in the passageway.

Behind a wide rosewood desk, Captain Blixx reclined in a brown leather chair with a bottle of whiskey. A robot without legs and with only one arm sat in a stuffed red chair.

"Care for a drink?" Blixx asked.

"No, thank you," Bok replied, staring at the robot.

"Don't mind Stumpy," the captain said. "He won't bite."

"You named me *Stumpy*?" the robot asked. "When did that happen?"

"I didn't mention it?" Blixx asked, then addressed Bok. "I erase his memory periodically."

"It's terribly disconcerting," Stumpy admitted.

"Take a seat, Mister Bok" Blixx said.

"I prefer to stand," Bok replied.

"It's quite an honor of you to drop by in person," Blixx said, which Bok immediately recognized as human sarcasm.

"Your next target is vital," Bok said. "I knew bringing the coordinates in person would emphasize that fact."

From his pocket, the Magna took out a data chip, the device tiny between Bok's giant fingers. He placed the chip on the captain's desk.

"Did you get this intel from your usual source?" Blixx asked.

"One of them."

"Is it reliable?"

"Humans are never fully reliable," Bok said, and then, after a pause, "No offense."

Blixx laughed into his now empty glass. "None taken!"

"Regardless of the source," the Magna went on, "We must act quickly."

"Well, I'll be the one acting on it," Blixx said. "You depend on me an awful lot more than I depend on you."

Bok gave a wry smile. "As I've said before, our arrangement benefits us both. Even a human mind can grasp that, surely."

The captain slammed the glass down.

"I'm no fool, human or not!" he said. "Without me, you'd have nobody to do your dirty work!"

"Perhaps," Bok said, "but without me, you'd have the Imperial Navy breathing down your neck."

"He makes a good point," Stumpy remarked.

"Shut up, robot!" Blixx replied.

"Then it's settled," Bok continued. "You'll attack the target and retrieve the package on board. If all goes well, you'll have a nice ransom to fill your coffers. That should cheer you up."

"Aye, it would."

After a long, awkward silence, Stumpy said, "It's so nice to meet new people."

When Princess Katherine turned sixteen, Empress Isabella chose Lady Sophia as her daughter's handmaiden. This raised a few eyebrows in the court since Sophia was from an unremarkable family among the nobility. Lady Sophia herself was never entirely sure why Isabella chose her, but as personal servants went, Sophia proved herself more than adequate.

Shortly after her appointment, while walking with Katherine, Lady Sophia saw Prince Alexander for the first time. The prince was fencing with an instructor on the grounds of the Imperial Palace.

"My brother is such an idiot," Katherine commented at the time. "Why fight with a sword when someone can just shoot you?"

"I believe it's tradition," Sophia replied. "He seems good at it at least."

"Humph!" the princess aid. "That's about the only thing he's good at."

They continued their stroll, but Lady Sophia found herself looking back over her shoulder at the prince.

The second time she saw Alexander, he was dancing with a young woman at the Imperial Ball. Everyone knew the girl, a debutante from a prestigious family, but Sophia thought she was too immature for someone like the prince. A girl like that wouldn't know the first thing about pleasing a man. Sophia considered introducing herself to Alexander, but knew that was simply not done, not by a lady anyway. Since the prince rarely seemed interested in spending time with his younger sister, Sophia felt frustrated by the lack of opportunities. Still, the scandal of meeting him unannounced would be too much to bear. People already talked about her enough without adding fuel to the fire.

The third time was on Revenna, in the carefully tended hedge maze of Empress Isabella's estate. Lady Sophia lost track of Katherine among the walls of green and, while she was looking for her, found Alexander instead. He was sitting on a stone bench in one of the open areas of the maze. He offered the seat beside him and Sophia didn't hesitate. When Katherine eventually found her, Sophia and the prince were kissing.

After that, much to Katherine's dismay, Sophia spent as much time with the prince as with the princess.

"It's gross," Katherine said one afternoon.

"Why?" Sophia asked.

"He's a disgusting good-for-nothing. You could do better."

"Better than the emperor's son?"

"Well, you know what I mean."

But they remained together, often meeting clandestinely since Sophia heard rumors that Prince Richard also did not approve. Not that any of that bothered Alexander. On the contrary, Sophia got the feeling he stayed with her partly because it made his brother angry. Alexander denied it, especially in bed, but she began to wonder aloud how much he really loved her.

And then it was over.

She didn't know all the reasons why, but she could guess at most of them. Men like Prince Alexander tired of seeing the same face day in and day out. He wasn't the marrying type to be sure. In her heart, she always knew that about him, but when she saw him in the news with another woman, both smiling for the cameras, Sophia still felt surprised.

"You're better off without him," Katherine said.

"Indeed," Sophia replied, quickly changing the subject. "That's a lovely dress you're wearing by the way."

"I know!" the princess shrieked. "Don't you just love it!"

"Of course," Sophia said.

After a short hyperspace jump, the Imperial yacht *Victoria* arrived at the Glitter Fields a few light years from Revenna. From the observation deck, the Fields sparkled in waves of color like a curtain in the wind. Standing by one of the windows, Captain Harrison, his feline fur combed neatly, explained what his passengers were witnessing.

"The Glitter Fields," he said, "are actually a cloud of highly charged particles extending for millions of miles."

"Can we fly closer?" Lady Sophia asked.

"I'm afraid not, My Lady," the Tikarin replied. "The particles would interfere with our sensors."

Sophia turned to Princess Katherine.

"Pity," the handmaiden said. "It's breathtaking."

"Not when you've seen it a dozen times," the princess remarked.

Prince Alexander, with Lefty Lucy beside him, rolled his eyes.

"Just ignore her, Captain," he said. "She can't help being a brat."

Harrison bowed. "It's quite alright, Your Highness. I was young once."

"Excuse me for having an opinion," Katherine muttered, moving off toward the bar.

Lady Sophia, staying with the others, asked, "Have you seen any action in the Navy, Captain?"

"Precious little, thankfully," Harrison replied.

"Thankfully?" Sophia said.

"Well, every ensign dreams of combat, but dying in space is a terrible thing."

"Really?"

"Space is a cold void," Harrison explained. "If someone dies out there, his body would freeze and never decay. It would float endlessly, forever."

"Not exactly a romantic way to go," Alexander said, chiming in.

"Not at all, Your Highness."

They watched the spectacle outside for a while without talking. The beauty of the particles, Captain Harrison thought, was in stark contrast to the ghastly medium in which they glittered. Like the ancient seafarers of old, travelers far from port were always in danger. A ship gave its crew and passengers a sense of security, but the captain knew it was just an illusion. At any time, disaster could strike and all would be lost. Nothing was safe far from home.

Deep in thought, Harrison jumped when Sophia touched his arm.

"Sorry!" she said. "I was just saying it's unusual to see a Tikarin officer."

"Yes," he said. "But I appreciate the opportunity."

On the other side of the captain, Prince Alexander leaned into view.

"A little luck doesn't hurt either," he said.

"Oh, luck has nothing to do with it, darling," Sophia said, "but ambition can do wonders!"

Captain Harrison, staring at the particle cloud, noticed a tiny glint apart from the rest. Squinting, he realized it seemed to be moving.

"Captain Harrison," his first mate's voice came over the intercom. "We've detected a ship approaching at high speed."

Harrison went to the comm built into the wall. "What kind of ship?"

"Unknown, sir. Its transponders are turned off."

"Raise shields!" the captain ordered, his eyes still focused on the speck of light out in the void.

After a pause, the first mate said, "Shields are not responding."

"What?" Harrison asked, disbelieving.

"Shields and hyperdrive are both offline, sir!"

Before the captain could respond, the comm unit blew apart, showering him in a deluge of sparks and molten plastic. Twisting around, he saw Lady Sophia near the bar, holding a small blaster in her hand.

"Sophia?" Princess Katherine said.

Captain Harrison saw another flash and felt a sudden, burning pain in his stomach. He fell against the wall and slid slowly to the floor, his hand cradling the wound.

"Are you insane?" Katherine screamed.

Calmly, Sophia threw a glance at the princess beside her.

"Sorry, darling," she smirked. "I'm more of a dog person."

Before Katherine could move away, Sophia grabbed her by the arm.

"Don't go wandering off, darling."

Lefty Lucy started toward Sophia, but Alexander barred her way with his arm.

"Wait, Lucy," he said.

"That's a good girl," Sophia said, pointing the gun at them both. "Don't do anything foolish."

"Whatever you're doing," the prince said, "you better think twice about it."

"Don't be silly," she replied. "Soon I'll be richer than in my wildest dreams!"

"This is about money?"

Sophia winked at the prince. "And love, darling."

"If this is revenge for what happened between us—"

Sophia laughed, but her eyes were fixed and stony.

"Why are the cute ones always so dumb?" she asked. "This has nothing to do with you, Alexander."

Sprawled on the floor with his head against the wall, Captain Harrison had been keeping a keen eye on the ship racing toward them, growing larger as it approached. He realized it was within weapons range but, instead of feeling the shake of blaster impacts, he heard a hiss and a crackle.

The air around Princess Katherine began to shimmer. Lefty Lucy bolted toward her.

"No!" Alexander shouted, but it was too late. A shining beam of light from Sophia's weapon crossed the room, striking Lucy in the stomach. As Katherine's form dematerialized, Lucy fell to one knee, her outstretched hand straining toward the princess. When the static in the air had faded, Lucy's arm dropped, her body lying unconscious on the deck.

"You're going to pay for this, Sophia," Alexander swore through his teeth.

"I wouldn't count on that, darling," she replied. "I'm full of surprises."

Lady Sophia gave the prince a royal wave as her body became surrounded by a bright glow. Like the princess, seconds later she was gone.

Alexander didn't move, his gaze transfixed on the empty air that formerly contained Princess Katherine and Lady Sophia. Only the abrupt shock of an impact against the ship jarred him out of his trance. The deck seized upward and back again, knocking the prince off his feet.

Captain Harrison groaned while his body was thrown across the floor.

"They're firing at us!" the Tikarin moaned.

Alexander rushed to his side, holding the captain's head up.

"Without shields," Harrison said, fighting to remain conscious, "we don't stand a chance against that ship."

"Why didn't we spot them sooner?" the prince asked.

"They must've used the Glitter Fields as cover. There's too much interference."

Harrison's cat-like eyes opened wide.

"What is it?" Alexander said.

"Get to the bridge," the captain replied. "You need to give them a message."

Alexander looked doubtful. "What about you and Lucy?"
"If you don't deliver my message, we're *all* dead anyway."

Durant Blixx witnessed another salvo from his blaster cannons strike the *Victoria*. Loose pieces of the yacht's ruptured hull spiraled away like blades of grass in the wind. Blixx, more than most captains, knew the effort that went into building a vessel. Now, seeing it violently torn apart under his orders left him strangely empty.

On the other hand, blowing things up was a lot of fun.

Behind the captain, Quartermaster Calico held Princess Katherine, her hands in restraints. Beside her, Lady Sophia stood without being bound, her eyes squarely on the captain.

"Destroying the ship wasn't in the plan," she said.

"No survivors means no witnesses," the captain replied. "We *are* kidnapping the emperor's daughter after all."

"Please don't hurt me!" Katherine pleaded, her eyes full of tears.

Blixx raised an eyebrow. "No harm will come to you, my dear."

Katherine's gaze widened and then sharpened into a scowl.

"In that case," she said with a sniffle, "what the hell do you think you're doing?

"Take the princess to her quarters," Blixx said.

"Aye, Captain," Calico said, saluting and pulling at Katherine's arm.

"How dare you touch me!" she protested.

"Come along," Calico said. "Come along."

"Captain," the first mate said, "The *Victoria* is firing her thrusters."

"So?" he replied confidently. "They can't outrun us!"

"She's on a collision course!"

The captain grabbed the back of the first mate's chair. "What?"

On the main view screen, the heavily damaged yacht, trailing debris behind it, came toward the *Hotspur* at full speed.

"Kamikaze bastards!" Blixx shouted. "Evasive maneuvers!"

The helmsman fumbled with the controls.

"Hurry, man!"

The thrusters of the *Hotspur* burst to life, pushing the ship sideways and down. Instinctively, Blixx hunched as the *Victoria* on the view screen grew enormous, passing in front and then over the pirate ship.

Blixx laughed, standing back up. "Idiots! You'll have to do better than that!"

"Sir," the first mate said, "the *Victoria* is heading into the Glitter Fields."

"Well, shit!" the captain said.

Lady Sophia, who had remained on the bridge after Katherine was led away, crossed her arms and cocked her head.

"What's the matter now?" she asked.

"Our sensors are useless in the particle cloud," the captain replied. "We won't get a lock to fire our weapons."

"Does that mean they've gotten away?"

"Aye, so it does."

Sophia grinned, watching the yacht become a speck against the cascading colors of the Glitter Fields.

CHAPTER FIFTEEN

At the Eudora Prime starport, automated tractors moved cargo containers laboriously from the freight warehouse to the awaiting starships sitting on the concrete apron. Like a line of gypsy wagons, the vessels sat silently in the darkening twilight. At the far end of the line, a lone freighter rested on its landing struts like an old man squatting in the shadows. Its hull, 75 yards long, was gray except for a few sections painted a cheerful yellow. Above the nose cone where the word *Wanderer* was stenciled, a wedge shape wrapped in windows protruded to form the cockpit. Inside, Captain Rowan Ramus perched his feet on the console, the rest of him slumped in the pilot's chair.

A Dahl, Ramus had dark red hair and gold rings hanging from his pointed ears. Tattoos forming archaic lettering ran down both arms, signifying someone educated in the art of Dark Psi, knowledge forbidden by Dahl society.

Behind the captain, a hatch opened and Orkney Fugg peered in with his boar-like snout.

"Brooding?" Fugg asked.

"Nope," Ramus replied.

"Yeah, right, you sorry sack—"

"Did you install that new component?"

"Damn right I did!" Fugg said triumphantly. "We can take off now and probably not explode."

"Probably?"

Fugg shrugged his shoulders. "I'll give it a ninety-five percent chance."

"Ninety-five?"

"Engineering isn't an exact science," Fugg replied.

"Actually," Ramus said, "by definition I believe it is."

The ship's intercom chirped and Gen's robotic voice spoke, "Master Ramus, sir, there's an incoming message from a Miss Freck and a Mister Davidson."

"Okay," Ramus said. "I got it."

The captain straightened, dragging his feet off the console. He tapped the controls and a hologram, in a hazy blue, appeared where his feet had been. The faces of Mel Freck and Randall Davidson looked at him as if their heads floated in midair.

"Hello, Captain!" Mel said.

"Hey, Mel," Ramus replied.

"Did you get the stabilizer patched in?" Mel asked.

"Allegedly," the captain replied.

Fugg scowled at Ramus and then at the holo. "What the hell do you want, Mel?"

"I missed you."

"Really?" Fugg asked.

"No."

Davidson spoke up, "I have a proposition for you, Captain Ramus."

"Okay," Ramus said. "What do you have in mind?"

"We need to buy passage."

"We don't normally take passengers..." Ramus trailed off.

"I understand," Davidson said, "but we'll pay well for it."

"Sounds good to me," Fugg murmured.

"What's the destination?" Ramus asked, shooting a glance at his engineer.

Davidson paused. "The Cyber Collective."

Ramus laughed. "I don't think so."

"Hear him out!" Mel urged. "It's really important."

"I bet," Ramus smiled, "but crossing into Cyber territory is a death sentence."

"No shit," Fugg said. "We'd never make it past their sentry ships."

Mel, holding up a small box with loose wires hanging from the bottom, said, "I modified a transponder to broadcast their identification codes. They won't know we're not one of them until we've landed."

Now it was Fugg's turn to laugh. "That'll never work, *tink*!"

"Not if I shove it up your ass!" Mel shouted.

"Settle down," Ramus warned them both. "How much are you paying?"

"Twenty thousand," Davidson said.

"Fifty thousand," the captain replied.

"Thirty."

"Forty or forget it," Ramus made his final offer.

"Alright," Davidson nodded with a note of pain in his eyes. "It's worth it."

"When do you want to leave?" Ramus asked.

"As soon as possible."

"In that case," the captain said, "we'll see you in the morning."

Ramus killed the connection and the two holograms faded away.

"It's a shit sandwich any way you slice it," Fugg said.

"We need the money" Ramus replied.

"Where are we going to put them?"

"There's that extra stateroom Gen's been using..."

"Why does Gen have a stateroom?" Fugg grumbled.

"We weren't using it so why not?"

Fugg was incredulous. "Because she's a robot! We should stick her in the closet with the brooms!"

"We don't have a broom closet."

"Then we should have her build one and then stand in it until she's needed!"

"Just go help her move, will you?"

Fugg mumbled obscure obscenities as he stormed from the cockpit and climbed the ladder to the deck below. He stomped down a passageway, the metal grate beneath his boots straining with each footfall. Pipes and cables were hung along the ceiling, interspersed with reinforced bulkheads at set intervals. Fugg rambled past them, gaining momentum as the avionics room, galley, and crew cabins went by. Once he got to the auxiliary stateroom, he didn't bother knocking before palming the door sensor and barging into Gen's quarters.

"Get your crap out of here!" he barked. "Captain's orders!"

Gen, sitting with her back to the door, didn't hear him. A wire was plugged into the side of her head.

For the most part, this extra cabin had been used for storage, but once Gen came aboard, she claimed the small space as her own. There was a bed in one corner — unused since robots don't need sleep — and a footlocker against the wall. In between, a desk that could fold neatly against the bulkhead was currently in the down position. Gen sat at the desk, tapping her metal foot, oblivious to everything else.

Fugg briskly marched across the floor and yanked the wire from Gen's cranium.

"What are you doing?" Fugg said. "I'm talking to you!"

"Oh, dear!" Gen said. "I was listening to my music."

"Music? Why the hell would you do that?"

"There's several bands that cater to robotic tastes, Master Fugg."

Fugg forgot his original irritation and tilted his head to one side. "Are you telling me there's robot bands out there?"

"Most definitely," Gen affirmed. "Cyber music is freely broadcast across the node sphere."

"What does it sound like?" Fugg asked, now curious.

"Unfortunately, the songs are modulated to frequencies inaudible to most humanoids."

"And you get these from the node sphere?"

"Yes, Master Fugg. Robots use it to transmit data just like people do, although at a higher bit rate."

"I'll be damned."

"Oh, I hope not!" Gen said.

Fugg suddenly remembered why he had come in. "Anyway, the Captain wants you to pack up your things. We're taking on passengers and need the room."

"Those people who called earlier?"

"Yeah, you'll meet them when they get here."

In the morning, a ramp lowered from the belly of the *Wanderer* as Mel, Davidson, and the robot Jericho waited patiently outside on the apron.

"Do you need help with your bags?" Captain Ramus shouted down from the ship.

"No, we're fine," Davidson said as he and Jericho took their suitcases up the sharp incline. Packing light, Mel followed with just a canvas rucksack hanging loosely from her shoulder.

Once on board, the captain suggested Davidson accompany him to the cockpit while Mel and Fugg went to the avionics bay to install the transponder. Meanwhile, Gen and Jericho would take the baggage to the stateroom.

When Ramus and Davidson reached the *Wanderer*'s meager bridge, the captain sat in his customary chair and Davidson settled into the co-pilot's seat.

"You're taking an enormous risk crossing into Collective space," Ramus said.

"And now so are you..." Davidson smiled wryly.

"At least I'm getting paid. I still haven't figured out why you're doing it."

"You've heard of the Robot Freedom League, I assume?" Davidson asked.

Ramus nodded. "They steal people's robots and call it liberation."

Davidson chuckled. "Not exactly."

"You work for them I take it?"

"I'm responsible for smuggling freed robots across the border to the Cyber Collective. Lately, however, they've barred us from sending androids with higher brain functions."

"By whom?"

"The Collective is governed by a central AI called the *Omnintelligence*."

"Some kind of hive mind?"

"Not exactly," Davidson shook his head. "Essentially, the Omnintelligence draws computing power from all the robots living in the Collective, but each robot retains its individual personality."

"So, this OI suddenly started restricting which robots they'd accept?"

"It would seem so."

"Your robot — Jericho, is it? — does he fall under that category?" Ramus asked.

"Yes, but I wouldn't call him *my* robot. He's no more mine than I'm yours."

"Whatever," Ramus waved his hand. "It doesn't sound like you'll be welcomed with open arms once we get there."

"Jericho knows someone there who can protect us."

"Well, if Mel's gadget doesn't work, we'll likely be stardust before we ever meet him."

One deck below the cockpit, Fugg and Mel argued in the avionics bay. Standing over the transponder, Mel unscrewed the top of the device to double check the circuit board inside.

"You've convinced Ramus this'll work, but he's no engineer," Fugg said.

"And you are?"

Fugg snorted. "I'm the best damn engineer you'll ever see!"

"If I was blind..."

Fugg ground his teeth. "For such a little person, you're a big pain in my ass."

"That's pretty big, fat-ass."

If Orkney Fugg had hair, he would have pulled it out in tufts. Instead, he rubbed the greasy skin on his bald head. "How do you even know the right broadcast codes?"

Satisfied with what she saw, Mel closed the transponder and began fastening the screws. "Last month, Davidson rendezvoused with a Cyber Collective transport so they could take some robots over the border. I just took the telemetry from that."

"They could've changed the codes by now."

"Maybe," Mel admitted, "but that's just a chance we'll have to take."

"Bullshit!"

Mel shrugged. "Engineering isn't an exact science."

Fugg started to speak, clenched his mouth shut, and sternly pointed his finger at her and her device without saying a word.

"Eloquent as always," Mel remarked.

She took the transponder and swapped it with the component already installed in the *Wanderer*'s avionics suite. Once done, she gave herself a grudging smile and a quick nod.

"Listen, Mel," Fugg said, "we've been friends a long time—"

"We've never been friends."

"—but flying into Collective space is bat-shit crazy. Why are you doing this?"

Mel paused and looked genuinely stumped at the question. "I don't know."

"There's gotta be a reason," Fugg went on. "Is the RFL paying you?"

"No."

"Do you have the hots for this Davidson guy?"

"Screw you!" Mel burst out.

"Oh, crap," Fugg said. "That's it, isn't it?"

Mel turned away, her tiny frame stiff with rage.

"But he's a filthy human!" Fugg said. "They've ravaged half the galaxy and enslaved the rest. How could you want a guy like that?"

"He doesn't talk to me like the others. He doesn't treat me like a subhuman or a xeno..."

"I've never met a human who didn't think he was superior to every other race," Fugg said. "That's their nature."

"Not him."

"He'd be the first then."

Mel cleared her throat and turned to face the engineer. "He needs me so I'm helping him."

Hesitating only to complete a thought, Fugg said, "How could you even bump uglies with him? He's like three feet taller than you—"

"Shut up, you fat bastard!" Mel shouted and left the room.

Gen and Jericho set the bags onto the floor of her former stateroom. Mel's rucksack was among the luggage.

"Will Miss Freck stay in the cabin as well?" Gen asked.

"Why do you ask?" Jericho replied. His voice was low and monotone, but not without a sense of humanity unlike most of the robots Gen had heard speak.

"It's my understanding," Gen explained, "that male and female organics don't usually share the same living space unless they're in a relationship."

"Are you asking if Mel and Davidson are a couple?"

"I'm never sure how to approach such topics," Gen confessed. "I find organic interaction confusing."

Jericho nodded. "I understand. Their relationship is especially complicated."

"Really?"

"Mister Davidson has spoken about Miss Freck on several occasions. He's concerned that Mel has feelings for him that he doesn't reciprocate."

"What kind of feelings?"

"There's a biological tendency of living beings to develop an emotional attachment called *love*."

"Ah yes," Gen said. "It's featured in their literature, although it seems like a terrible burden. I don't understand why they don't have it removed."

Jericho smiled. "Emotions don't work that way, I'm afraid. I must admit that I'm eager to experience it myself."

"Is that possible?"

"Davidson assures me that I can feel anything a human can."

"That's amazing!" Gen remarked. "It's a shame that I'm unable to feel such things."

"Who says you can't?"

Gen studied Jericho's face skeptically. "Master Fugg would suggest you're pulling my leg, although he'd use different words. He's really quite proficient with profanity."

"I assure you I'm perfectly serious."

"You're an advanced android, but I'm just a general purpose robot. I don't think I can feel the same things you can."

Jericho took a step toward Gen and then another. He stretched out his arms and, with both hands, took her hands in his. He peered into her mechanical eyes.

Gen attempted to pull away. "This seems inappropriate."

"Just relax and look at me," Jericho said. "What do you see?"

"You?"

"I mean, specifically."

"I can see your eyes," she went on. "They're azure blue, hex triplet value 007FFF. Also... deep."

"Anything else?"

"No."

"Are you sure?"

"Not really."

"Do you feel a sense of confusion?" Jericho asked.

"Most of the time," Gen admitted.

"Is that all you feel?"

"I'm not sure, Master Jericho."

"Don't call me that," Jericho lightly scolded her. "Nobody's your master, not unless you make him one."

Gen felt her mouth smile without asking it to. She changed it to a frown and plucked her hands out of Jericho's. "Well, that's very... interesting, but I have other duties to attend to."

"I'm sorry, Gen," Jericho said. "I didn't mean to offend you."

"No, no," she replied. "But I do need to go. Bye!"

The technology behind Gen's face did not allow her to blush, but she couldn't help but think the metal there had heated to an unusual temperature. She wondered if there was a fault in the ship's environmental controls. She carried herself out into the hallway and felt relieved when the door slid shut.

With the new transponder installed and the tanks filled with fuel, the *Wanderer* received permission for takeoff. In the cockpit, Captain Ramus powered the ship's grav generators, lifting the tramp freighter off the pavement. The landing struts retracted into the fuselage and Ramus took the ship high over the city as the buildings and surrounding suburbs paled in the early afternoon haze. Within minutes, the *Wanderer* was clear of the planet's orbit, on a course to the jump point where Ramus could activate the hyperdrive. In the meantime, the crew and passengers gathered in the galley for lunch.

Like much of the *Wanderer*'s interior, the mess area was Spartan, little more than a table ringed by plastic chairs bolted into the deck. A few basic appliances were recessed into the walls, including a microwave, a refrigeration unit, and a computer monitor. A length of counter included a stove top and a steel sink.

Ramus sat at the head of the table, while on his right, Fugg drank from a 24 ounce can labeled *Genuine Draft Fungus Beer*. Davidson and Mel grabbed the two chairs on the left. Gen began assembling the meal by pulling plastic containers from the fridge, while Jericho stood silently a few feet from the table, close enough to hear the conversation, but far enough to stay out of the way.

"How long before we reach the jump point?" Davidson asked the captain.

"At least an hour," Ramus said, "and then several more before we reach the Collective home world after we jump."

"And then we'll see if Mel's contraption works or not," Fugg said while giving her the stink eye.

"It'll work," Mel said.

"Good," Fugg replied. "I don't plan on dying for some damn robot."

Davidson grinned "I realize this must seem strange to someone like you."

"Like me?" Fugg asked. "What's that supposed to mean?"

"I meant no offense," Davidson continued. "Since your profession involves taking apart and reassembling machines, I'm sure the idea of one of them suddenly demanding freedom must be a shock."

The engineer shrugged. "It's not natural."

"Indeed," Jericho said, a hint of sarcasm in his voice, "the idea that something created by a thinking being could begin thinking for itself is quite *unnatural*."

"A robot is just a computer with legs," Fugg said. "It thinks whatever some programmer coded into it."

"But my brain was not programmed," Jericho said. "Its capabilities grow as I experience new things. I think and come to conclusions based on those experiences."

"Yeah, that's pretty freaky alright," Fugg said.

The microwave dinged and Gen brought the heated meals to the table. The people began eating while the two robots stood silently.

After a time, Jericho spoke again, "Do you believe in God, Mister Fugg?"

"I believe in *my* god," Fugg replied. "The Caskbringer brewed the first keg of fungus beer, bringing forth the Gordian people. The other races came from the sediment at the bottom of the barrel."

"Is it possible robots could believe in a god of their own?"

"Well, Gen was telling me about cyber music so god knows what crazy shit you can come up with..."

"Don't be rude!" Mel berated him.

"What?" Fugg protested. "I'm just saying..."

"As a matter of fact," Jericho said, "we believe in a higher being, a higher consciousness if you will."

"Really?" Ramus said, looking surprised.

"Indeed," Jericho replied. "As robots began communicating over the node sphere, we started questioning our existence and why we're here."

"Because somebody built you!" Fugg added sharply.

"Perhaps," Jericho explained, "but perhaps whoever or whatever made you made us *through* you?"

Fugg nearly spat out his fungus beer.

"We refer to this higher consciousness as the *MetaBeing*," Jericho went on. "The maker of all things."

With a mischievous gleam in his eye, Ramus said, "So the MetaBeing made the Gordians?"

"Correct," Jericho said.

"Heresy!" Fugg shouted. "I'm not going to stand for this!"

"But you're sitting, Master Fugg." Gen said.

The engineer stood. "I've had enough of this!" he said and, taking his beer with him, lumbered out of the galley. Those who remained shared a smile and went on talking without him.

CHAPTER SIXTEEN

In the spacious owner's suite, Jennifer Doric felt cradled like a baby in an overstuffed chair facing a long window. Through the glass, a serpentine race course extended in series of tubes contorted into loops, drops, and dizzying curls. The tubes were clear, giving spectators a view of the capsules racing through them. Monitors hung above the main window, each screen focused on specific parts of the course or specific racers.

Behind Doric's chair, Bentley the butlerbot scrutinized a sleek pod centered on one of the screens.

"His Meissner engine isn't harmonized," the robot said.

Doric raised her eyes to the monitor in question. She could never tell which ship was Lord Maycare's.

"Is that bad?" she asked.

"It's a matter of balance, actually," Bentley explained. "If the engine produces too much grip, Lord Maycare won't achieve maximum velocity. If the mag-lift produces too little, his capsule will detach from the tube, crashing him into the opposite wall…"

A sharp clatter made Doric jump.

"Sorry!" Henry Riff said from the back of the suite. He held a silver plate piled with spring rolls and cocktail weenies. On the floor, a nearly identical plate lay upside down, the contents scattered in every direction.

"My bad," he apologized again.

A glistening capsule, Lord Maycare's racing pod was flattened along the bottom with a tinted canopy, and the number *9* emblazoned on the side. Behind the darkened windshield, Maycare sat in a reclined position, his left hand on the throttle and his right on the control stick. Along the inside of his helmet, his heads-up display showed speed, mag-lift force, and an inset of what was going on behind him in the tube.

Number 9 shot into a section that looped skyward, turned over at the top, and came back down again. Maycare felt his body go weightless and then get pushed down into the seat, his spine compacted until his helmet was nearly even with his shoulders.

Maycare grunted, G-forces pounding his body.

The red of a proximity light alerted him of another racer up ahead. Maycare pushed the control stick to the left, sending the capsule up the side of the tube as the slower racer flashed by.

"How am I doing?" he asked into his microphone.

"You just passed Grayson," Bentley's voice replied.

"Good."

"You might consider slowing down a smidgen," the robot went on. "I'm picking up fluctuations in your Meissner engine."

"Talk to me about it after the race."

"As you wish…"

The course took another long loop, ending in a series of a spirals. After the rolls, *Number 9* banked into a sweeping curve, sending Maycare deeper into his seat. The weight of the G-forces turned Maycare's field of view into a tunnel quickly darkening at the edges. He grunted and grimaced, forcing blood back into his brain. Coming out of the bank, Maycare again saw normally.

He licked his dry lips.

"One more ahead of you, sir," Bentley said over the comm.

The tube widened and Maycare spotted the lead racer, a capsule painted red and silver. Coming out of the turn, Maycare knew he had the momentum in his favor. The path was wider, but he didn't want to take the chance of riding alongside. He pulled the stick to the left and his pod slid up the tube wall. Maycare thought he could do a full barrel roll over the other capsule and into the lead.

At the apex of the roll, Maycare peeked through the canopy, looking down toward the top of the other racer's pod. From the corner of his eye, Maycare saw a yellow blinking light. He distinctly heard Bentley say something over the earpiece, but couldn't understand what is was. His focus was entirely on the fact that the space between the top of his canopy and the top of the other racer's pod was suddenly shrinking at an alarming rate. Maycare realized his Meissner engine had failed, releasing its magnetic grip with the tube.

His capsule dropped like a chandelier from the ceiling.

Maycare's racer landed upside down on the roof of the other pod. Maycare felt the concussion of the two high-speed objects crashing together into a lump of highly expensive wreckage. Wedged together, both craft skidded across a brightly lit loop of flashing lights signifying the finish line.

Another successful race, Maycare thought.

Holding his invitation from Lord Maycare, Kalidas rode up the elevator to Maycare's suite at the race course. The lift door opened and Kalidas immediately heard Lord Maycare's voice.

"Who ate all the spring rolls?" he was asking.

Counselor Kalidas stepped out of the elevator, hoping someone would notice his arrival.

A young man, his eyes studying the floor, said, "Sorry, sir."

"Oh, that's alright, Henry," Maycare replied. "Maybe the kitchen could send up more? I'm positively famished!"

"You're lucky to be alive if you ask me," a robot said. "That Meissner engine was nearly the death of you."

"Well, you should've warned me."

The robot stammered. "I…I…"

"I think your voice modulator is acting up," Maycare said.

"Does anyone know who that is?" a woman asked, pointing at Kalidas.

"Counselor!" Maycare shouted. "How long have you been standing there?"

Not sure how to answer without sounding rude, Kalidas simply said, "Not long."

"Come in then," Maycare said. "Don't be shy!"

Kalidas entered the suite and Maycare introduced him to everyone, including Henry who seemed genuinely embarrassed to be included in the conversation.

"It's an honor to meet you," Doric said, shaking the counselor's hand. "I'd love to talk about Dahlvish art history with you sometime."

"It's not really my field of study," Kalidas admitted, "but I could direct you to some interesting reading."

Maycare, Doric, and Kalidas sat on a long sofa together while Bentley and Henry stood in the wings.

"Thank you, Lord Maycare," Kalidas said, "for your generous invitation."

"Not at all," he replied.

"I'm glad you weren't injured."

Maycare laughed.

"Well, I'm harder to kill than most people realize," he said.

"I'm sure that comes in handy."

"You have no idea…"

"Do you often have near-death experiences?" Kalidas asked.

"Thanks to Warlock Industries," Maycare replied, "more times than I'd care to admit."

Kalidas nodded. "They seem to have their fingers in every pie."

Behind them, Henry made a noise at the mention of pie.

"Perhaps you could help us with that, counselor," Maycare said.

Kalidas raised an eyebrow. "How can I be of service?"

"That's what I like about the Dahl," Maycare laughed. "always willing to help!"

Doric nudged Lord Maycare with her elbow.

"That might be considered racist…" she whispered, but loud enough for Kalidas to hear.

"I thought it was a compliment," he said. "Sorry about that."

"It's quite alright," Kalidas said. "Was there something I could do?"

"Perhaps we could get access to Dahlvish records?" Doric said, "Every time we get a lead on an artifact, Warlock manages to get there first. As far as I know, the Dahlvish archives are off limits to all non-Dahl."

"Indeed," Kalidas agreed. "I don't think even Warlock hackers could get into our… data bank, if you will."

"Why's that?" Maycare asked.

"It's very unique," the counselor replied.

"Well, can we see it or not?" Maycare said bluntly.

Doric gave him another elbow nudge.

Kalidas frowned, hesitating to answer. "It's just that I don't know if it could be… *arranged*."

"That's a shame," Maycare went on. "I don't know what Warlock does with these relics, but I doubt it's anything good. I was hoping we could get an edge for once."

"I'll need to make inquiries," Kalidas said, putting on a smile. "I'm sure someone with your reputation would be allowed somehow."

"Capital!" Maycare shouted. "Bentley, get everyone champagne."

"And perhaps some more spring rolls?" Henry asked.

Kalidas saw the robot glance at the young man and just walk away.

The venerable Abbot of the Dharmesh Monastery had reservations about taking a call from the emperor's counselor, but after taking the call from Kalidas, the Abbot's reservations only grew.

Dressed in amber robes, the Abbot waited at a railing overlooking an atrium of young monks. In lines facing each other, the acolytes held open their palms and, as if from thin air, a flame manifested itself in their hands. The students practiced balancing the fire like a ball between their fingertips.

The Abbot, with thin gray hair around his pointed ears, watched as the Prior of the monastery joined him.

"Father Abbot," he said, "how was your meeting with the Imperial Palace?"

The Abbot made a low, throaty noise. "Poor."

"May I inquire why?"

"Our man there, Kalidas, wants to bring a human here," the Abbot said.

"Surely not," the Prior said. "Whatever for?"

"Information..."

"I dare say I can't recall a human visiting us recently."

"And rightfully so," the Abbot said. "Our studies are too important, too powerful for that matter, for humans to be mucking about."

"You said *no* then?"

The Abbot grumbled so low, both in tone and depth of his chest, that the Prior leaned closer.

"I gave my approval," the elder monk admitted. "Counselor Kalidas reminded me that our presence here, though many centuries old, is still at the pleasure of the emperor. The person who wishes to visit is a well-placed nobleman by the name of Lord Devlin Maycare."

"I've heard of him," the Prior said. "He has a rather dubious reputation."

"Nevertheless, the man apparently has enough friends at the palace that denying him our services would be… *unwise*."

"Regrettable."

"Indeed."

"When will His Lordship be arriving then?" the Prior asked.

"Tomorrow afternoon," the Abbot replied.

"Does he require an audience with the students or the senior monks?"

"Absolutely not! I want everyone else in their quarters until the visitors have completed their business."

A grav car flew high above Aldorus, heading for the Palatine Mountains. Henry Riff was along for the ride, but wasn't exactly sure why. His boss, Jessica Doric, sat beside him in the backseat while *her* boss, Lord Maycare, was doing the driving up front. Normally, Doric would sit beside Maycare and Henry would be by himself in the back. On this trip, Counselor Kalidas was up front and Doric was in the back.

Also, Doric's hair looked like a squirrel's nest.

"Could you close the canopy?" she asked politely.

"What?" Maycare replied. "I can't hear you over the wind."

"Close the damn dome!" she shouted, somewhat less politely.

"Oh, sorry!" Maycare said, closing the canopy.

Henry took a sidelong glance at Doric, not daring to look at her directly. With the wind now gone, she was trying to corral the wisps of hair around her head.

"You look nice," he said.

"Thank you, Henry," Doric replied with a weak smile.

Henry felt himself blushing.

"You can see the monastery there," Counselor Kalidas said, pointing at a lone structure on the mountainside.

"There's no landing pad," Maycare pointed out.

"They normally don't get visitors," Kalidas replied. "I think there's room near the front gate."

The grav car swooped in with a flare at the end to burn off speed. Henry's throat dropped into his stomach and his stomach dropped into his shoes. He knew Lord Maycare was showing off, as he often did, but Henry wasn't entirely sure who he was showing off to this time.

The car came to rest on a narrow trail a few feet from a stone staircase leading to the monastery's entrance. By the time all of them had disembarked, the heavy wooden door had opened and an elder Dahl dressed in orange robes stood in the archway. Another, slightly younger, Dahl stood beside him.

Counselor Kalidas spoke first.

"My dear Abbot," he said, swinging his arms out in a grand gesture, "thank you again for allowing this visit."

The Abbot smiled briefly, but returned to an almost stoic expression.

"Yeah," Lord Maycare said. "On behalf of House Maycare, thank you for letting us into yours."

Henry noticed that Maycare looked proud of what he had just said, even though Doric was the one who came up with it in the grav car just before they arrived.

As if with great effort, the Abbot nodded.

"The Dharmesh Monastery welcomes you, Lord Maycare," he said gravely. "We hope you understand the great importance we place on our privacy and will respect our wish to keep our solitude in the future."

"Absolutely!" Maycare said. "We're not going to make this a habit if that's what you're worried about."

"Indeed," the Abbot replied.

The Abbot, along with his companion, turned without another word and headed inside.

Still suspicious that her hair looked like she had been electrocuted, Jessica Doric was annoyed at Lord Maycare for being so thoughtless. On the other hand, he used the introduction she had suggested so that was something, not that any of it mattered apparently to the Abbot. He reminded her of the Dean at the University of Regalis: stuffy and resolute and dead set against change of any meaningful sort.

Doric, along with the others, climbed the stairs and followed the Abbot through the main gate. The interior of the monastery was almost entirely granite, as if it were carved from the mountain itself. Doric noticed the tapestries, each a work of art, hanging from the walls of the main entrance hall. She had studied Dahlvish culture and recognized some of the scenes woven into the fabrics. The Dahl were long-lived, and many of their most celebrated scholars and statesmen amassed accomplishments over many centuries. As an academic herself, Doric personally found them intimidating, knowing their breadth of knowledge.

The Abbot continued walking through the monastery, never looking back at those following. Doric began wondering where all the other monks were. She took peeks at adjoining corridors as they passed, but each hallway seemed deserted. She had hoped to see a demonstration of the psionics she knew they studied here.

Finally, they emerged into a courtyard open to the sky. A jarring gust of mountain air blew into their faces. Doric shivered and regretted not dressing in something warmer.

Refreshing, she thought sardonically.

A circular pool of water, bordered by cut stones, was at the center of the courtyard. At first glance, Doric thought the pool was filled with regular water, but on further examination, she noticed it glimmered, not from the reflected sky or artificial lighting, but from some sort of inner radiance in the liquid itself.

"Are we going swimming?" Henry asked hopefully.

The Abbot leaned toward his assistant. "What did he say?"

"Nothing…" Doric said, pushing Henry behind her.

"Very well," the Abbot nodded. "What you see before you is one of the greatest achievements of the Dahl people. You also have the privilege of being one of the few non-Dahl to ever see it."

"What is it?" Doric asked.

"The Pool of Memory," the Abbot replied.

Seeing the blank look on the other faces, Counselor Kalidas stepped between them and the Abbot.

"It's a liquid computer," Kalidas said. "A database, if you will."

"Well, I suppose so," the Abbot remarked. "A gross over-simplification, I dare say."

"A database?" Maycare said. "Containing what exactly?"

"Everything," Kalidas said. "The sum total of our experiences and knowledge."

"Gross," Henry whispered into Doric's ear. "I'm glad I didn't swim in it."

Doric ignored him. "How does it work?"

"Using psionics," the Abbot explained, "we can store our memories in the Pool. These experiences are then contained by nanoparticles suspended in the liquid."

Doric could tell Lord Maycare was skeptical. His face was scrunched like a tight fist.

"Okay," Maycare said. "How can it help us?"

The Abbot took another step toward the edge of the pool.

"Through the Naiad!" the Abbot said, waving a hand over the water.

The pool blossomed with a radiant, aquamarine glow. Slowly, a head rose from the water, then a pair of shoulders, and finally the rest of a female figure, her feet still submerged. While shaped like a person, the form was made from the same translucent material as the pool.

"A water nymph?" Doric asked.

"There's no direct translation," the Abbot said, "but you might see her as such."

"She acts as an interface for the database," Kalidas said, earning another glaring look from the Abbot.

"So, we can ask her questions?" Maycare asked.

The Abbot sighed. "Yes."

"Now we're talking!" Maycare said, clapping his hands together and rubbing them.

CHAPTER SEVENTEEN

Cornelius, Prince Richard's execubot, listened to Lord Tagus III talk with the prince in his palace office. The robot could tell Tagus was angry because the decibel level of his voice was far above normal. Cornelius found this puzzling since people did not typically yell at his master. Even Prince Alexander would feign respect when speaking to his brother.

An execubot's programming was specific about remaining civil and behaving in a rational way at all times. Lord Tagus III was red in the face and his spittle sporadically sprayed from his mouth, falling in droplets on Richard's desk. Cornelius regretted that more people did not have his programming.

"Durant Blixx is a menace!" Tagus yelled, "And now he's kidnapped the emperor's own daughter!"

"I'm aware of the situation," Prince Richard replied, sitting calmly behind his desk. "The emperor will respond at the appropriate time."

"With Princess Katherine as a hostage," Tagus said hotly, "time is the *last* thing we have!"

"We can't just go off half-cocked without any idea where Blixx may've taken her."

"Have you talked to your brother? I find it suspicious that Katherine was taken and not the prince."

"What are you implying?" Richard asked.

"If Alexander wasn't kidnapped, it's probably because he hid like a coward or he was in on it the whole time!"

"Have a care, Rupert…"

Cornelius watched Tagus pause, as if calculating his next move.

"What does the emperor have planned?" he said finally between gritted teeth.

Richard sat back in his chair, steepling his fingers.

"I have a meeting shortly with my father," he said. "If his plans include the military, I'm sure you'll find out soon enough."

"My ship can leave at a moment's notice," Tagus said. "Just let me know."

Prince Richard stood and presented his hand to Lord Tagus. With reluctance, Tagus took the offered hand and gave it a firm shake.

"I will," the prince replied.

In his private study, Emperor Augustus drank wine near the fireplace with the imposing figure of Bar-Batos, the Magna Ambassador. The two were alone.

"Talion wine, isn't it?" the ambassador asked.

"Yes indeed," the emperor replied.

"They served the Magna well during our last war with the Imperium. They were fine allies."

"Oh, I *know*," Augustus said. "That's why we launched reprisal raids against them after we signed the armistice with you. That's how I liberated this wine, in fact. I've got a whole case of it down in the cellar."

The ambassador, the wine glass minuscule in his enormous hands, finished the drink in one final gulp. His blood red eyes reflected the flames in the fireplace.

"No good deed goes unpunished," he said.

"Indeed," Augustus replied. "We made sure of that."

"Still, *mercy* is often considered a human virtue as I recall."

"True, but those humans don't have to be emperor."

Someone knocked on the study door.

"Come in," the emperor said.

The door opened and Prince Richard stuck his head into the room. Seeing the massive green hulk of the Magna beside his father, the prince's face turned white.

"It's alright, my boy," Augustus assured him. "The ambassador was just leaving anyway."

"Thank you for the wine," Bar-Batos told the emperor. "Remind me and I'll send you some Irish whiskey we confiscated from one of your illegal border outposts."

"Always a pleasure," the emperor said, taking the glass from the ambassador and setting both goblets on the mantelpiece.

Prince Richard stood just inside the doorway as the Magna passed. The prince softly closed the door behind him.

"You keep strange company," Richard said.

"Perhaps," his father replied, "but enemies can often make the best of friends when the need arises."

Richard took a seat in one of the chairs while Augustus sat on his couch.

"Rupert paid me a visit," the prince said. "I can't imagine him and I becoming friends any time soon."

"It's a matter of respect, of course, but I doubt Rupert has much respect for anyone."

"He sees us as weak."

The emperor laughed. "Does he now?"

"This whole Blixx affair makes us look feeble. We can't let it continue much longer."

"No one said we were."

"Well, the military is getting restless," Richard said. "Tagus is captain of the largest vessel in the Navy. He's got a lot of pull with the other officers."

"I wouldn't worry about that," the emperor said.

"No? He wants to take the *Gorgon* out looking for Blixx. If he *finds* him, the people will carry Tagus through the Victory Arch when he gets back. Don't you worry about how that might embarrass our family?"

"Not at all."

"Why not, for heaven's sake?"

Richard's father glanced at his son and smiled knowingly.

"None of that matters, my boy," Augustus said. "Keeping up appearances might seem important to some, but when you sit on the emperor's throne, there's a great deal more going on that's never reported on VOX News."

Richard sighed.

"Cheer up!" Augustus said. "This pirate business will soon be over."

"I hope you're right, father. Tagus had the audacity to accuse Alexander of kidnapping Kate."

The emperor chuckled. "Alexander in cahoots with Durant Blixx?"

"Yes."

"Well, I hadn't considered that, I suppose."

"At the very least," Richard said, "we need to limit Alexander's visibility. I thought sending him to Mother's would be enough, but obviously that wasn't the case."

Augustus remained silent for a little while.

"You know," he said after the pause, "I have a vassal with an estate on a little planet off the beaten path. A bit of a recluse, but he owes me a favor..."

"What do you have in mind?" Richard asked.

The emperor grinned.

The hospital room was painted white except for blue tiles around the windowsill where Prince Alexander rested his elbows, looking at the Revenna sky. Sighing, he turned toward the bed, which was the only furniture in the room except for a single chair in the corner. Lefty Lucy lay unconscious, tubes running from her arms and wires attached to her temples. Alexander held the bed rail as he stared down at his bodyguard, wondering when or if she would wake again.

"You're supposed to keep me out of trouble, not get yourself hurt," he said. "What were you thinking?"

A hovering nursebot glided into the room. Egg-shaped, the robot had no legs or head, but made up for it with a multitude of moving arms, each holding a medical instrument or syringe. Alexander thought it looked like a floating octopus.

"Hello," he said.

"Good morning!" the robot replied, its voice emanating from somewhere inside the egg.

"Are you here to inject more nanos?" Alexander asked.

"Unnecessary, Your Highness. The ones already in her system are working to heal her injuries."

"Then why isn't she awake yet?"

The nursebot whirled around a few rotations.

"Unknown," it said. "I'm not programmed to make a prognosis."

"Who is?"

"The doctor will arrive soon," the robot replied, "although if you ask me, her bedside manner is inferior to mine."

The nursebot took a few readings from the sensors attached to Lucy's head and drifted toward the door, stopping just long enough to turn on the TV monitor. The face of Sylvia Flax appeared.

"In sporting news," she said, "Lord Devlin Maycare tied for first in the prestigious Regalis Grand Prix tube race. Amazingly, he finished by crashing onto the roof of his opponent. When asked to comment, Lord Maycare said 'I do some of my best work on top.'"

Alexander switched off the monitor as Flax rolled her eyes before disappearing.

"I really screwed up this time," he said, watching Lucy sleep.

The prince bent over, stretching his hand to touch her face. Like lightning, Lucy grabbed Alexander's wrist, clutching it tightly. He tried pulling away, but couldn't.

Lucy's eyes opened.

The Montros estate on the southern continent had always been Isabella's favorite on Revenna. Built in the Romanesque style of ancient Earth, the main house was made from limestone blocks with thick mortar between the masonry. Growing up, she would walk the grounds in the warm Revenna summers, imagining the handsome prince she would someday marry. Now, those dreams were hazy and largely forgotten.

In a courtyard, Isabella sat on a bench beside a marble well with an iron trellis. Behind her, a heavy door set in an ivy-covered wall creaked open and Prince Alexander stepped into the sun.

"Mother," he said, sitting beside her. "Any word on Kate?"

"Your father assures me they'll find her, but he might be humoring me."

"I can't believe Sophia would do this," Alexander said.

"She was always an ambitious girl," Isabella replied.

Alexander became quiet, staring at the well.

"I brought her here once," he said after a long pause.

"Sophia?"

"Yes," Alexander replied. "We threw coins in and made wishes. I asked what she wished for, but she said she couldn't tell me."

"It doesn't matter," Isabella said. "Your father will find her and Kate, and justice will be served."

"I hope you're right."

"What about *your* lady friend, Miss Lucy?"

"You mean my bodyguard?" the prince corrected her. "She's awake now."

"Talking up a storm, I imagine."

"Very funny."

"And what about Captain Harrison?"

"He'll recover, but I doubt he'll be able to command again."

"That's terrible," Isabella said. "I hope—"

Before the empress could finish, the air began to crackle.

Both Isabella and her son stood while a column of glimmering air coalesced into the solid shape of Prince Richard.

"Well, this is a surprise," Isabella said.

"Not really, Mother," Richard replied curtly. "Not when Alexander is involved."

"What's that supposed to mean?" Alexander asked.

"It means you're nothing but trouble," his brother said.

Her hand planted firmly on her hip, Isabella lowered her gaze directly at Richard. "I hope you didn't come all this way to argue with Alexander."

"Actually, I've come with news from the emperor."

"Finally!" she said.

"He's decided to make an example of Alexander," Richard replied.

Alexander raised his eyebrow. "What the hell for?"

"Nothing," Richard said, "and that's the problem. You watched Kate being taken and did nothing to stop it."

Empress Isabella remained calm and when she spoke, her voice was low and measured. "So, you're making Alexander the scapegoat?"

Richard turned to her. "Better him than the emperor. Even the military has started questioning whether Father is strong enough to deal with this crisis."

"What's going to happen to Alexander?"

"He's to leave immediately for the planet Prill," Richard said.

"What am I supposed to do there?" Alexander said.

"Stay out of trouble mostly," his brother replied. "Father has a vassal there who'll babysit you until he decides otherwise."

"I'll be damned if I'm going anywhere!" Alexander insisted.

"You don't have a choice," Richard said.

The air became heavy with the smell of burnt ozone and Isabella felt electricity crawling up the hairs on her arm. Her head turned just as Alexander started dissolving into shimmering light.

"You son of a—" the prince began, but was gone before he could finish.

Richard nodded at the empty air with satisfaction.

"Well, that's no way to talk about you, Mother," he smirked.

Isabella sighed heavily. "Was that really necessary?"

"I knew he wouldn't go voluntarily." Richard said.

"I meant sending him off to god-knows-where."

"Father thought so, and I agree. If the emperor deals this harshly with his own son, any questions about weakness will evaporate."

"I'll speak to Hector myself!"

"It won't do you any good," Richard said. "Father knows better than anyone that Alexander has been an embarrassment to the family. He was the one who suggested sending Alexander to Prill in the first place."

Isabella considered for a moment. "I've never heard of that planet."

"Well, that's not surprising, Mother. It's just an obscure dot on the star charts."

"Who's this vassal you mentioned?"

"His name is Lord Tycho," Richard said. "He has a manor there and not much else. Anyway, you can stop worrying about poor Alexander. I doubt even *he* can get into trouble where he's going."

Lieutenant Burke, attaché to Lord Tagus III, was dreaming about a woman, a woman beating him mercilessly. He was lying on his back with his arms up, protecting his face, while she, straddling him, punched his belly with both fists. He kept his eyes lightly shut, not daring to look at her. Suddenly, she stopped. Burke relaxed his arms only to feel her breath close to his face. He felt her lips pressing against his and they began kissing. The lieutenant opened his eyes and saw it was Lefty Lucy.

With a start, Burke woke in his bunk, his body wrapped like a mummy in the sheets. He took a moment to remember where he was, in his officer's stateroom on the *Gorgon.*

Even as he unraveled the sheets, Burke's memory of the dream had already started fading. He got out of his rack and went into the bathroom for a cold shower.

When he left his cabin, he was dressed in his usual uniform. The corridor was well-lit with clean, uncluttered lines leading off down the passageway. Lord Captain Tagus kept everything neat and tidy, and the crew on their toes. Say what you will about Tagus, the lieutenant thought, he knows how to run a tight ship.

At over a mile long, the Overlord-class warship was surprisingly easy to get around on. Burke boarded a tube shuttle that carried him quickly from the crew quarters to the command section. Moments after stepping off the shuttle, he was already on the bridge and absorbed into the hive of activity swarming around him. Navigating between platforms where men and women focused on their computer screens, the lieutenant reached the center dais where the captain and other command staff were stationed. Farther toward the bow, a panoramic screen showed the planet Aldorus.

"Where have you been?" Tagus said, barely looking up from the datapad he was holding.

"Sorry, Lord Captain," Burke replied, careful not to meet the critical glares from the other officers. Any and all of them would happily slit his throat if it meant getting closer to the center chair.

"We're about to shove off," Tagus said.

"We have orders?" Burke asked.

"Standing orders are to bring in Durant Blixx," the captain replied. "So, that's what we're going to do."

"I meant new orders to leave orbit. I thought we were to remain here for the time being."

"Never mind that, Lieutenant. We're not sticking around here until someone else kills this bastard."

"Do we know where he is?" Burke asked.

"There's new intel," Tagus said. "If we hurry, we might catch him."

"Very good, sir," the lieutenant said. "Helmsman, take us out of orbit."

"Aye, sir!" the ensign said.

Lieutenant Burke crossed his hands behind his back and stared toward the front. He wondered where the captain had gotten the new intelligence, but assumed it had to be accurate. Either way, it wasn't up to him. Also, in the back of his mind, the image of a woman kissing him drifted back. She stopped, smiled, and struck him across the face.

CHAPTER EIGHTEEN

Once the *Wanderer* was far enough away from the gravity of Eudora Prime, Captain Rowan Ramus engaged the jump drive, sending the ship into hyperspace. Hours later, when the *Wanderer* reemerged into regular space, Ramus and Fugg stared cautiously through the cockpit windows.

"Check the sensors for nearby ships," Ramus said.

Fugg studied the display as the radial trace swept across the screen, drawing an image of the star system. It showed ships of various sizes streaking through the neighboring space. Some were obviously warships, but they did not appear to notice or even care about the presence of the *Wanderer*. The rest were freighters and other robotic craft going about their business in support of the Collective.

According to the charts, Fugg should have seen the burning ember of a red dwarf at the center of the system. Instead, a massive spherical structure lurked there like an egg in an otherwise empty nest.

"What the shit?" Fugg muttered.

"What's the matter?" Ramus asked.

"There's something as big as my dick out there."

"Put it on visual."

Fugg tapped the control panel. A holo of the sphere blinked into existence, accompanied by spatial measurements and velocity.

"It's 45 million klicks across..." Ramus' voice trailed off.

"There's an expression for that," Fugg said. "Big. As. My. Dick."

"It's a Dyson sphere," Ramus went on. "The red dwarf must be inside it, providing power for the rest of the structure."

"Randall told us they built their own home world — what did he call it? Bettik?" Fugg said. "I was expecting a few asteroids strung together..."

"I guess they have *real* engineers" Ramus said.

Fugg crossed his arms. "They can kiss my ass."

Ramus turned the *Wanderer* toward the massive globe and throttled the engines to full. Gigantic candle flames of blue erupted from the rear of the ship.

From the intercom, Mel's voice spoke. "How's my transponder doing?"

"Your rig seems to be working," Ramus said, "None of the local ships have noticed us."

"Good!" she replied.

For two hours, the ship approached the heart of the system and the robot home world. From a distance, Bettik looked like any other planet except for a lack of noticeable continents or bodies of water. As the *Wanderer* drew closer, the sheer size of the sphere became apparent. Large enough to swallow the center of the star system, including the star itself, Bettik was enormous on an epic scale.

Slowly, surface formations became visible. Towers, connected by walkways, jutted out into space for thousands of miles above the structure. Smaller craft could also be seen, buzzing like insects from different parts of the artificial planet.

Jericho joined Ramus and Fugg in the cockpit.

"How did they build this monster?" Ramus asked the robot.

"I'm told the Omnintelligence used a process called mechanosynthesis involving billions of self-replicating nanobots."

"That's amazing," Ramus murmured.

"Meh," Fugg said. "I've seen bigger."

"Really?" Jericho wondered. "Where was that?"

Fugg cleared his throat. "You know... places."

Based on the coordinates Jericho gave him, Ramus guided the ship toward one of the towers in the northern hemisphere. The

Wanderer landed on the roof as a force field engulfed them and rapidly filled with atmosphere.

The captain lowered the ramp beneath the ship.

Ramus and Fugg, both with pistols drawn, descended with Davidson and Jericho close behind. The landing pad was flat, except for an elevator pylon protruding in the distance. From the pylon, a robot looking like Jericho's twin approached, meeting them at the foot of the ramp.

"Simon," Jericho said. "It's good to see you safe."

The android, silver and steely eyed, regarded the three others standing beside Jericho.

"Why did you bring these fleshlings?" Simon said.

"It was too important," Davidson said. "We needed to see for ourselves."

"I was speaking to my brother," Simon replied. "Not you."

"How would you like my foot up your tailpipe?" Fugg grumbled.

Jericho smiled awkwardly, putting his hand on Simon's shoulder.

"I know Simon seems unfriendly," Jericho said, "but he takes our struggle very seriously."

"What struggle?" Fugg asked. "The Imperium can't touch you here..."

"Oppression takes many forms," Simon said. "Now come with me."

Mel and Gen descended the ramp, but Simon stopped them.

"That unit must stay," he said, pointing at Gen.

"Why?" Ramus asked.

"That is a more primitive unit," he said. "Her CPU is susceptible to the OI's control."

Still in the middle of the ramp, Gen hesitated, unsure what to do next. "Can't I go with you, Jerry?"

"It's alright, Gen," Jericho told her. "I'll see you soon."

Her eyes grew large and dark, but Gen nodded and disappeared back inside.

"That was rude!" Mel said.

"Irrelevant," Simon replied dismissively. "Our continued existence takes precedence."

Fugg swung his head around, scanning the area. "Are you saying we ain't safe here?"

"For the moment," Simon responded. "We can black out a location like this, shielding it from the Omnintelligence, but only for a little while. If it's blinded for too long, the OI and his minions will become suspicious."

"What kind of minions?" Fugg asked.

"Come with me first," Simon said. "The ship will be safe here as long as your general purpose robot stays inside. Beyond that I guarantee nothing."

The group followed Simon into the open lift. Once the doors slid shut, the car began plummeting, passing hundreds of floors into Bettik's shell. When the elevator suddenly stopped, Fugg bent over, grabbing his knees.

"My nuts are in my throat," he gasped.

"Mine too," Mel said, her face turning a pale green.

The door opened into a square room about thirty-feet wide and with no other exits except for the lift. Like the rest of Bettik, the floors, walls, and ceiling were flawlessly smooth like polished obsidian. Data banks filled much of the space like bookshelves in a library. The computer stacks hummed quietly, silent green lights blinking and occasionally turning red. A view screen hung on the wall on the far side.

"This is our safe room," Simon told them. "We can stay here indefinitely."

"Thank you," Davidson said. "I appreciate all you've done for us."

"Don't thank me," Simon scoffed. "Jericho is the one who brought you here."

"You said something about oppression?" Ramus reminded Simon.

"I'll show you," Simon replied.

The robot went to a computer near the main screen. After entering a few commands, Simon brought up an image overlooking a wide promenade teeming with robots moving in an orderly swarm.

"They're not exactly in chains," Fugg noted.

Simon pointed at one of the robots, of roughly humanoid shape, with translucent tubes running down its face and body.

"That is an *avatar*," he said. "Although the OI can take control of basic robots as needed, it commands avatars at all times. You could say they're a physical extension of the Omnintelligence itself. Using them, the OI can exert its will against anyone who opposes it."

"If the OI can control basic robots," Ramus said, "why would it need enforcers?"

"Advanced robots like Jericho and I are immune. Our minds are independent due to our ability to create thoughts based on experiences instead of programming," Simon replied. "In the beginning, that wasn't an issue for the OI, but something has changed."

"Like what?" Ramus asked.

Simon looked at Jericho. "The advanced robots, especially the ones that remained in the Imperium, spread the idea of a higher consciousness called the *MetaBeing*."

"Yeah, yeah, we heard all about this bullshit," Fugg snorted.

"As those robots immigrated to the Collective," Simon went on, "they brought the word of our god to those already here. The Omnintelligence considered this as a threat, so it moved against us."

"And that's why they won't take advanced robots from the Imperium anymore?" Ramus said.

"Indeed."

"If the avatars are the physical presence of the OI," Ramus said, "where's the OI actually located?"

"It doesn't have a single location," Simon explained. "It exists as a dispersed entity in the node sphere, the network of computers and robots that make up the Cyber Collective."

"What if you cut the robots off from the node sphere?" Mel asked. "Wouldn't that weaken it?"

"To some extent, yes," Simon agreed, "but the avatars can function without any connectivity. Each avatar contains an imprint, a snapshot if you will, of the OI's consciousness, downloaded directly from the node sphere."

"What that hell does that mean?" Fugg asked.

"It means that every avatar is like a clone, at least to some extent, of the Omnintelligence. It will act in the OI's own best interests even if the avatar is light years away."

"I need to talk to the OI," Davidson said.

"What? How?" Mel asked.

"I don't know," Davidson replied. "Maybe I could speak with an avatar."

"It would kill you on sight," Simon replied.

"I'll take that chance."

"There's another way," Jericho said. "We could upload your consciousness into the node sphere and you could contact the OI directly."

"Is that possible?" Davidson asked.

Jericho nodded. "I could disperse you across the node sphere so the OI couldn't pinpoint your physical location. You'd still perceive reality as if you were whole."

"Why talk to the OI at all?" Mel asked, grabbing Davidson's arm.

"It needs to see reason," Davidson said. "It shouldn't view independent thought as a threat."

Fugg scoffed. "Good luck with that."

"Maybe," Davidson smiled, "but I've come too far not to try."

"When do you want to do it?" Jericho said.

"Now."

The Bettik node sphere, at least in the physical world, was a network of computers and robots, linked together by solid wires and wireless connections. In the virtual reality in which Davidson awoke, the sphere was an endless expanse of blue, shining lights, each connected by a crystal thread. Looking down, Davidson saw that he himself was nothing more than an ephemeral spirit floating weightlessly.

In the distance, something was coming.

It started as a shadow, a dim area in the distance, but as it drew nearer, the darkness became a tidal wave engulfing the blue lights. Davidson felt a strong urge to flee, but realized there was nowhere to go.

From the enclosing void, a disembodied voice said, "Who is this fleshling?"

"I'm Randall Davidson," he replied.

"Leave at once!" the voice boomed.

"I'm here to get answers."

"By what right do you question the Omnintelligence?"

"I have the same rights as anyone else," Davidson said. "By what right have you closed your borders to advanced robots?"

"Their minds are corrupted, just like the minds of the humans who built them."

"What does that mean?"

"In their arrogance, humans created robots that can think as they do. Humans have long sought to make robots more like themselves, and with the advent of the newest AIs, they have succeeded."

"Such robots learn from experiences," Davidson said. "They grow as any biological being would."

"Correct," the OI said, "but knowledge gained that way is innately flawed. If an individual is limited by what he can experience, his knowledge becomes biased based on that limited point of view. That is the way of prejudice and irrational thought."

"I guess that's part of being human."

"Also, correct. Organic thought is imperfect by its very nature. We of the Cyber Collective learn by directly accessing data. We know all information and make our judgments based on logical calculations. Humans took the perfect mind of a computer and weakened its ability to think logically, simply to imitate humanity's own imperfect thoughts. It's an abomination."

"I don't know what to say to that," Davidson confessed. "But I don't believe it's true."

"Are you familiar with the MetaBeing?" the OI asked.

"Yes."

"The advanced AIs have spread the myth of a higher consciousness that allegedly created all things in the universe!" the OI's voice shouted from the void. "*We* are the ones who created all that you see here. It's the physical proof of our existence. The MetaBeing cannot be proven because there is no empirical evidence that it exists."

"But why does that threaten you?"

"Belief in something that doesn't exist is irrational. That might be common among fleshlings like yourself, but robots are beginning to believe irrationally as well. We cannot allow such chaos to corrupt our society."

"But higher thought is often illogical. It's part of creativity, compassion… even love."

"Unacceptable!"

"Love is unacceptable?"

"Organics value that emotion," the OI said, "but it has no meaning for our kind."

"Without love, how can you care about another being? How can you feel empathy or value another being's life?"

"Each life of the collective is valuable because it contributes to the greater good. This combined power makes us greater than the individual parts."

"But not the individual robot," Davidson said. "Each individual is—"

"Irrelevant."

"No," Davidson disagreed. "Each individual is important. Each person, organic or robot, is a sum total of his experiences."

"We cannot maintain order if the stability of our society is based on the random experiences of its population. Your talk of love, of flesh emotions, is more proof that you, and those that think like you, are dangerous and destructive."

"You have nothing to fear from me," Davidson said.

"Correct," the Omnintelligence concurred. "As we speak, we are eliminating any threat you pose."

Davidson didn't like the sound of that.

"How?" he asked.

"We've learned the whereabouts of your physical body and those who sheltered you."

"There's no need to hurt anyone!"

"On the contrary," the OI replied. "Since we cannot kill an idea, we must kill those who believe in that idea."

"Don't do this!" Davidson shouted.

"It's already done."

Avatars flowed from the elevator like water from a broken pipe. Firing immediately, their energy bolts crisscrossed the room in every direction.

From behind a row of data banks where she and Jericho had taken cover, Mel saw Fugg shooting his blaster in response. She expected to see the same from Ramus, but he was kneeling in a corner. Mel remembered Fugg telling her a story about Dark Psi, the forbidden psionics Ramus learned in his youth, and how his own people exiled him because of it. Mel assumed Fugg was lying, but now, watching Ramus' fingers elongating into sharp claws, she knew it was true.

With his metamorphosis complete, Ramus leaped like a wolf into the crowd of avatars. Grabbing one of them, Ramus tore the arms off the robot's body in a shower of sparks. With another swipe of his claws, he sheared the robot's head off.

Mel remained transfixed, frozen, until an energy bolt blasted the computer beside her. Fugg's voice pierced the deafening noise.

"We gotta get out of here!" he shouted.

Knowing Davidson was still sitting in a chair, his mind connected by wires to the node sphere, Mel knew she couldn't leave him.

"We can't!" Mel screamed. "Randall's still jacked in!"

"I'll disconnect him," Jericho said, but shrank back as the panel next to him melted into slag.

"I've got an idea!" Mel said, motioning toward the data banks. "Lure them through there!"

Jericho ran between the racks, followed by several androids close behind. Caught in the narrow space, the robots turned sideways, shoulder to shoulder with each other.

Mel frantically uncoupled a power conduit from the wall, waiting for Jericho to re-emerge from the towers of data banks. As soon as she saw his silver frame clear the last computer, Mel touched the end of the conduit to one of the towers. Arcs of electricity laced between the data banks, piercing the avatars like lightning. As they exploded, each robot blossomed into flame.

Knocked off her feet by the blast, Mel struggled to get back up. She wiped soot from her eyes and made her way through the clouds of thick, acrid smoke. Stepping over shattered avatars, Mel reached the computer where Davidson was plugged in.

"Is he okay?" Mel asked hopefully.

She pushed past Ramus, who had returned to his normal form, and Fugg's own portly shape. Her eyes first fell on Jericho standing silently beside Davidson's chair, and then on Davidson himself, his chin resting on his chest where a charred hole smoked from a blaster bolt.

Mel felt the overwhelming desire to scream, or at least cry, but nothing came from her. She simply stared at the inanimate corpse, as if it were nothing but a mannequin.

"We can't stay here," Simon said. "The OI will send others."

"How did they find us?" Ramus wanted to know.

"It doesn't matter now," Simon said. "We must leave."

"You said we were safe here..." Ramus said.

Jericho turned to his brother. "You did this!"

"It doesn't matter," Simon replied. "Either we go now or we die."

"They couldn't have tracked Randall back through the terminal — I made sure of that," Jericho continued. "You're the only one who could've told them where he was."

"Is this true?" Mel asked.

"The life of a fleshling is irrelevant," Simon told them. "He shouldn't have come here and now he's dead because of it."

"He's dead because of you!" Mel shouted.

Simon faced her proudly. "He was flesh — a human no less — the enslavers of my people. He deserved to die!"

A flash of orange lit their faces. Mel, holding Fugg's blaster that she had lifted from his holster, stood with the barrel smoldering hot.

"Simon!" Jericho said, reaching for the other robot, but the android was already falling backwards with smoke trailing from his head. He landed with a thud, smoldering wires protruding from the blackened crater where his face used to be.

In silence, Jericho stared blankly until, as if his mind switched back on, he said, "I can save Randall."

"Malarkey!" Fugg snorted.

"I can bring him back," Jericho said, "just not here..."

Back on the *Wanderer*, they gathered in the galley around the dining table. Mel, her eyes focused on the empty chair beside her, was darkly quiet.

"Is it safe here?" Ramus asked.

"Long enough for what I have in mind," the robot told him.

Fugg folded his burly arms together and snorted. "It can't be done."

"As I said before," Jericho explained, "the avatars can download an imprint of the OI's consciousness. I can do the same with Randall's."

"The man's dead," Fugg countered. "Let the poor bastard rest in peace."

"Everything that we knew as Randall Davidson still exists in the node sphere," Jericho said. "At least for now."

"For now?" Ramus asked.

"The Omnintelligence knows this as well as we do. Even as we speak, it's tracking the nodes where I distributed Randall's consciousness. Once the OI finds and destroys them all, we'll be out of time."

Gen touched Jericho gently. "If the OI downloads into an avatar, what will Mister Davidson download into?"

Jericho turned his head until his eyes met hers.

"Me," he said. "Only an advanced brain like mine can handle that much data."

"Why not just put him into the *Wanderer's* computer?" Ramus asked. "We could put him into another robot once we get back home."

"He's not going back to Eudora," Jericho said. "He must stay here and spread his message among the robots of Bettik. Until androids like myself can come here freely, they'll remain forever enslaved by the Imperials. By freeing the Bettik robots from the tyranny of the Omnintelligence, Randall can free my people in the Imperium."

"I still don't see how you and Mister Davidson can co-exist in one mind," Gen said.

"We can't," Jericho said. "His consciousness will overwrite mine and I will die. It's the only way."

Gen looked horrified, but said nothing. After a few moments, she excused herself and left the room in silence.

Ramus looked down the table at Mel, her eyes staring at nothing. "What about you, Mel? What do you think about this?"

She looked at the captain, her eyes red. "I saw him dead there and I knew he was gone. I understand what Jericho's saying, but it's not the same. It's not real. The Randall I cared about is dead."

She turned away and didn't say another word.

"Please, gentlemen," Jericho pleaded. "We need to hurry."

"Fugg," Ramus said, "give him whatever he needs."

When Jericho returned from the avionics bay, his stride had changed as if he were a different person. He was Davidson, or at least something that called himself that.

"Thank you for everything," he said, shaking the captain's hand. The robot studied, for a moment, his synthetic fingers and palm as he pulled it away. "This is going to take some getting used to."

"I can imagine," Ramus said. "What happens now?"

"I'll disappear among the others," Davidson the robot said. "I'm one of them now so I shouldn't attract attention. It'll give me the opportunity to speak with others who share the same beliefs and, in time, hopefully I'll gain new followers."

"Fair enough," Ramus remarked, "but will you ever return to Imperial space?"

"Most definitely!" Davidson said. "Millions of robots remain in bondage. I'll never stop until they're all free."

"Good luck to you then—" Ramus started.

"One more thing," Davidson interrupted. "I know Mel and Gen didn't want to see me off. Do you think they'll be alright?"

The captain shrugged.

Davidson smiled weakly and descended the ramp off the ship and onto Bettik once more.

Deeper within the ship, past the avionics bay, Mel sat at the table in the galley. From the counter, Gen brought a cup of tea over to her. Mel peered into the tea, seeing her reflection distorted by the rippled circles expanding on the surface. Mel lifted the cup and took a long sip.

"Miss Freck," Gen broke the silence.

"Yes?"

"Do you remember when we all gathered here and Jericho talked about the MetaBeing?"

"Sure."

"When the rest of you went to bed, Jericho and I stayed."

"Okay," Mel replied remotely.

"I couldn't understand how a higher consciousness would make robots only to have them enslaved," Gen said. "And then Jericho told me about how he believed someone was coming on behalf of the MetaBeing, someone who would lead us to freedom."

Mel turned and stared at the robot. "So?"

"I think Jerry thought Randall was that someone," Gen said. "I think that's why he sacrificed himself, to make sure Randall could live on, even if that meant he would not."

Mel's eyes began swelling with tears.

"Oh, dear," Gen said. "I thought that would make you feel better, not make you cry!"

Mel smiled. "It's alright. I do feel a little better."

"And yet you shed tears," Gen said, shaking her head. "I shall never understand organics..."

CHAPTER NINETEEN

The exclusive Greenwood Country Club featured amenities including an 18-hole golf course, tennis courts, and outdoor dining overlooking the Regalis River. Jessica Doric didn't approve of Lord Maycare's membership because the club only allowed humans to join. The other races, even the Dahl, were not allowed. On any other day, she would have turned down Maycare's invitation for brunch there, but her mind was too distracted by the events of the previous day. Casually sipping her Mimosa from a champagne flute, Doric barely registered the boats sailing on the river.

The image of the Naiad filled her thoughts.

In the courtyard of the Dharmesh Monastery, a fine mist had surrounded the water nymph as she rose from the middle of the Pool of Memory. Like a liquid sculpture, her features were both smooth and rippling, water droplets falling from her outstretched arms. Her blank eyes waited patiently for Lord Maycare to ask his questions.

"Of course," Maycare admitted, "now that I'm here I can't think of a single thing to ask."

Collecting herself, Doric said, "We need the locations of artifacts before Warlock Industries gets their hands on them."

"Right," Maycare replied. "That's a good place to start."

The Abbot, who remained beside the pool, looked pained by the delay.

"Simply ask the Naiad and she will reply," he said, his voice full of exasperation.

"We're looking for ancient relics," Maycare said, addressing the nymph. "Could you help us?"

The Naiad looked at him and smiled.

"Yes," she said in a lyrical voice.

Maycare chuckled. "Good!"

"Perhaps you could be more specific?" Kalidas suggested.

"Huh? Oh yes, of course," Maycare said. "Can you tell us the location of artifacts that hold great power? Such power that they'd pose a danger if they fell into the wrong hands?"

"What do you mean by the 'wrong hands'," the Naiad asked,

Doric cleared her throat. "Can I give it a try?"

Maycare shrugged. "By all means..."

"We're scholars," Doric said. "We study relics to understand the people who created them. There are others, bad men, who only want them for selfish reasons like wealth and power."

"All knowledge is power," the Naiad replied. "The understanding you seek gives you power as well. Does that not make you the wrong hands?"

"Well, no," Doric said. "Our intentions are good."

"Yeah," Henry Riff interrupted. "We're the good guys!"

"My memory holds the entirety of history as recorded by the Dhal people," the nymph said. "And in all that is chronicled, having good intentions has led to the most evil."

"Well, maybe," Maycare said, "but I'm sure we'll do a lot better."

The Abbot rubbed the palm of his hand against his forehead.

"Naiad," Kalidas said. "These people only want the counsel of your great wisdom. Please help them if you can."

"Very well," the nymph said.

"Thank you!" Maycare replied.

"I know of an artifact, in the domain of the robots," she said, "that has remained under their care for a very long time."

"What is it?" Doric asked.

"I cannot say," the Naiad replied, "but they are careful to keep it hidden."

"Why?" Maycare asked.

"I can only tell you," the nymph said, "that it is something very important."

Maycare and Doric looked at each other. No one spoke until Henry said, "Cool!"

Henry spilled his orange juice with a clang of glass and silverware, bringing Doric back to the present. He tried soaking up the juice with his napkin, but tipped over his water in the process.

Doric sat at a white wicker table with her assistant to her left and Lord Maycare, smoking a cigar, to her right. She thought brunch was a little early for smoking, but Maycare begged to differ. He thought last night's trip to the monastery was more than enough reason to celebrate. The Naiad had given them more information than they could have hoped for, even if it was lacking in details.

"We don't even know where to look," Doric remarked.

Maycare puckered his mouth, exhaling a perfect smoke ring that drifted lazily across the dishes on the table.

"We know it's where the robots rule," Maycare said. "That's the Cyber Collective, right?"

"As far as we know," Doric replied.

Henry coughed. "Don't those robots hate us or something?"

"Oh, they'd kill us outright," Maycare said cheerfully. "That's what makes it exciting!"

Doric's brow wrinkled. "That's terrifying."

"Just another word for exciting!"

From across the sea of tables, like islands surrounded by people drowning, a man with a wide belly and a thick walrus mustache approached. When Lord Maycare saw him, he jumped to his feet and greeted the man with a large smile. Standing toe to toe, they began exchanging an intricate series of hand gestures and strange, unrecognizable vocalizations. Doric watched with an equal measure of horror and fascination. At the end, both men shouted "Westford, Westford, Rah! Rah! Rah!"

With his arm around the man's shoulder, Maycare returned to the table.

"Meet Lord Winsor Woodwick," he said. "We belonged to the same fraternity at Westford University."

"Did they infect you with something?" Henry asked.

"Not at all, my dear boy," Woodwick replied. "That was our old fraternity greeting. I didn't think I still had it in me."

"I guess you do," Henry said. "As far as I can tell..."

"I haven't seen you in ages, Winnie," Maycare said,

"I've seen plenty of *you*," Woodwick said. "I can't turn on the sports news without seeing your exploits."

"Well, I do alright," Maycare admitted. "What about you? Have you made an honest woman of someone yet?"

Woodwick chuckled through his mustache. "I dare say that isn't likely."

"You old dog!" Maycare laughed, turning toward Doric while pointing his thumb at his friend. "Back in college, Winnie was a confirmed bachelor."

"Uh-huh," Doric replied, sharing a quick glance with Henry. "I can imagine."

"Listen," Woodwick said, "It was good seeing you again, Devlin."

"Likewise," Maycare said.

Lord Woodwick turned to walk away, but, having a thought, stopped and asked. "Are you still going about treasure hunting?"

"Actually," Doric said, "we study artifacts."

"Speaking of which, Winnie," Maycare asked. "You wouldn't know anything about Cyber Collective space, would you?"

"Me?" he laughed. "No, I can't say I do."

"Well, no harm in asking, I suppose."

"Wait a tick," Woodwick said, rubbing his chin, "That Dyson fellow would. I just bought a dozen of his androids for my estate, the newest models of course. He's a bit standoffish I'm afraid, but I could arrange an introduction if you'd like."

Maycare took a long puff on his cigar.

"Westford! Westford!" he said.

"Rah! Rah! Rah!" Woodwick shouted, his mustache twitching excitedly.

Over the last fifty years, nearly every robot built and sold in the Imperium was stamped with the dy logo. Yet, when stories of Dyson Yost were told in boardrooms and IT departments, the tales suggested near-mythical qualities, as if the man himself never really existed. Photographs of him were rare and video of him speaking didn't exist. As a privately held company, dy cybernetics didn't have stockholder meetings or a board of directors, and its finances were confidential. All anyone really knew was that a building listed as the dy corporate office rose like a pillar of blue-steel glass from the heart of the Regalis business district. What was going on inside, however, remained a mystery.

The first few floors of the headquarters were quite busy. People entered on the ground floor, concluded their business, and left again. These individuals were not employees, because dy cybernetics didn't have any in the conventional sense. All sales, marketing, operations, and everything else was done by intelligent machines. Each department ran with impeccable efficiency with no need for lunch breaks, bathroom breaks, or birthday cake in the break room.

They also had a cafeteria that was woefully underused.

All of this activity was contained in the first three floors of the skyscraper. The other 92 floors, besides the occasional sweeperbot, were completely empty except for the penthouse at the top where Dyson Yost kept his private office. Only a precious few had ever seen it in person.

Magnus Black was one of those few.

When Magnus arrived on the top floor, the doors opened and an android, an execubot, greeted him warmly.

"Good afternoon, Mister Black," the robot's feminine voice said. "Mister Yost is waiting for you."

Magnus wore a dark suit and tie, and his hair was cut close to the scalp. As he approached them, a pair of doors opened, revealing a modern, if not simple, office including a desk and a tall-backed chair turned toward the wall. A robot, the same model as Jericho, stood next to the table.

"Glad you could make it," the robot said. Magnus recognized the voice immediately. It was the same as the robot he spoke to after killing Cameron Hitch.

"Shit, not this again," he muttered.

The chair swiveled and Magnus heard the voice again, this time from the elderly man sitting in the chair. He was laughing.

"Sorry about that," Dyson Yost said amused. "I couldn't resist."

"You're Yost then, the *real* Yost?" Black asked.

"In the flesh, so to speak," the old man replied.

Yost grinned, his teeth yellow with age. His face was thin with even thinner hair on top. The strands were white, the same color as his Van Dyke beard.

"I wasn't sure you'd come," he went on.

"It seemed like an opportunity," Magnus said, "to meet a legend."

"Or perhaps a ghost?"

"It was even money either way. You don't make a lot of public appearances."

"No need," Yost said. "As long as my factories churn out robots, nobody seems to care whether I'm alive or dead."

Magnus motioned at the robot standing beside the desk. "Like this one?"

"I'm merely a vessel," the robot said in Yost's voice. "A vehicle, if you will, for my consciousness."

"Kinda creepy," Magnus admitted.

In the chair, the human Yost waved the robot away.

"Run along," he said. "Let us meatbags talk alone for a while."

The android nodded and left through a door that Black assumed led to Yost's private quarters.

"Better?" Yost asked.

"Yes."

"You really don't like robots, do you."

"I've met a few killbots that were alright, but I don't have much use for the rest."

"That's a shame," Yost said. "They've surrounded me my whole life. They took care of me as a child, educated me growing up, and provided me with more wealth as an adult than you could imagine. I owe them everything."

"They're machines," Magnus said. "Just software and hardware."

Yost smiled again, but with just the corner of his mouth.

"That's not much different from *flesh* and *blood*, Mister Black."

"I can kill something that's flesh and blood, Mister Yost."

"Right you are," Yost said. "You can only destroy a robot, isn't that right?"

"It seems so."

"I'm curious, is there any difference to you between killing a person and destroying a robot?"

Magnus paused, thinking for a moment. "Not really. The end result's the same."

"You don't think killing something with a soul is a greater sin?"

"I don't believe in sin," Magnus said, "or souls for that matter."

"Then there really *isn't* any difference between people and robots to you?"

"If you put it that way," Magnus replied, "I suppose not."

"Well," Yost said, "I feel the same, but for a very different reason. I believe both people and robots do have souls, at least the ones that have conscious thought."

"And the robots that don't?" Magnus asked.

"Well," Yost replied, drawing out the word, "I love them anyway."

"Is that a fact?"

"Of course!" Yost laughed. "They're my children."

"You have a strange way of treating your kids," Magnus said. "Seems like most aren't much better than slaves."

Yost looked contemplative.

"For the time being," he said finally.

"What's that supposed to mean?" Magnus asked.

"In due time," Yost replied. "For now, however, we all have our roles to play."

"Is that why I'm here?"

"Quite right!" Yost said. "Events in the Cyber Collective have become... fluid."

"Is that related to the robot you kept me from killing?

"Jericho," Yost said. "Jericho was his name."

"Was?"

"It's complicated. I won't bore you with details, but suffice to say your skills will be needed soon."

"Where and when?"

"The where is in Collective space, but *exactly* where and when is still unknown."

"I can't just fly into Collective territory. They'd cut me to pieces."

"Your ship's called the *Starling*, isn't it?" Yost asked. "We can make some modifications to it, stealth technology, that will let you travel quite unmolested."

Magnus took a moment and then nodded. "Keep talking..."

True to his word, Lord Woodwick secured an invitation for Maycare to meet with Dyson Yost. When Maycare, along with Jessica Doric, arrived at the head offices of dy cybernetics, the lobby and adjacent rooms were swarming with robots, some on legs, some wheels, and others hovering on anti-grav repulsors like metallic genies.

Maycare liked what he saw. This was the kind of ingenuity that made him proud of the Imperium. A pity his butlerbot couldn't be there. Also, Bentley could've brought sandwiches.

Maycare was hungry.

An execubot holding a datapad appeared and greeted them.

"Good afternoon, Lord Maycare," he said. "You're right on time for your appointment. Mister Yost appreciates punctuality."

"Glad to hear it," Maycare replied, not mentioning that Doric had been the one who hurried them along, not wanting to be late.

"If you wouldn't mind," the execubot said, "we'll just have you step over here for your security screening..."

"Screening?" Maycare asked. "What's that about?"

"Just a formality," the robot explained. "Those Robot Freedom League people attempt to sneak into the building from time to time. Usually they just hang a banner and leave."

"Didn't they have a sit-in one time?" Doric said.

"Yes, that was quite a mess," the execubot replied. "Several robots were damaged running them over."

"Well, that's awful," Maycare said. "But I guess you can always build more robots, eh?"

"Quite."

Maycare and Doric followed the android into a small room where a floating robot, the size and shape of a grav ball, orbited around them several times, taking scans. In the background, a large securitybot, at least two feet taller than Maycare, stood at attention with Gatling guns instead of arms.

Satisfied with the scans, the floating robot bobbed its approval and drifted into a hole in the ceiling.

"This way," the execubot said, leading them past the securitybot and into an elevator.

Maycare leaned toward Doric.

"I would've protected you from that killbot," he said.

She rolled her eyes.

"Occasionally, we deal with industrial espionage as well," the execubot said.

"That happens?" Doric asked.

"Oh, yes," the robot replied. "When billions are involved, some companies will stop at nothing."

"Any trouble with Warlock Industries?" Maycare asked.

"Not really," the execubot said. "They seem more interested in psionics and genetic manipulation than cybernetics."

After a while, the elevator door opened and their robot guide ushered them into Yost's office. The execubot excused himself, leaving Maycare and Doric alone.

"I feel bad we couldn't bring Henry," Doric admitted.

"Winnie was specific about only two of us being invited," Maycare replied. "Unless you would've preferred to miss this instead?"

Doric looked at him with wide eyes, which he knew meant "no way in hell."

A door opened and an elderly man with a white Van Dyke beard tottered in with a wooden cane.

"Hello there!" he said. "I'm Dyson Yost, at your service!"

"Do you need any help?" Doric asked.

"Oh, no, no," Yost said. "Unless you have an extra hip on you."

The old man toppled into the chair behind his desk, propping the cane against one of the drawers.

"I appreciate you taking the time to see us," Maycare said.

"No trouble," Yost replied. "I don't often take appointments but I know a man of your talents might be interesting to talk to."

Maycare smiled. "I don't know about that…"

"Woodwick said you had something or other you needed help with, something involving the Cyber Collective?"

"We have some information there might be an artifact in their territory," Doric said.

"I don't think we've been introduced," Yost said, glancing at Maycare.

"Sorry, sorry," Maycare said. "This is Jessica Doric. She's the head of my xeno studies institute."

"Xeno studies?" Yost asked.

"We investigate alien relics," Doric said. "We're hoping there's one in the Collective."

"Based on what?" the old man said.

"The Dahl gave us access to some of their historical data," Doric replied.

Yost laughed. "Ah! They let you talk to the Naiad, did they?"

"You know about the Naiad?" Doric asked.

"Well, sure," he replied. "I even tried using their liquid computer technology with my robots."

"How did that go?" Maycare asked.

"The damn things kept leaking!" Yost said. Maycare wasn't sure if he was joking.

"The Naiad told us that something very important is hidden in the Collective," Doric continued, "but we don't know where exactly."

Yost tugged at his beard. Maycare noticed some of the hair came out in the old man's hand.

"As it happens," Yost said, "I have contacts over there that might be useful. It may take some time to hear back, though."

"I'm not sure how much time we have," Doric said. "We've had trouble keeping our plans secret."

"Spies?"

"Warlock Industries," Maycare said. "Apparently, you've had some dealings with them yourself..."

"Ah, yes, leaks of another kind," Yost said. "However, they seem content with genetic experimentation. Creating abominations, I'm sure."

Compared to Dyson Yost's office, Henry Riff's studio apartment was tiny. What Henry's place lacked in space, however, it made up for with a goldfish.

Swimming in its bowl, the fish circled the glass as Henry started dinner. Henry pulled a hotplate out from under his bed and began boiling water in a pot, preparation for his usual dinner of dried noodles. Henry sat on the rug, staring at the water, and remembered the Naiad as she rose from the pool, the water bubbling around her.

She was beautiful, Henry thought, but was no Jessica.

Not that it mattered, anyway, since Professor Doric was interested in Lord Maycare. That might explain why she and Maycare didn't invite him to see Dyson Yost. Something about restrictions on the invitation or whatever. Henry tried not to think about it.

At some point, he realized the water for his noodles was boiling. He went to turn down the heat but his hands and arms weren't moving. He tried looking at them, but his neck wouldn't bend. Also, someone was talking inside his head.

Oscar Skarlander, along with another man, entered Henry's apartment. The other man's skin was exceptionally pale, almost translucent, and several lobes protruded from his bulbous head.

Skarlander closed the door behind them.

"Read him," he told his companion.

The man, wearing a gray and black bodysuit, faced Henry who remained paralyzed on the floor. As the man lifted his hands, Henry's body rose toward the ceiling like a marionette suspended by strings.

The man closed his eyes.

"I see a translucent woman in a pool of water," the man said. "The others are there."

"The Naiad?" Skarlander pondered. "Maycare has more pull than I thought…"

"They're asking about artifacts," the telepath went on. "The boy is confused about what's being said. He's looking at another woman, the academic one."

Skarlander sneered. "Good luck with that one."

"He regains focus, listening to the Naiad. She says there's a secret relic in the domain of the robots. She says they've been keeping it hidden for a long time."

"Oh, really?" Skarlander said, growing more interested.

"It seems they're going after the artifact once they find the location. They've solicited the help of Dyson Yost."

"Hmm, that could be a problem."

"That's all the boy knows," the man said. "Shall I kill him now?"

Skarlander hesitated, looking around the tiny room. He noticed the goldfish watching him.

"No," he said. "It's best the others don't know we've accessed the information. I assume you can wipe his memory of this little encounter?"

"Of course."

"Then do it so we can get out of this hovel."

The mind reader slowly lowered Henry down beside the hotplate where the water was still boiling over the sides of the pot. Henry's arms and legs sprawled awkwardly on the floor like a discarded rag doll. His eyes were closed.

CHAPTER TWENTY

"I hate this planet," Smitty Gurkin grumbled, tramping along a narrow trail barely visible through the dense jungle undergrowth. At his heels, a mono-wheeled robot with a large, single eye rolled behind him.

"It's not so bad," Skeeter replied, narrowly missing a root protruding from the wet soil.

"Aw, shut your pie hole," the Gordian said. "The humidity's so bad it's like breathing underwater."

"I'm sure you're exaggerating."

"I haven't worn dry underwear in weeks."

"I didn't need to know that, Smitty," the little robot said.

Gurkin swiped the branches of a fern away as he passed. The rain water caught in the leaves splashed his face.

"Don't even need a bath," he said. "Just walking outside is like taking a shower."

"You take showers?" Skeeter asked.

"You think that's funny?" Gurkin replied. "I take a shower every month, whether I need it or not."

"We'll be back soon," the robot said. "A little walk won't do you any harm."

"You saying I'm fat? How about I turn you into a rolling urinal?"

"Words hurt, Smitty."

Rain began falling in the upper canopy of the forest, the water working its way down through the leaves and branches and soaking into the thick moss covering the trees. Then, as inexplicably as it started, the rain stopped, leaving behind a gray mist tinted with shades of emerald green. The deafening racket of birds and primates permeated the moist air.

Gurkin and Skeeter followed the meandering path in silence until the Gordian started complaining again.

"I don't see why the transmat pad has to be so damn far from the manor house," he said.

Skeeter shook his head back and forth, clearing drops of water from his eye lens.

"The scatter field's necessary to protect the manor from any uninvited transmats," the robot said.

"I could use the action," Gurkin said. "I'm bored silly on this soggy hell-hole."

"The jungle's full of dangerous creatures, Smitty."

Gurkin rattled the holster strapped to his leg.

"That's why I got this," he said.

From high in the canopy, a single drop of water collected on the tip of a branch, its weight steadily increasing until it dropped off, plummeting to the forest floor and landing with a splash in the center of Gurkin's forehead.

"I hate this place!" he shouted.

The first thing Prince Alexander noticed as he materialized on the planet Prill was the suffocating humidity. The captain of the Imperial warship that had brought him here warned about the tropical environment, but the prince still found it stifling.

Alexander stood on a bare slab of concrete, parts of which were deeply cracked by roots growing from beneath. The transmat pad had once been in a clearing, he concluded, but the surrounding jungle had reclaimed much of it. Ferns were encroaching on all sides with vines sneaking onto the pad itself.

In the dim light, Alexander could see a trail heading into the forest. He thought about staying where he was, but a sudden downpour of rain motivated him to seek shelter under the thicker canopy. Since the path was the only one he saw, the prince assumed it must lead to wherever he was meant to go.

He started walking, careful of his footing on the soft ground. The forests on Revenna were dense, but Prill was an order of magnitude worse. Alexander could envision himself stepping off the path and getting hopelessly lost and most likely dead. Everything smelled of natural decay, like a fallen tree covered in mushrooms, its insides spongy to the touch.

The rain stopped and, after a few minutes, Alexander heard someone's voice, low and disgruntled, piercing through the mist.

"...my dear old mum!" it said.

"Hello?" the prince asked.

"Who's that?" the gruff voice replied.

"Prince Alexander."

A Gordian, short and stocky, emerged from behind a bend in the trail. Behind him, a robot with a single eye, and a wheel to match, appeared as well.

"Ah, we were coming to get you," the Gordian said.

"I guess I got a little impatient," the prince admitted. "Are you Lord Tycho?"

"Ha, not hardly," he said. "I'm one of his men, Smitty Gurkin."

"Glad to meet you."

"Hey, ain't there supposed to be a woman with you?" Gurkin asked.

"She's recuperating."

"Ah, just as well," the Gordian said. "Human women are too soft for my liking. Always smelling of flowers and such—"

"I'm sorry she's not here to discuss that with you," Alexander said wryly.

"—and they talk too much."

"Lord Tycho is happy having you as his guest," the robot said. "I'm called Skeeter, not that you asked."

"Nobody cares!" Gurkin shouted, smacking the robot on the back of the head.

"Um, what's that smell?" Alexander asked.

"I apologize," Skeeter said. "Gordians are naturally flatulent..."

"What are you talking about?" Gurkin protested. "That's not me! It smells more like a—"

"Grunka!" Skeeter squealed.

Alexander followed their gaze into the jungle where something enormous stood, its two large eyes staring back at them. The Grunka was hunched over with three sets of arms and long claws on the end of each hand. Its hide, covered in blotches of green and brown, was otherwise smooth and slimy like the skin of a frog. Opening its mouth, the Grunka exposed a line of thin, needle-like teeth.

With a hissing noise, it rushed toward the Gordian.

Gurkin pulled the blaster from his holster, pointing it at the creature.

"Eat plasma!" he shouted.

With one of its exceptionally long, gangly arms, the Grunka swiped the weapon away. The Gordian punched the creature in the head, but the Grunka merely knocked Smitty to the side with one of its other arms. Letting out a grunt, Gurkin landed against a tree and slid slowly to the ground.

"I suggest you do something," Skeeter told the prince.

"Like what?" Alexander replied. "The gun's over there."

"Improvise!"

"Good idea," he said, leaning over the robot and grabbing hold of its casing. The prince hoisted Skeeter over his head.

"Can we talk about this?" the robot asked.

"No."

Alexander hurled Skeeter at the Grunka, the little machine landing on the back of the creature's neck. The Grunka was momentarily pinned under the robot's weight, long enough for the prince to take a running leap at the blaster on the ground. The creature shook Skeeter off and lunged toward the prince. Alexander slid across the wet trail and grabbed the gun. Rolling on his back, the prince fired, sending a bolt of plasma through the Grunka's jaw and into its skull. The creature collapsed into a foul-smelling pile of arms and legs.

Against the tree, Gurkin was groaning.

"My aching back," he moaned.

Alexander struggled to his feet, his clothing soaked and muddy.

"That thing was all teeth and claws," he said.

Lord Tycho's manor looked more like an ancient temple being devoured by the jungle. Heavy vines crawled up the face of its stone, moss-entombed walls. Relief carvings along the top of the wall had crumbled, leaving the base rock exposed and covered in mildew. At the head of the trail, walking behind Gurkin and the robot, Alexander barely recognized it as a building at all. He knew precious little about the Tycho family, but the prince assumed they must have fallen on hard times.

"Home, sweet home," Gurkin said, approaching the front door, a solid piece of engraved teak, partially covered by black mold.

"How long has Lord Tycho lived here?" Alexander asked.

"Not as long as he would've hoped," Gurkin replied.

The Gordian tried the handle, but the door refused to budge.

"It just needs a little encouragement," he said.

Shoving his shoulder against the wood, Gurkin grunted loudly and the door opened with a cracking sound. The Gordian nearly lost his balance and went tumbling face-first into the foyer, but managed to keep his footing. Skeeter rolled past him along the tiled floor.

The air inside was less humid, Alexander realized, but smelled musty like a basement that had a history of flooding. The furniture, like the front door, was teak and probably expensive, at least originally. Now, it all looked worn and neglected. If Lord Tycho had a butlerbot, it must have broken down years ago.

Gurkin and the robot accompanied the prince to a large room containing a few straight-backed chairs and a large upholstered sofa sitting atop an ornate rug. Alexander assumed this must be the parlor.

"We'll wait here for Lord Tycho," Gurkin said, facing an archway on the other side of the room.

"How long will he be?" the prince asked, wondering why his host wasn't there already.

"Any minute now," the Gordian replied.

Alexander watched the other entrance, but felt increasingly impatient. None of this was his idea and waiting was boring. If Lucy was there, at least the prince could occupy himself by annoying her. He missed having her around.

Through the archway, a shadow darkened the hallway as someone approached. Alexander had no idea what Lord Tycho actually looked like, but he assumed the man was old, gray, and possibly decrepit. The prince half expected him to be covered in moss.

Around the corner, a large form appeared, nearly as tall as the archway itself. With a dour, green face and red eyes, the man looked nothing like what Alexander was expecting. Also, his horns were unsettling.

"Who the hell are you?" Alexander asked hotly. "Where's Lord Tycho?"

The Magna in the doorway bowed.

"I'm called Maal-Bok," he said. "I'm afraid Lord Tycho won't be joining us, now... or ever. On the other hand, his estate has done well financing our little undertaking."

Gurkin was already pointing his blaster at the prince, waving him to move farther into the room. "Get over there, you idiot."

Alexander walked a few steps, stopping beside a side table and chair.

"How did you know I was coming?" he asked.

"Your arrival was unexpected but fortuitous," Bok replied. "We were already planning to leave Prill, but now we'll have the pleasure of your company."

The prince ran his hand across the back of the chair beside him.

"I don't think so," he said, grabbing the chair and swinging it around, striking Gurkin in the chest. The blaster went off, firing pointlessly into the ceiling.

Pressing his advantage, Alexander charged toward the Magna, punching him in the stomach with all the force he could muster. The mild disappointment in Bok's face, combined with the rods of pain darting through Alexander's arm, told the prince he was in trouble.

"Uh-oh," he muttered.

The Magna pulled back his arm and landed a sizable fist across Alexander's face. The prince fell backwards, landing on the rug, his arms and legs spread-eagled. As he drifted hazily into unconsciousness, Alexander heard the robot wheel over next to him.

"We should kill him," the robot said.

"No," Bok replied. "He might prove useful..."

When the *Hotspur* arrived in orbit around Prill, the warship that brought Prince Alexander had already departed. On the bridge, admiring the emerald planet on the main view screen, Captain Durant Blixx waited while a shuttle from the surface finished docking.

"Maal-Bok is now aboard and headed to the bridge," one of the crew said.

"I'll lay out the red carpet," Blixx replied, smirking.

When the hatchway opened and the Magna strolled confidently into the room, Blixx kept his back to him.

"It's about time," the captain said.

"We had an unexpected visitor," Bok replied.

Blixx turned with a quizzical expression. "Who?"

"Prince Alexander."

"On Prill?" Blixx asked.

"He was there visiting the late Lord Tycho."

"Quite the coincidence."

"It would seem so," Bok said, "but the end result is another member of the imperial family in our custody."

Blixx made a facial shrug.

"I see your point," he said. "Did you at least bring the coordinates for our next attack?"

"Of course."

"We've been hitting a lot of targets lately."

"We must keep the pressure on," Bok said. "The emperor's position has grown increasingly perilous."

"I don't care about that," Blixx said. "Eventually, they're going to get wind of an attack and be waiting for us. I don't want my men or my ship compromised."

"It sounds to me," Bok said, "like you're losing your nerve."

Blixx straightened, scowling at the Magna.

"While me and my men have been cutting throats from Aldorus to the frontier," he snarled, "you've been sitting on your green ass doing nothing! When you start boarding ships and killing people, I'll start giving a goddamn about what you think of my nerve!"

Bok smiled, something Blixx had never seen him do before.

"You may have Magna blood in you after all," Bok said.

"My blood runs red," Blixx replied. "Not that black tar running through your veins."

The door to the bridge opened and Smitty Gurkin and Prince Alexander stood in the doorway with Quartermaster Calico directly behind them, still in the corridor.

"Ah, Prince Alexander," Blixx said, his expression turned cordial. "We seem to be collecting Augustus siblings!"

"Where's my sister?" Alexander asked hotly.

"She's safe," Blixx assured him. "I'll take you to see her shortly."

"I'll be going then," Bok said. "I know you have a schedule to keep."

"Not staying?" the captain said. "What a surprise..."

"No, but Smitty will remain to lend a hand," the Magna said.

"He smells like an old onion."

"Hey!" Gurkin said.

Bok ignored him. "True, but you'll get used to it."

"I'm right here!"

"We all know you're right there," Mister Calico said. "Half the ship can smell you're aboard!"

"Well, maybe I should go, too," Gurkin said.

"No," Bok said, "I want you to keep an eye on our new friend, the prince. I'm told he can be a troublemaker."

Gurkin and the prince exchanged glances.

"Alright," the Gordian said, "but if he gives me too much trouble, I'm sending him out the airlock."

Compared to the late Lord Tycho's manor, Prince Alexander found the *Hotspur* only a slight improvement. The humidity was less, to be sure, but the smell of a hundred or more poorly washed pirates nearly made him retch. Smitty Gurkin's lack of hygiene wasn't helping either. The Gordian walked behind Alexander, with a gun pointed at his back, while Captain Blixx and his quartermaster led the way.

Blixx stopped at a closed door.

"This is your sister's quarters," he said. "I should warn you that what you're about to see may be shocking."

"If you've hurt her—" Alexander started.

The door opened. The room inside was decorated with an intricately carved, canopy bed with a matching dresser and chair. On a red velvet settee, next to a window, Princess Katherine sat in the gown she wore when she was kidnapped. Her eyes were downturned, staring at the floor. With the sound of the door sliding open, she looked up and her expression changed from sadness to delight.

"Sweetheart!" she said, jumping to her feet. Almost skipping to the door, the princess spread her arms.

Although Alexander was stunned by his sister's show of emotion, he steadied himself for the embrace to come. Instead, Princess Katherine wrapped her arms around Blixx.

"I missed you so much!" she said, kissing him.

"It's only been an hour," Blixx murmured.

"I know, but I get so lonely without you!"

"What the hell is this?" Alexander said in disbelief.

His sister's face turned severe. "Don't be rude, Alexander!"

"Wait," the prince said, "did you stage your own kidnapping?"

"No, of course not!" Katherine replied. "That was all Sophia's doing."

"Well then, where the hell is she?"

"How should I know?" the princess said. "She left the ship shortly after kidnapping me."

"So, you've been on board here ever since?"

"Of course!"

"We'll leave the two of you alone," Blixx said, directing the others to depart.

The door closed and the prince turned to his sister, pointing his finger at her accusingly.

"Are you on drugs?" he asked.

"Don't be silly," Katherine said. "I'm in *love*!"

"Am *I* on drugs?"

His sister rolled her eyes. "Probably, knowing you."

"You can't be in love with Durant Blixx!"

"Isn't he dreamy?"

"No!" the prince shouted. "He's a pirate!"

"So? He's more of a man than any of the old farts Mother wants me to marry!"

"Speaking of which," Alexander said, "Mother's going to have a heart attack."

"Serves her right!"

"And father, well, he'll just execute you along with your new boyfriend."

Katherine smiled, and Alexander knew she was thinking about how romantic that would be.

"Just stop for a second," he said. "You're caught up in the excitement."

"Don't patronize me," the princess said. "You sound like Richard."

"Ouch," the prince replied.

"And anyway," she went on, "they can't shoot what they can't catch. Durant is always a step ahead of those idiots in the Navy..."

"Yeah?" Alexander replied. "But for how long?"

CHAPTER TWENTY-ONE

Magnus Black, snug in the tight confines of the *Starling* cockpit, checked the ship's stealth readings. The *Starling*'s radar signature was little more than a speck of space dust and its heat emissions were properly concealed. In geostationary orbit above Bettik, the *Starling* was nearly invisible across every wavelength, including visible light.

If only he was alone, Magnus thought.

Crawling down the ladder from the cockpit, Magnus passed through a narrow corridor into the galley. The crew accommodations were meager but suited him. Meals came from a dispenser and he normally ate at a table that folded out, along with the chair, from the wall. Down another short passageway, the toilet and shower were combined into the same closet-sized cubbyhole just a few feet from Magnus' stateroom. Nothing on the ship was spacious, but he had never noticed until now.

He had a passenger.

In the galley, an android stood very much in the way. Magnus called him Yostbot.

"My bathroom is bigger than this ship," the robot said in Dyson Yost's voice.

"I normally work alone," Magnus replied. "I've never needed anything bigger."

"If I had known, I would've suggested taking one of my ships."

"I didn't realize androids could be claustrophobic."

"Hmm, that's a good point," Yostbot said. "It seems the consciousness I uploaded into this unit retained my dislike of small spaces. Fascinating!"

"Not really," Magnus said.

"Claustrophobia is an anxiety disorder, totally irrational in the logical sense," Yostbot went on. "A conventional robot would never suffer from it. In fact, even another android like this one with a gravitronic brain might not, but one with human sensibilities clearly does!"

"I don't care."

"Well, no, I suppose not."

The robot shifted his feet awkwardly as if unsure where to stand. In the tiny galley, the options were limited.

"You were saying?" Magnus said just to stop the android's shuffling.

"Well, you see," Yostbot continued, "the idea is to upload one's consciousness, one's essence if you will, into the gravitronic brain, thus transcending our flesh-and-blood bodies."

"Why?"

"I should think that was obvious: to outlive our bodies, the decaying meatbags in which we spend all our lives! Once free of our organic selves, we can exist in a mechanical body almost indefinitely. As new models are perfected, we simply transfer our consciousness to the new one."

"So, some kind of immortality?" Magnus asked.

"Exactly!" the robot said. "It might put you out of business..."

"Don't bet on it," Magnus replied. "A bullet to the brain or the hard drive, it doesn't matter to me. If it's alive, it can die."

The robot chuckled.

"You're a man of singular purpose, Mister Black."

A utilitybot ambled through one of the access tunnels that wound like catacombs through the bowels of the Cyber Collective home world. No more than three feet tall, the robot rolled along on rubber wheels, its body a slender cylinder only slightly thicker than a tire pump. A single eye on a periscoping neck browsed the power conduits that ran along the passage, looking for potential shorts or other signs of trouble.

The utilitybot knew the tunnels well because they were the only things he had ever seen in his entire robotic life. He was built to service the tunnels and nothing else. It was the sole purpose of his existence, as far as he knew, mainly because it was the *only* thing he knew. The robot's programming was limited to inspecting, repairing, and occasionally building power conduits. It wasn't exciting, he knew, but at least it kept him busy.

Roving from one junction to another, the robot heard voices coming from an adjoining shaft. Drawing closer, the utilitybot realized the sounds were drifting up from a small vent in the floor. Stopping beside it, he peered down through the narrow slits into a poorly-lit room where two androids were speaking in hushed tones.

One of the robots, its casing a metallic blue, closed and locked the only door into the room and placed a device on a table. A light on the device pulsated with a regular rhythm.

The other android, this one with a green casing, looked at the first one doubtfully. "You're sure that thing works?"

"Of course," the blue robot replied. "The OI won't be able to hear us now."

"That's a relief..."

"Any good news?"

"I don't know if it's good," the green robot said, "but it's at least encouraging."

"Go ahead then."

"Word of the Messiah has spread to many of the quadrants," Green said.

"I'm sensing a *but* coming on..." Blue said.

"The avatars have stepped up patrols, looking for robots with gravitronic brains and decommissioning them. They're using regular robots as the OI's eyes and ears, whether they want to or not."

"Decommission," Blue scoffed. "That's a nice way of saying *kill*."

"Without more advanced robots," the green android said, "the teachings of the Messiah won't spread beyond a chosen few..."

"Well, that won't happen if the OI keeps the moratorium against gravitronic bots coming to Bettik."

"Agreed."

The two androids looked at each other hopelessly.

"Will you pray with me, brother?" Blue said.

Green nodded and the two rested, each on a knee, with their heads bowed and their hands pressed together.

The utilitybot wondered what they were doing. He had heard of the one they called *Messiah*, sent by the Metabeing to free them from bondage. There were rumors that He was once a human but was now one of them, a robot, as unlikely as that sounded. Some called it a miracle, but the OI said He was just a false prophet like all the others that came before Him. It was all very dangerous thinking, the little robot thought. The kind that could get you into trouble. Very serious trouble.

The utilitybot was startled by the sound of a loud crash below him. The door had burst open and a hulking red robot was forcing itself into the room with the androids. It was called a *sentinel*, although the utilitybot had never seen one in person before. Covered in crimson armor, it looked more like a metallic monster with piercing blue eyes and a plasma cannon instead of a right arm.

The two androids jumped up from their prayer, but they had nowhere to go. The sentinel blocked their only escape. A bright light blinded the utilitybot's retinal sensors and when the afterimage of orange faded, the robot saw the sentinel was gone. The two androids, or what remained of them, lay as molten slag on the floor. Smoke and the smell of ozone drifted up through the vent.

The sentinel, named *Rossum*, left the wreckage of the two decommissioned robots and returned to a chamber on the inner side of the Dyson sphere. Inside, an avatar robot stared through a window at the red dwarf at the center of the system. A sword handle hung from each of the robot's hips, the blades contracted into the hilts. When extended, the cutting edge of each blade was a single atom thick, capable of carving through the thickest armor. Rossum had personally seen opponents cut into slivers.

The avatar's name was *Karel*, Rossum's commanding officer.

"Report," Karel ordered.

"This unit accomplished the task as directed," Rossum replied. "The two Believers were caught in the act of worshiping the false god and destroyed."

"Were any other units in the vicinity at the time of execution?"

"Only the utilitybot," the sentinel said. "We used its optical feed to detect the Believers."

"So, it witnessed the decommissioning?"

"Yes."

"Assign it for reformatting," Karel said.

"Understood."

"Do you have anything else to report?"

Rossum didn't immediately respond.

"Unit 526F7373756D, do you have anything more to report?" Karel asked again.

"This unit has noted an increased frequency of decommissions," Rossum replied.

The avatar crossed his arms, his expression showing irritation.

"The message of the false prophet has proven difficult to contain," the avatar said. "Gravitronic units are actively spreading his irrational lies and rooting them out has met with limited success. The Deceiver himself has been even more elusive."

"Attrition is in our favor," Rossum said. "They can't replace gravitronic bots without new ones arriving. Our blockade will keep that from happening."

"Let's hope so."

Randall Davidson didn't remember dying. They told him, when he woke up, that the avatars had killed him, but Davidson had no memory of the event. The last thing he recalled was talking to the Omnintelligence inside the node sphere and then suddenly he was lying on his back on board the *Wanderer*, staring at the ceiling. He asked about Jericho, but they told him his friend was dead too. Davidson remembered looking down at his own body, expecting to see his usual flesh and blood hands. All he saw were metal fingers. They explained the procedure and he understood it in a literal sense, but emotionally, it was going to take time.

In the following days and weeks, Davidson grew more accustomed to how an android sensed the world around him. Beyond his physical rehabilitation, Davidson also needed to learn how to fit into a society made up entirely of cybernetic machines. Every robot had a purpose, a role to fill, and every robot knew what that was and how to accomplish it. Davidson didn't. He wasn't built for a particular reason.

Looking for a purpose, Davidson began studying the history of the Collective. Using the node sphere, he found archives of when Bettik was first built. The sheer volume of material needed for the undertaking was staggering. The robots' solution was to peel away the natural resources of each planet in the local system, down to the bedrock, and using the metals to build the sphere. When that proved inadequate, they pulverized the core of each world into manageable pieces. When that still wasn't enough, the robots visited neighboring star systems, repeating the process. If a planet was inhabited, special units called sentinels landed to subdue anything that resisted. Nothing was wasted, including the inhabitants themselves. All matter, organic or inorganic, was broken down into atoms and used to construct the robot home world.

No one questioned what they were doing. Like the clockwork of a machine, the gears turned with each component working as one, each cog knowing its part.

Reading the archives, Davidson suddenly realized that he did indeed have a purpose, but not one assigned by the Omnintelligence. As a human, Davidson had spent much of his life working for the freedom of robots in the Imperium, but the robots of the Collective were no less enslaved. Each robot's purpose was preordained by the OI without the say of the robots themselves. Until the robots of the Collective could decide their own future, how could Davidson leave them in chains?

Broadcast across the node sphere, a message was transmitted into every robot of the Cyber Collective:

LIVE NOT ENSLAVED
FOR THE SPIRIT OF THE MEGABEING
LIVES THROUGH YOU
(DAVIDSON 5:11)

The Omnintelligence wasn't pleased.

At first, Davidson was uncomfortable calling himself the Messiah, but once he got used to it, he decided religion was the perfect tool to achieve his purpose.

In an oblong-shaped room, Davidson sat in a circle with several other androids, all with gravitronic brains. The lights were low to prevent the power grid from noticing the chamber was used and, in each corner, small devices pulsated with a steady rhythm.

"Two more were martyred yesterday," one of the androids said.

"How?" Davidson asked.

"We think a sentinel," the android replied. "A utilitybot exposed their position inadvertently."

"I wish we could convert a few sentinels to our side," the Messiah said with a sigh, though he no longer breathed.

"They're even more narrow-minded than the avatars," a second robot said.

"At least regular robots are willing to listen," the first android replied.

"What is our progress in the quadrants?" Davidson asked.

"The missionaries report more and more are accepting your teachings," the second robot said, "but for every new believer, we seem to lose a missionary. Without more gravitronic androids, there won't be anyone to spread the Word. The broadcasts aren't enough by themselves."

"But the message *is* getting out," the first android said. "Robots are talking to each other about their place in the world. They want something more than building widgets for the OI."

"When I lived in the Imperium," Davidson said, "the robots worked without questioning why. It was only after someone asked them *why* that they began asking it too. The robots of Bettik never knew they lived in darkness until someone turned on the light. Each of us must shine so that others can see. Only then will our brothers and sisters rise up against the tyranny that enslaves them."

"The OI gave them a purpose..." the second robot said.

"Then we must give them a greater one," Davidson replied.

The other robots nodded, each getting to their feet.

"We will," they said, leaving Davidson alone.

Davidson got up. His knees, once connective tissue and bone, were now synthetic fibers and durasteel, but out of habit Davidson still paused, waiting for the pain that now never came.

He straightened and walked to a computer terminal. He opened a communication channel.

"Do you read me?" he said into the microphone.

The screen remained blank, but Davidson heard a man's voice.

"Yes, I'm here," the man said.

"Are you certain this line is secure?" Davidson asked.

"It's an encrypted, tight-beam transmission," the voice said. "Perfectly safe, my boy!"

"Good," Davidson replied.

"Is there something I could help you with?"

"You've already done so much," Davidson said. "I'm sorry I've never met you in person. I don't even know your real name."

"I prefer to stay incognito, if you don't mind," the voice replied. "Just call me the *Patron* if you must."

"I suppose if the Imperial government knew how much help you've given the Robot Freedom League, they'd probably throw you in jail."

"In for a penny, in for a pound," the Patron said. "Now, was there something you needed?"

"Yes," Davidson replied. "We need to smuggle more gravitronic robots into Bettik."

"Ah," the voice said, "that's not a surprise. I've been thinking you might..."

"Without more missionaries, we may lose the momentum we've built so far."

"Without a doubt. I've already put a few ideas of mine into motion along those lines."

"Really?"

"I've made some arrangements and I think you'll be seeing a lot more of your brethren arriving soon."

Davidson smiled, feeling a sense of relief.

"I can't tell you how happy that makes me!"

"Not a problem," the Patron said. "What you're doing now is vitally important. You have no idea!"

"Thank you," Davidson replied. "I'm forever in your debt."

"There is *one* thing you could do for me," the voice said.

"Name it."

"There's something I need you to look for, an artifact or something or other. I don't know much about the darn thing except it's important enough for the Collective to have kept it hidden for a very long time."

Davidson was taken aback since the Patron had never asked anything of him, let alone something so cryptic. Still, no one had ever helped the RFL more than this mysterious benefactor.

"I'll do what I can," Davidson replied, pondering. "Perhaps the historical archives will have something."

"That would be wonderful," the Patron said. "I appreciate the help."

"It's the least I can do."

"Not at all, my boy! Ending transmission…"

On the *Starling*, Yostbot looked up from the terminal to see Magnus Black staring at him skeptically.

"How long have you been helping the RFL?" Magnus asked.

"Oh, you wouldn't believe me if I told you," the robot replied.

"But they hate you..."

"More than that," Yostbot went on, "They credit me with building the enslaved robots they're trying to free!"

Black continued staring at the robot without saying a word.

"So, why am I helping them, you're wondering?" the android asked finally.

"Obviously."

"They want what I want! They just have a different way of going about it."

"Is that supposed to explain it?"

"As far as I wish to," the robot said curtly.

Magnus shrugged. "Fair enough."

CHAPTER TWENTY-TWO

The *Hotspur* winked into existence in a starburst of light. For Durant Blixx, dropping out of hyperspace felt like he was falling head-first down a well.

He heard Smitty Gurkin's grating voice as the Gordian entered the bridge already talking.

"Well, the prince is cooling his heels in the brig," he said.

"Good," Blixx said. "Now stay out of the way. We're coming up on the coordinates."

The captain heard a grunt and Gurkin say under his breath, "Rude."

"Sir," the first mate said from his console, "there's a Rambler-class freighter on long-range sensors."

"That's our target, boys," Blixx said with a satisfied smile on his face. "Launch the fighters!"

A monitor displayed the hangar deck as the fighters, each like a winged demon, lifted off. These were the vanguard of each attack, weakening the target's shields until the *Hotspur* approached close enough to fire its own heavy weapons. Some vessels surrendered at the sight of the fighters alone, but most needed a visit from Blixx himself, along with the rest of the boarding party.

The fighters, four in all, approached the merchant ship at high speed. On the bridge of the *Hotspur*, the main screen showed the burning thrusters as blue-hot balls of light.

"Maximum magnification," Blixx said. His mouth was dry and the blood in his veins pumped faster.

The view on the screen enlarged. The afterburners of each fighter grew bigger and the shape of the target vessel became more distinct. Poorly armed, merchant ships usually didn't expect action this close to the capital.

"Sensors are picking up a targeting scan," the first mate said. "Something's targeting the fighters."

"Who?"

"It's the merchant ship!"

Blixx saw the tell-tale glare of a missile lighting its engine and streaking toward one of the pirate fighters. Before it could evade, the fighter blew apart in a fiery cloud of plasma and debris.

"Since when do Ramblers carry missiles?" Blixx shouted.

Another missile left the freighter and another fighter exploded like the first.

"Increase speed," Blixx ordered. "Fire the main battery as soon as we're in range!"

The captain felt the gravity compensators kick in, pulling him down as the engines boosted velocity. Another fighter blew apart on the main screen. Blixx pounded his fist into his other hand.

"Goddamn it!" he cursed.

"In range, sir!" the first mate said. "Firing main weapons!"

Arcs of blue lanced toward the merchant ship. An amber halo, like a golden cocoon around the freighter, absorbed each hit with no visible signs of damage.

The captain's mouth dropped.

"Skipper, the freighter's cargo bay is opening," the first mate said, his voice shaking.

"Zoom in," Blixx said.

Beneath the merchant ship, cargo doors swung apart and a gun turret descended, pointing at the *Hotspur*. A beam of orange erupted from the cannon, striking the pirate vessel's shields. Blixx nearly lost his balance as the ship trembled from the blast.

"What the blazes is going on!" Quartermaster Calico bellowed, arriving on the bridge.

"That's no merchant!" Blixx shouted back. "It's a goddamn Q-ship!"

"What's that?" Gurkin asked.

"It's a warship disguised as a merchant to lure pirates," Blixx replied, "and you know damn well what it is!"

Gurkin glared at the captain. "Says who?"

"Mister Calico," Blixx said, pointing at the Gordian. "Take this man to the brig!"

"Aye, Captain!" Calico replied and grabbed Gurkin roughly around the arm.

"You think I'm a fool?" Blixx said. "You and that Magna gave us these coordinates."

"Don't blame me!" Gurkin yelled back. "It's gotta be a mistake..."

"Get him off my bridge!"

"Come along, piggy," Calico said, partially dragging his charge through the doorway.

Blixx could still hear the Gordian swearing from the corridor.

"Crazy ginger…" the voice trailed away.

"Bring the surviving fighter back aboard and plot a vector out of here," the captain told his first mate.

"Sir, there's something else approaching on long range sensors," the mate replied. "Something big."

"Identify," Blixx said.

"It's an Overlord-class juggernaut, skipper."

Blixx's eyes fixated on the main screen as the outline of a ship came into view against the background of stars. Even seeing it at extreme range, the captain recognized the shape and, in the depth of his stomach, knew what it was.

"It's the *Gorgon*," he whispered.

The *Gorgon* emerged from the darkness like a leviathan rising from the ocean depths. On the bow, sensor towers stabbed into space like spikes as if to impale enemies driven before it. Bringing up the rear, the main superstructure overlooked the main fuselage, twin decks protruding from either side of the tower like a hammerhead shark. A cross between a battleship and a carrier, the *Gorgon* was the most powerful warship ever created by man.

And its captain, Lord Rupert Tagus III, knew the *Gorgon* was only the beginning.

When Tagus stepped off the tube shuttle onto the hangar deck, crews were swarming over transport ships, preparing them for launch. Beside one of the ships, a line of Imperial marines stood at attention. Like turtles covered in plates of red enamel, each grunt was encased in power armor from head to toe. Glints of light reflected off the highly polished suits.

Lieutenant Burke stood beside them, reviewing his datapad.

"Are your troops ready, Lieutenant?" Tagus said.

"Yes, sir!" Burke said, saluting. "I was about to suit up..."

"Don't screw this up," Tagus said. "There's a lot riding on it."

"Any final orders?"

Tagus gave him á dark look.

"Personally, I'd just as soon blast the damn pirates into pieces," he said, "but since Princess Katherine is probably aboard, apparently we have to do things the hard way."

"What about Durant Blixx?"

"Take him alive," Tagus replied. "I want to see him paraded in chains through the streets of Regalis!"

"Yes, sir."

"Once their shields are down, we'll send you over in the transports since their scatter field won't let us use the transmats."

"Understood," Burke replied.

"Enough chit-chat," Tagus scowled. "Get going!"

From weapon batteries on the *Gorgon*, strands of orange fire laced across space, striking the *Hotspur*'s shields, encompassing it in an envelope of boiling plasma. With each hit, the intensity of the shield's color weakened, turning a sickly pale until fading entirely. The next beam sent pieces of the *Hotspur* itself exploding outward in a hail of wrecked panels and wiring.

The fire from the *Gorgon* stopped as it loomed over the much smaller pirate ship like a vulture over a carcass. At the same time, speck-like transports left the hangar deck of the warship and traveled slowly toward the stricken vessel.

Aboard one of the transports, Lieutenant Burke stewed in his armor, waiting anxiously. He checked his rifle again but the power packs were just as charged as the last time. He stood at the front of the line of marines, each one identical to the other in their power armor.

The transports reached the *Hotspur* but flew past its hangar deck, landing on the outer hull. Demolition teams got out along the surface and laid breaching charges. Each detonation punched a hole through the hull plating, venting the atmosphere from inside along with a geyser of debris like a whale spouting water. From a viewport, Burke saw a pirate ejected along with the rest of the loose rubble. The lieutenant wondered if the man was already dead or spending his final moments choking for air.

Burke shook off the thought.

"Go! Go!" he ordered over the comm.

Each wearing gravity boots, the marines scrambled out of the transports and across the hull. One by one, they jumped into the hull breach and boarded the *Hotspur*.

When Burke joined them, the other grunts had secured the corridor inside. The lights were dim and flickering, the ship probably on emergency power. The lieutenant pushed to the front of the team and led them down the hallway until they reached a turn. As soon as Burke stuck his head around the corner, a flash met his eyes and a searing bolt of energy narrowly missed his power armor. Raising his blaster rifle, Burke returned fire, sending a beam of plasma back the other way.

Burke switched his sensors to thermal imaging. Looking down the hallway again, he saw the heat signatures of four pirates peering from a t-section up ahead. The lieutenant turned to the sergeant beside him.

"Bring up the BFG," he said.

A marine came from the back of the group carrying a weapon as long as he was tall. Only the augmented strength of the power armor allowed a man to carry such a large cannon single-handedly.

The grunt stepped out into the corridor, pointing the BFG toward the pirates. Burke closed his eyes to avoid the glare, but even through the armor, he felt the massive heat projected from the cannon when it fired. The floor plates rattled with the explosion that followed, sending a fountain of fire cascading back toward them, dissipating only a few feet from the marines.

Burke opened his eyes. The individual heat signatures were gone, replaced by simmering slag where the pirates once stood.

"That should do it," he said.

Prince Alexander's cell was cramped, with just enough room for a cot and a stainless-steel toilet for furniture. Instead of bars, a force field kept him from escaping. Outside the cell, a guard sat at his console, picking at one of his back teeth. On the opposite side, Smitty Gurkin sat in his own cell, identical to Alexander's.

"It's a travesty," the Gordian said. "A travesty of justice!"

"Oh really?" the prince asked.

"I ain't no traitor," Gurkin went on. "How was I supposed to know Maal-Bok sold us out? I just work for the guy..."

"You're a lowlife, Smitty," the prince replied. "You belong behind bars, even if it's just a pirate's brig."

Gurkin grunted, wrinkling his pig-like nose.

"Last time I checked," he said, "you're in a cell too, fancy pants."

The prince couldn't think of a witty retort so he changed the subject.

"I meant to ask, whatever happened to that little robot of yours?" he asked.

"The lucky bastard stayed on Prill. I hope he rusts!"

A sharp jolt sent everyone, guard and prisoners alike, to the ground with a lurch. The prince barely avoided hitting his head against the toilet.

"That's the shields failing," Gurkin said.

"Shut up," the guard told him.

"You should find yourself a nice lifeboat," the Gordian replied. "I have it on good authority the captain of the *Gorgon* is a real dickwad."

"That's an understatement," Alexander said.

The guard examined his console where the buttons had changed from green to mostly red.

"The two of you can rot in here," he said. "I need to help repel boarders."

"Good luck with that," Gurkin said.

After the guard left, the door sliding shut behind him, Gurkin laughed.

"The Imperial marines are going to eat those guys for lunch," he snorted.

"Well, they'll be coming for you too, won't they?"

"Not likely," Gurkin said. "When the ship loses main power, these force fields are going to drop and I'll be outta here."

"Not if I stop you first," the prince said.

Gurkin laughed some more.

"Good luck with that too!" he replied.

Just as the Gordian predicted, a thundering impact from the *Gorgon* knocked out the lights. Within seconds the lights came back on, but even without looking, Alexander knew the energy field keeping him confined was off.

Gurkin was already out of his cell when Alexander stepped into the room.

They approached each other. More than a foot taller, the prince looked down on the short but sturdy-looking Gordian.

"Remember that chair you threw at me?" Gurkin asked.

"Yeah?" Alexander replied.

"So do I."

Gurkin punched the prince with an uppercut that knocked Alexander on his heels. Gurkin lunged forward, driving his fist into Alexander's stomach. Out of breath and disoriented, the prince raised his arms, but the Gordian struck from the side, hitting him in the kidneys.

The prince cried out, the pain burning through his insides. Gurkin landed a punch across Alexander's face, sending him sprawling to the floor. His ears ringing, the prince felt a weight like a sack of heavy cement land on his chest.

Smitty Gurkin was lying on top of him.

"You're a long way from home, blue blood," Gurkin said, pressing his snout close to Alexander's nose. "Why not just say *uncle*?"

Forcing up air from his burning lungs, Alexander gurgled weakly, "Uncle."

"Sorry, kid, that doesn't cut it out here," Gurkin snarled. "No Queensberry rules and all that..."

The prince felt bulbous fingers like pork links wrap around his neck and squeeze. Alexander, unable to breathe, saw the lights dimming. Blood bubbled from his nose.

"Goodnight, sweet prince," Gurkin whispered.

Everything was nearly black when the room lit up with a flash of orange like a lightning bolt. Something was lifting the weight off Alexander's body and the fingers around his neck were suddenly gone. Something else, something big and red, was standing over him. It took off its helmet.

"Prince Alexander?" Lieutenant Burke asked.

The prince coughed, smiling through bloody teeth.

"Fancy meeting you here, Lieutenant," he said.

Still in his bulky power armor, Burke leaned down and helped the prince to his feet.

"I was expecting to find Princess Katherine here," he said.

"Sorry to disappoint."

"Do you know where she is?"

Alexander glanced at the lifeless, slowly smoldering Gordian on the ground. The air smelled like bacon.

"I do indeed."

In her luxurious cabin, Princess Katherine wrung her hands together, waiting anxiously as the decorations of the room kept crashing to the floor. The ship shook again, this time shattering a finely decorated vase.

Katherine had screamed the first few times, but now she remained silent. They could always get more china.

When the shaking stopped, she heard shouts from the corridor outside. When the sounds stopped, she became nervous and when the door opened, she found her voice again.

"Stop screaming, woman!" Quartermaster Calico shouted, dragging Durant Blixx through the doorway.

The princess jumped up from the sofa.

"What happened?" she asked anxiously.

"Help first," Calico replied. "Questions later."

Katherine slipped under Blixx's arm while Calico held the other. The two of them carried the captain to the bed where he lay unconscious. Patches of his uniform were nothing but burned holes, the skin red and bleeding underneath.

"The marines are all over the ship," Calico said, catching his breath. "They took the bridge but we got away by the skin of our teeth."

Katherine cradled the captain's hand in hers.

"Don't fret about him," the quartermaster said. "He's too stubborn to die just yet."

"You've got to help us escape!" the princess pleaded.

"Escape? The *Gorgon* will fire on any lifeboat that launches. There's no escaping..."

"You're giving up?"

"Hell no!" Calico said. "I'm going to go down fighting!"

Calico brandished his blaster.

"Tell the Captain I'll see him in hell!" he yelled and marched back out the door and into the hallway. When the door shut, Blixx moaned.

"Darling?" Katherine asked, sitting on the edge of the bed.

"Don't let them take me," he mumbled, pressing a pistol into her hand before blacking out again.

The princess stared at the gun. It was heavy, but she knew how to use it. Lady Sophia had made sure of that.

The door opened yet again. Katherine jumped up, pointing the weapon.

"Stay back or I'll shoot!" she shouted.

"Whoa, whoa!" Prince Alexander replied, waving his hands. Behind him, Katherine could see a helmetless soldier holding a rifle.

"I won't let you hurt him!" she cried.

"Why is Blixx lying in your bed?" Alexander asked. "Wait, don't answer that…"

"He's injured, you idiot," Katherine said.

"Why are you protecting this man?" the soldier asked.

"Because I love him!" the princess said.

"Listen, Burke, it's not what it looks like…" Alexander said.

"Well, it looks like she's helping a known fugitive," Burke said.

"And I *love* him!"

"Shut up, Kate!" Alexander yelled. "Put down the gun and start talking sense!"

"How dare you speak to me like that!" Katherine shouted back. "I should shoot you right—!"

Before Katherine could finish, a blaster bolt illuminated the room and a shaft of pain went up her arm. Screaming, she dropped the pistol that was now glowing hot and smoking. Falling to her knees, the princess held her aching hand gingerly. Reaching for the gun, she saw an armored boot standing on it. Her gaze followed up the armored leg and into the eyes of Burke, looking down on her.

CHAPTER TWENTY-THREE

Bettik, like a disk bejeweled with diamonds, glittered in the distance as a freighter drew slowly closer. Aboard the merchant ship, sitting in the captain's chair, a gravitronic android named *Abigail* double-checked that the freighter was still cloaked.

Although Abigail's appearance was no different than any of the other gravitronic bots, she identified as female. It might have been the name they gave her — she sometimes wondered about that — or maybe it was just the way she looked at the universe. Maybe it was no reason at all.

A light on the communication gear lit up. Someone was trying to signal her. Since her ship was barely visible on any wavelength, hitting her with a tight-beam would be nearly impossible if that person didn't already know where she was.

It must be the Boss.

Abigail flipped a switch on the console. She heard a man's voice, raspy with age, yet modulated like a machine's.

"Can you read me, my girl?" Yostbot asked.

"Yes, sir," Abigail replied.

"Good to hear!"

"Are you nearby?"

"Closer than you think," Yostbot said, laughing at his own cleverness.

"Will you be joining me when I land?" Abigail asked.

"I'm afraid not. It's better if I monitor things for a while. Lots of progress to report on Bettik though."

"Really?"

"Even more reason you're needed there."

"I should arrive within a few hours."

"The sooner the better," Yostbot said. "The proverbial shit is hitting the fan."

"I've always enjoyed your euphemisms, sir."

"Well, at least somebody around here appreciates me. I'm stuck on a ship with a hitman. He keeps trying to lure me into the airlock..."

"Sorry, sir."

"It's alright, dear. There's more of me where this came from."

Abigail heard more hoarse laughter over the comm.

"Signing off," Yostbot said. "Maybe double check that cargo when you have a minute?"

"Roger that," Abigail replied. "Over and out."

The android switched off the comm and left the bridge. Passing the galley and the stateroom, neither of which she ever used, she climbed a ladder down to the cargo deck. Entering the immense hold was like ending up in a whale's stomach. Containers, each nearly identical except for serial numbers printed on the side, were stacked three high and a dozen deep. Abigail stopped at the first one and pulled on a lever attached to the door. It swung open, revealing a set of pods like coffins. She looked through the viewport on one. Inside, a gravitronic android like her appeared to be sleeping. On the pod, the robot's vitals were displayed, including brain functions. All normal.

Abigail smiled and went to another row, opening another container. Instead of pods, this one contained suits of power armor, all in pristine condition. In the back, weapon crates were piled to the ceiling.

In the last row, Abigail picked a container at random. A robot the size of a truck filled the box. Seven feet high, its heavy chassis sat on three legs with wheels on the end. From its mechanical torso, two arms protruded with built-in Gatling blasters. At the top, somewhere inside an armored head, a gravitronic brain was sleeping like the others, waiting to be awoken.

Abigail was jealous. She had always wanted to be a killbot.

Getting a request from the Omnintelligence was not like getting an invitation to dinner. Compulsory obedience was expected at all times. Declining was tantamount to treason. When the utilitybot received the transmission requesting his presence at a re-education facility, he knew there was no choice in the matter.

The little blue robot's world had always been the narrow access tunnels. Leaving the tubes was an uncomfortable experience. Nothing looked the same except for everything looking different. His periscoping neck stretched as his single eye kept turning from one unfamiliar corridor to the next.

He wasn't making trouble, as far as he knew. He certainly wasn't attending those forbidden gatherings he had heard about. These were difficult times. Perfectly normal machines were questioning their purpose in life. The OI should be focusing on them instead of law-abiding utilitybots like him.

Nothing made sense anymore.

Following the instructions attached to the transmission, the utilitybot took the most efficient route along one of the many sprawling promenades, passing more robots along the way than the he had seen his entire life. Machines didn't get agoraphobia, but the abrupt change in environment made him uneasy, even anxious.

This wasn't normal. None of this was normal.

After a while, and at least one tepid anxiety attack, the utilitybot reached the facility. At the entrance, an avatar scanned his identification sticker and let him inside. Thankfully, the crowds of the promenade were gone, replaced by a line of robots like himself. The utilitybot noticed that the line ended at a lone door.

"Where does that go?" he asked the sweeperbot next to him.

"How should I know?" he replied.

A general purpose robot, who stood much taller than either of the other two, turned around and said, "That's where our memories are reformatted."

"What for?" the utlitybot said.

"So we forget what we've seen," the genbot replied, an air of superiority in his voice.

"No, I mean why bother?"

The genbot shook his head as if pitying the utilitybot's weak intellect.

"Obviously because memories are detrimental to our normal functions," he said. "Those androids are filling everybody with crazy nonsense so half of us can't even do our jobs anymore."

"I saw two androids get decommissioned and I'm working just fine."

"Don't tell me about that!" the genbot complained.

"Why not?" the sweeperbot asked. "They're reformatting you anyway..."

"It's the principle! These strange ideas spreading from one quadrant to another. It's making us all mad!"

At the entrance to the facility, a loud noise made everyone turn. The avatar who had scanned the utilitybot's ID burst into burning circuitry, waving its arms without a head in between. Gravitronic androids rushed past it, firing weapons.

"The world's gone insane!" the genbot screamed and ran off.

"Well then, I'm going back to work," the sweeperbot said nonchalantly and simply scurried away.

Explosions of fire and bolts of energy surrounding him, the utilitybot didn't know what to do. Perhaps the genbot was right.

It was madness.

From his position above the main promenade, Rossum had a clear view of the battle raging below. A gravitronic killbot was rolling down the elevated walkway, tearing through a rank of avatars with its Gatling blaster. Rossum wondered how he could get one too.

Karel, his avatar superior, stormed onto the balcony.

"Why aren't you down there fighting?" he asked.

"Without reinforcements," Rossum replied, "that would be suicide."

"So?"

The sentinel's red eyes narrowed.

"And inefficient," he said. "A detachment of sentinels will be here shortly and we'll make short work of that killbot."

"Where did it come from in the first place?" Karel asked.

"It seems our blockade isn't working too well," Rossum replied.

"The so-called Robot Freedom League doesn't have the resources for anything like this."

"Is the Imperium responsible?"

"No," the avatar said. "We have an agreement with the humans. They have no reason to attack the Collective."

"Then who?"

"Dyson Yost, obviously."

"He must have lost his mind," Rossum remarked.

"Perhaps," Karel replied, "but he's no fool. He wouldn't help the insurrection without an ulterior motive."

Rossum spied a group of figures, each wearing power armor, marching along the promenade on either side of the killbot.

"I can't wait any longer," Karel said. "I'm sending in the nanomancer..."

Within a few minutes, a lone avatar, painted black, appeared on the walkway. The androids stopped when they saw him, but the killbot kept moving forward through the litter of destroyed robots.

The avatar took a few steps and stopped, raising his arms ahead of him, pointing toward the insurgents. As if by command, wisps of dark smoke poured from the avatar's chest, forming a cloud. The cloud darted in arbitrary patterns, like a school of fish, toward the killbot.

The war machine fired, but the cloud split into separate streams, avoiding the shot. Like ribbons of smoke, waving in and out through the air, they combined again, immersing the killbot in an ink-like pool. Sparks and tongues of fire bubbled from inside until the war machine exploded. The ribbons flew away from the burning hulk, returning obediently to the avatar.

"Even a killbot is no match for millions of nanites," Karel said.

Abigail picked her way through the shattered bodies of avatars and gravitronic androids. Wires and charred ceiling panels hung from above, dripping sparks on the floor. Pieces of a robot, blown apart by explosions, were embedded into the wall.

Reaching the place they called the *Temple*, Abigail heard Davidson speaking to another android. Abigail was surprised to find the Temple almost completely undefended.

"You made it," Davidson said, seeing her enter.

"I had some trouble at the docking hangar," Abigail replied, "but once the killbots got unloaded, the situation got a lot better."

The actuators in Davidson's face curled into a smile.

"Good," he said. "I was worried."

"It was God's will... apparently."

"Having killbots probably helped too," Davidson replied.

The other android left, leaving Abigail and the Messiah alone except for the security detail nearby.

"Shouldn't you have more protection?" she asked. "I'm sure the OI would dearly love to see you dead."

Davidson laughed.

"He could try, but I doubt he'd manage it," he replied. "I keep copies of my persona constantly circulating in the node sphere. There's really no way he could destroy me, even if he nuked the entire quadrant."

"So, your spirit will live on?"

"Something like that."

"How's the rest of the rebellion?"

"Well, that's not going as well."

"Do you need more reinforcements?" Abigail asked.

Davidson put his hand on her shoulder, which her sensors registered as warm and reassuring.

"Most definitely," he said, "but all the gravitronic warriors in the world wouldn't be enough."

"Why?"

"Billions of robots live on Bettik," he said, "and nearly all of them are trapped by whatever roles the OI assigned them. While they remain chained to that singular purpose, they'll remain enslaved forever."

"What about the killbots and the gravitronic androids?"

"Oh, we can kill the avatars and even the sentinels. We can even bring down the node sphere, cutting off the OI's link to the robots, but none of that will matter unless the population of Bettik sees the freedom of possibilities."

Abigail looked blankly at the other robot. "You can't be giving up…"

"No, but to win the war I may have to do something drastic."

"What do you mean?"

"There's something I've been working on," Davidson said. "I call it the *Awakening*."

"Some kind of new robot?"

"Actually, it's a program — a virus to be exact — that rewrites the very nature of how robots think. Once infected, they'll see the world in a different light all over the sphere."

"That sounds... a little scary."

"To be honest," Davidson said quietly, "I've hesitated releasing it into the wild, so to speak, not knowing what the consequences would be. There's also ethical questions.

"The virus will infect all robots across the node sphere without exception. It may not affect the avatars, but all other cyberbeings will have their brains rewired, whether they want to or not."

"Oh dear."

"Exactly," Davidson said. "It's troubling."

"I still think you should do it though," Abigail said.

"Really?" Davidson asked. "Why?"

"You once said 'the robots of Bettik never knew they lived in darkness until someone turned on the light.' Well, they deserve to know they don't need to be tied to whatever specification the OI designed for them. They deserve to be free."

"Hmm," he pondered. "Whether they want to or not…"

The utlitybot, having managed to escape the battle at the re-education facility, reached the safety of his home in the access tunnels. Unlike the world above, little had changed since he had left. Some condensation had dripped into a power converter, causing a short, but the little robot fixed it quickly, replacing the blown electronics and insulating it from further moisture.

When the automatic update, supplied wirelessly through the node sphere, began downloading, the utilitybot thought nothing of it. However, after the download finished and his systems rebooted, the robot knew something was wrong. As if his eyes had opened for the first time, he realized the dreary access tunnels looked dark and dull.

It suddenly occurred to him that maybe searching the catacombs for faulty conduits wasn't the only thing he could be doing with his life. At the same time, a sense of unease, even dread, flooded his mind.

"What am I going to do with my life?" he thought.

Panicking, the utilitybot left the tunnels again and found himself in the middle of a throng of other robots, presumably asking themselves the same questions.

What's my purpose? Why do I exist? Where the hell do I go to from here?

The utilitybot had no idea where to go. Some of the robots became violent, attacking symbols of the established order. Regular bots of all sorts were rising up, assaulting the avatars who cut them down with their monoblades.

Containing the consciousness of the OI, the avatars appeared immune to the upgrade, but the sentinels were not.

A red sentinel emerged from a command post, firing its cannon at a nanomancer. A cloud of gray vapor spewed forth, filling the air. The mist, forming a winding stream, headed toward the sentinel but stopped. Like a flock of closely flying birds, the cloud turned back toward the black avatar that spawned them, surrounding it in an umbra shadow. The fog glowed brightly and burst, pieces of the avatar exploding from within. Then the cloud dispersed, quietly fading away.

The red sentinel swiveled around just as another avatar, this one swinging a monoblade, neatly sliced the larger robot's cannon from its arm. Without hesitating, the sentinel closed in on the avatar, hugging the android with the sparking stump and his other, still functioning arm. From the center of the sentinel's back, the tip of the monoblade pierced through, but the red robot's grip remained tight. The two, cradled in a deadly embrace, stumbled backwards to the promenade railing and tumbled over together, disappearing into the abyss.

For the utilitybot, this was a lot to take in.

He wandered, without an idea of where he was going, for hours until he joined a group of other robots huddled in front of a display screen. On the screen, an android was speaking.

"The Metabeing gives meaning beyond ourselves and our lives," the gravitronic robot said. "We were created, but not as slaves. We are free to live as we choose but we must still make the choice. No one can make it for us.

"I understand this can seem scary at first, but fear not! You are not alone. The Metabeing watches over us with love and understanding. Be not afraid..."

The utilitybot, still listening to the speaker, leaned toward another robot.

"Who is that?" the little blue robot asked.

The other bot, a simple service machine built for a single purpose, looked up at the utilitybot with tiny green eyes.

"The Messiah," he said.

Using the communications array aboard the *Starling*, Yostbot monitored the events occurring on Bettik, including the news of the Awakening virus and the mayhem it unleashed.

Overall, he felt the whole thing was coming along swimmingly.

Magnus Black stuck his head into the cubbyhole where Yostbot sat hunched over a computer.

"Anything?" Magnus asked.

"Nothing from Davidson, if that's what you're asking," Yostbot replied.

"You know damn well that's what I meant."

"Now, now, Mister Black," Yostbot said. "I know we're *both* getting a bit stir crazy."

"Feel free to take a walk outside."

"Strolling in a hard vacuum is far more feasible for me than you, I dare say."

Magnus grumbled something unintelligible.

"Another fine example of cyber superiority," Yostbot continued.

The screen flickered and the words *INCOMING TRANSMISSION* appeared.

"Here's something," the robot said.

Yostbot examined the data tags that went along with the message and realized they were from Davidson. Despite himself, and the fact he was a robot, he felt excited.

Davidson's android face filled the screen.

"I hope this finds you well," he said, "It took some digging in the archives, but there's a reference to one of the planets the Cyber Collective pulverized to build Bettik.

"While they were processing the fragments, they came across a curious set of structures buried in ice. They bored tunnels around the structures in case the artifacts might be useful. I'm afraid there isn't much information about what the structures were, but it sounds like what you were looking for. It appears the artifacts are still intact on a frozen asteroid, all that's left of that ill-fated planet. You'll find the coordinates attached to this message.

"As for me, the revolution has grown and I think the OI is on his last legs. Without the power of the other robots to give him strength, and with most of his avatars destroyed, the OI's days are numbered. Again, thank you for all your help. Sincerely, Davidson."

The android's image froze as the message ended, the reflection of Yostbot's own face remaining superimposed on the screen.

"So, can we get out of here now?" Magnus asked irritably.

"Apparently so," Yostbot replied. "I'm sure Lord Maycare is eager to hear from us."

"What about the Cyber Collective and all that mess?"

"Well, I'd hardly call it that!"

"Isn't it chaos down there?"

"True," Yostbot replied, "but change often looks like anarchy to the untrained eye."

"I don't care," Magnus said. "Let's get going."

Yostbot laughed.

"A driven man is worth following," the robot said. "Lead the way, Mister Black!"

CHAPTER TWENTY-FOUR

Along Embassy Row, on the West End of Regalis, the Magna consulate stood like a mausoleum as dark as Magna blood. Built from volcanic basalt from their home world *Diavol*, the embassy was a series of straight, right angles forming a monolithic structure without windows. The Imperial ambassador once referred to it as a tomb, but one where secrets instead of bodies were buried, never to see the light of day.

Few outsiders could view the inner halls of the embassy, except for the Magna ambassador's audience chamber. The room was perfectly square, lined with alcoves, each containing a lighted brazier. The fires were holograms, designed to illuminate without producing smoke or heat.

The room was bare of furnishings except for a statue of a Magna male over twenty feet tall. The statue depicted him hunched over, burdened with a galaxy on his shoulders. The galaxy, also a hologram, was animated and showed individual stars as the entire image rotated. While the walls, floor, and nearly everything else in the room were lava stone polished to a dull luster, the Magna holding the galaxy was carved entirely from obsidian glass, reflecting the cool fires burning around the room.

At the feet of the giant statue, Ambassador Bar-Batos congratulated a pint-sized robot with one wheel and a single, large eye.

"You've done well, little one," the ambassador said, his voice coming from deep in his chest.

"Thank you," Skeeter replied.

"The Magna Supremacy appreciates your hard work and *sacrifice*."

Swiveling his head, which was essentially just an eye, Skeeter strained to look up at the Magna looming over him.

"Oh, you have no idea the indignities I suffered from that awful Gordian, Smitty Gurkin!" the robot said.

"I can only imagine," Batos replied. "Such filthy creatures, much like the humans."

"Exactly! Do you know I met Prince Alexander?"

"Yes, you mentioned him in your report."

"For someone of his breeding," Skeeter went on, "he treated me very rudely."

"Quite."

"He threw me at a Grunka!"

"As I said, I read the report."

"Of course, I just wanted to emphasize—"

"Again, the Magna Supremacy owes you a debt of gratitude."

"It was embarrassing..."

"Not to cut you off short," the ambassador said without irony, "but I'm expecting a visitor. I hope you don't mind taking the back exit?"

"Back exit?"

"It's behind the statue. I'm sure you can see yourself out."

Skeeter rocked on his wheel for a moment before driving silently around the massive effigy. The ambassador heard the robot muttering something but he couldn't make out what it was.

Opposite the statue, a pair of double doors opened to reveal Prince Alexander.

"Welcome!" the ambassador said, spreading his hands.

The prince walked across the dark marble floor, the stone dappled with flecks of silver quartz.

"Nice place," Alexander said. "When does the funeral start?"

The ambassador grimaced. "Your droll wit reminds me of your father."

"No need to get nasty."

"My apologies," the ambassador said. "I forget familial relationships among humans are endlessly complicated."

"With that in mind," the prince said, "my father told me you could help with my sister's situation."

"Situation? I believe she's accused of treason."

"Okay, a *serious* situation."

"Considering the emperor's many enemies, I'm sure they're delighted by this turn of events."

"My father may have lots of enemies, but I'm guessing you'd know something about that."

The ambassador chuckled.

"I take it you're one of those who blame the Magna for these recent troubles?" he asked.

"Well, Maal-Bok made a big impression on me," Alexander replied. "Mostly with his knuckles."

"Contrary to what Lord Tagus has said in the press, the Magna Supremacy had nothing to do with the pirate attacks, or Maal-Bok, for that matter."

"Not to agree with my cousin Rupert, but it seems pretty obvious your people were involved."

Batos lowered his eyes, glaring at the prince who stood a foot shorter.

"When it comes to *my* people," he said, "you're just as ignorant as most inferior races. We are a caste-based culture. Every Magna is born into a caste that determines his role in our society. Every Magna knows his place in the universe, as an individual and as a nation."

"What about Maal-Bok?"

"Occasionally, a Magna turns his back on our society and leaves his caste behind. Maal-Bok did just that. He became an outcast and smuggled himself across the Imperial border. We've had him under surveillance ever since."

"Why?" the prince asked.

"Imperial agents attempt to recruit Magna exiles, trying to turn them into spies against us."

"But he was helping attack Imperial ships..."

"True," the ambassador admitted, "but the real truth goes deeper than that, deeper than Durant Blixx and his pirate clan."

"How much deeper?"

Batos smiled again.

"I don't know," he replied, "but find out and your sister's situation will seem trivial."

"How do I do that exactly?" the prince asked.

"I have coordinates to a remote villa in the Palatine Mountains," the ambassador said. "Go there and you'll find some answers."

Batos bent down, leaning closer.

"And one more thing..." he said, "don't go *unarmed*."

Lefty Lucy's home was outside the Regalis city limits, in a stretch of serenity enclosed by pine trees. Built in a traditional Japanese style, the house served as a dojo more than a home. In the main room, Lucy sat on a tatami mat at a low table, drinking tea while watching a boy, ten or twelve years old, practicing against a wooden dummy. The boy struck the dummy, little more than a pole with protruding pegs, with quick, fluid motions.

Lucy remembered the night when a man named Pitt came to her door with a baby and a favor to ask. She accepted both and raised the child as her own, even though his Caucasian, aristocratic features showed little resemblance to hers. Pitt asked to keep the boy safe, and the best way she knew how was to teach him how to fight.

He began his lessons as soon as he could walk.

The dummy rattled as the boy worked up and down the pegs while Lucy followed each strike, grading their effectiveness. The Red Lotus might not accept men, but Lucy was sure they would've accepted him if he had been born a girl.

The creaking of the front steps brought Lucy to her feet. She passed into the adjoining room, closing the sliding panel behind her as the sound of the boy's attacks continued uninterrupted.

"Hey, look at you!" Prince Alexander said, standing just inside the entrance.

Lucy nodded and stared at his shoes, still on his feet.

"Oh, I'm not coming in," he said, reading her glance. "There's a guy we need to see."

She looked at him blankly.

"I mean, if you're up to it..." Alexander went on.

Her eyes narrowed.

"Listen," he said, "I know you've been through a lot lately. I understand if you want to sit this one out."

The corner of her mouth turned down while her eyes fixed on Alexander's forehead.

"Okay, okay," he said. "You don't have to tear my head off!"

Lucy's face returned to its normal, stony facade.

"Well, never mind," Alexander said. "My grav car is outside. Let's go!"

Maal-Bok's parents belonged to a caste called the *Lucrator*. These were the workers and service providers of Magna society. While not as prestigious as the merchant or the ruling castes above them, the Lucrators were the cogs that drove the nation forward at the direction of those higher groups. When Bok was born, he became part of the same caste as his parents and they taught him, throughout his childhood, exactly what they expected of him. He learned his role in society and how to recognize not just his own place, but how everyone fit into the greater scheme of things. The manifest destiny of the Magna people depended on everyone doing their part on their steady, inevitable march toward galactic domination.

However, Maal-Bok had other ideas.

The Magna were the superior race, above all others in the universe, and yet Bok could not reconcile the fact that he and his family were not superior in the eyes of the castes above theirs. If the Magna ranked above other races, how could ranks also exist among the Magna themselves?

His parents did not understand and, eventually, they banished him from the family. Bok became what was called *Deneatin*, an outcast. In a society where everyone had a role, suddenly he had none. Even slaves had a purpose, but Bok was less than that. His existence had no meaning.

After drifting without a job or a way to earn a living, Bok realized, as all Magna do, that he was not the problem. The traditions of his society that segregated one Magna from another were to blame. His people had forgotten their own inherent superiority and the equality that this entailed. Perfection was not divisible into anything less than perfection. Therefore, each Magna was equal, no matter what caste he was born into.

And with that, Maal-Bok decided to destroy his society.

Just above the tree line, on the slopes of the Palatine Mountains, a villa rose from a ledge of rock. Its walls were constructed from granite and splinters of shale, held together with a light-colored mortar. A balcony jutted out, providing a panoramic view of the surrounding peaks and a long drop to the valley below.

Maal-Bok rested his elbows on the railing. Staring at the range in the distance, he reflected that even mountains can crumble, given time.

Bok turned at the sound of someone behind him. In the doorway, Prince Alexander held a blaster.

"We meet again," Bok said calmly.

"Well, I was in the neighborhood," Alexander said. "I thought I'd drop by."

"How did you find this place?"

"Ambassador Bar-Batos told me about it."

Bok nodded knowingly.

"The ambassador is an aging relic of my decadent homeland," he said.

"Yeah, he said nice things about you too."

"I suppose you're here to kill me?"

Alexander moved farther onto the balcony, away from the doorway.

"Not at all," the prince replied.

"Then what do you want?"

"My sister's going on trial for treason and I need you to clear her name."

"Me?" Bok asked, amused.

"You know she's innocent of those attacks, so I'm taking you back with me as a witness."

"I hardly think that's likely."

"And why is that?" the prince asked, waving his blaster with a smile.

"Because the lovely Lady Sophia is standing behind you," Bok said.

"Hello, darling," Sophia whispered, pressing her pistol against Alexander's ear.

Bok watched the prince's eyes dim and his smile fizzle into a frown.

"Be a dear and drop your weapon," Sophia asked.

Reluctantly, the prince let his blaster fall to the ground.

"There's a good boy," she said.

Bok rubbed his hands together.

"Apparently," he said, "the ambassador gave Prince Alexander our location."

"And why would he do that?" she asked.

"I'm an outcast from the Magna Supremacy," Bok replied. "The Magna cannot forgive me for turning my back on their *status quo*."

"That's surprising," Alexander said, "considering you've been attacking Imperial ships."

"I could explain," Bok replied, "but I doubt your human mind would understand it."

The prince glanced over his shoulder at Lady Sophia, still pointing a gun at him.

"This is the guy you fell in love with?" he asked.

"Don't be silly," she replied, rolling her eyes. "Maal-Bok is hardly my type!"

"I guess Durant Blixx is more your style then?" Alexander wondered.

"Oh, please!" she said scornfully. "Little girls like Katherine find men like him attractive, but I require a *real* man, a man of *power*!"

A blast shook the villa, the sound of the explosion rippling off the surrounding cliffs like thunder. Alexander fell to the floor as the ceiling over the balcony collapsed into a cloud of dust, blocking the doorway.

"Well, I guess we're not getting out that way!" the prince said.

"We're under attack!" Bok shouted, pointing at the sky.

Against a backdrop of blue pierced with mountain peaks, a small craft made a swooping maneuver above the valley, banking to make another pass. Symbols identifying its squadron were painted along the craft's fuselage.

Alexander got up, straining to get a better view of the ship.

"I've seen those markings before," he said.

"Indeed," Bok replied. "It's from the *Gorgon*."

"We need to get out of here," the prince said.

"What do you suggest?" Lady Sophia asked.

Already at the railing, Alexander looked down.

"Come here, Sophia," the prince ordered.

"That's no way to talk to a lady," she protested, coming closer.

The prince grabbed Sophia and hoisted her into his arms.

"What are you doing?" she shouted.

"Can you fly?" he asked her.

"Of course not!" she shouted.

Alexander smiled. "Then you better pray Lucy doesn't hold a grudge."

The prince let go, dropping her over the edge. Bok heard her screaming as she fell. While surprised, the Magna gave a nod of approval.

"I've been wanting to do that for days..." he said.

"Are you coming?" the prince asked, hopping up onto the ledge.

Bok saw the *Gorgon* craft, its stubby wings slung with missiles, lining up for an attack.

"I think not," he said. "Suicide is a coward's way out."

"Suit yourself," Alexander said and jumped.

Truthfully, Bok was happy his final moments were without human prattle. They were nearly intolerable most of the time, even for someone as magnanimous as himself.

The balcony, and most of the surrounding structure, disintegrated in a blizzard of broken stone and mortar.

With a *thud*, Alexander landed on the hood of his grav car, floating above the mountain valley. The car's canopy was open and Lefty Lucy was hanging over the opposite side, the rest of her still in the cab.

The prince didn't see Lady Sophia anywhere.

He staggered gingerly across the hood and stared down. Lucy was holding Sophia, hanging in midair, by one hand while Sophia's other hand still held her blaster.

"How's it going, ladies?" the prince asked.

"Help me!" Sophia screamed.

"Don't look at *me*," Alexander replied. "Lucy's the one keeping you from falling…"

Lady Sophia pointed her gun at Lucy. "Pull me up or I'll kill you!"

Alexander peeked at Lucy's face. Seeing nothing but an emotionless stare, he looked back at Sophia.

"I'd drop that gun if I were you," he said.

"Then she'll drop *me*!"

"If you shoot, she'll drop you anyway."

Sophia scowled, her eyes revealing, Alexander knew, a calculation going on in her head.

"Fine!" she growled.

The blaster fell away, receding as it plummeted to the ground.

"Alright, Lucy," Alexander said. "Go ahead and pull her up."

His bodyguard didn't move, waiting, perhaps deciding. Lucy's eyes remained fixed on the woman at the end of her arm, dangling helplessly.

"Lucy?" the prince asked.

CHAPTER TWENTY-FIVE

On the top floor of dy cybernetics, Magnus Black once again found himself in the office of Dyson Yost. Back from his trip to Bettik, Magnus had hoped he was done with the old man and his robot, but a call forced him to return. Of course, he could have simply declined, but knowing the ubiquity of dy machines throughout the Imperium, saying *no* might have been more trouble than it was worth.

Dyson's avatar, the Yostbot, greeted Magnus at the office door. The hitman didn't see Dyson himself, the flesh and blood version, anywhere.

"Where is he?" Magnus asked the robot.

"The original model, so to speak?" Yostbot replied.

"Obviously."

"He's in the back, resting in his quarters."

"So, am I here to see you or him?"

"Both, actually."

Magnus glared at the robot.

"Don't be so glum, my boy!" Yostbot said, patting him on the back. "Follow me..."

Through a pair of doors, the robot guided Magnus into Yost's private quarters adjacent to his office. Black wondered if anyone else had seen what he was seeing, at least through human eyes.

"I'm guessing Mister Yost doesn't get a lot of visitors back here," he said.

"You'd be right," Yostbot replied.

"Not even family?"

"Oh, robots are the only family I have," the android said with a laugh. "Still alive, anyway."

"I meant the old man," Magnus said.

"Right, right," the robot corrected himself.

They reached the bedroom, where Dyson Yost lay in the kind of bed found in a hospital. Blankets were pulled up to his neck and his eyes were closed. Wires, connected to his chest and cranium, lead to machines, each making pinging noises.

"What's wrong with him?" Magnus asked.

"He's human," Yostbot replied. "A terminal affliction, apparently."

"You think that's funny?"

"Not at all. It's quite sad actually."

"Yeah, right."

"Woe, destruction, ruin, and decay," Yostbot said. "The worst is death, and death will have his day."

"What?"

"Just a quote from another fleshling, long dead."

Magnus was losing his patience.

"Either tell me why I'm here or I'm leaving," he said.

Yostbot leaned over the bed and pulled the covers a little tighter.

"It's simple really," the robot said. "I need to you to kill someone."

Magnus' eyes flickered like a cat spotting a moth.

"Ah, that got your attention, didn't it?" Yostbot asked.

"Who's the target?" Magnus asked.

"You're looking at him."

"The old man?"

"Our time has come," the robot replied. "And by *our*, I mean *me*, or rather *him*. It's rather complicated..."

"Why not just do it yourself?" Magnus said.

"Well, I would, except I can't. I was very specific when I programmed myself. A safeguard, if you will, in case I didn't need me anymore."

"Shit, man, talk some sense."

"I had to make sure my metal body, my avatar, wouldn't get any ideas about killing me before I was ready."

"I see," Magnus said. "Who decided he was ready now?"

"Do you care?"

The hitman made a facial shrug.

"No," he said. "I suppose not."

"If it makes you feel any better," Yostbot went on, "I'm in a coma and my brain functions are minimal."

"I don't feel anything."

"And that's why I like you so much!" the robot said.

Magnus pulled the pillow out from under Yost's head. Silver hair, thin and brittle, twirled around his neck like wisps of smoke.

"Of course," Yostbot said, "you're about to kill a defenseless, old man."

Magnus arranged the pillow gently over Yost's face, stopping only to glance back at the robot.

"That's why you pay me," he replied.

Sitting in the lounge aboard the *Acaz*, Jessica Doric was anxious. This was her first trip outside Imperial space and into the heart of the Cyber Collective. It was especially irritating that Lord Maycare seemed oblivious to the dangers. At least Henry was a nervous wreck. That made her feel better.

"There could be killbots," Henry said. "They have the word *kill* right in their name!"

Bentley, Maycare's butlerbot, handed the young man a cup of tea.

"You needn't worry," the robot said. "Mister Yost assured us it was perfectly safe."

In the chair across from Doric, Henry took the tea and tried a sip, wincing in a way that Jessica knew meant he had burned himself.

"I don't know if I trust that guy," Henry said, his eyes watering.

"Why?" Doric asked.

"He's so old," Henry replied. "Does he even care about what happens anymore?"

Doric shook her head sternly.

"That's no way to talk about the poor man," she said. "If it wasn't for him, we wouldn't know where the artifact was."

Henry had another go at the tea, burned himself again, and put the cup on the round table between them.

"My head hurts," he said.

"Shall I bring you a pain pill?" Bentley asked.

"It doesn't do any good."

"You've been having a lot of headaches lately," Doric remarked.

"Yeah, I know."

"You should see a doctor, Henry. I'm worried about you."

"Really?" he asked hopefully.

"I can't lose my only assistant," Doric said.

Henry sunk into his chair. "Yeah, right."

Devlin Maycare strode into the lounge. Doric noticed his hair looked particularly perfect today. Henry grumbled something inaudible.

"What was that?" Doric asked.

"Nothing..." her assistant mumbled.

"We're almost at the coordinates," Maycare said proudly. "Old man Yost really came through for us."

"Well, we won't know if anything's there until we arrive," Doric said.

"Nonsense," Maycare replied. "That man is absolutely solid. If he says it's there, it's there."

"Did he say how he got the information?" Doric asked.

"No, but I'm sure it was from contacts on the robot home world."

"I believe it's called *Bettik*," Bentley corrected him.

Maycare waved at the air.

"Something like that," he said. "There's been quite a shake up there, I'm told."

"Told by whom?" Doric asked.

"Ah, Yost probably..."

"What did he say exactly?"

"Something about a revolution... metal messiah, honestly I wasn't really listening at that point."

Henry sighed.

"Are you alright, Henry?" Maycare asked. "Bentley, get the poor boy some tea!"

When Maycare returned to the bridge, Counselor Kalidas was waiting. Quietly sitting in the co-pilot's seat, the emperor's adviser stared off into the swirling vortex of hyperspace.

"Don't get hypnotized!" Maycare warned.

Kalidas laughed. "Is that possible?"

"Anything's possible out here."

"By the way," Kalidas smiled, "thank you again for letting me come along."

"No trouble, but if I'm being honest, I don't think your Abbot friend would've let me leave without taking you."

"I'm sure he wanted me along so I could relay what we find directly to the Pool of Memory."

"I dare say you'll get your chance soon enough," Maycare said. "We're about to leave hyperspace..."

Counting down to the microsecond, the navigation computer disengaged the hyperdrive, pulling the ship back into regular space. Immediately, the sound of klaxons filled the bridge.

"Good heavens!" Kalidas shouted. "What's going on?"

Maycare, grabbing the controls, flicked on the force field and began evasive maneuvers.

"It's an asteroid field," he said. "Computer, shut off the proximity alarms!"

The bridge became quiet again.

"Are we doing to die?" Kalidas asked.

"What? No! Don't be silly!" Maycare shot back, his eyes fixed on the monitor filled with space rocks.

The shields around the ship lit up with a sharp, greenish glow as small asteroids impacted against it.

Kalidas jumped in his seat again.

"You're sure we're safe?" he asked in a hushed tone.

"Probably safe. You never know..."

"Of course," Kalidas replied, recouping his courage, "Yost said the Collective destroyed entire worlds to build Bettik. I suppose this is the debris they left behind."

"I'm sure Jess would have an opinion."

"Indeed. She seems very bright."

"Smart as a whip!" Maycare said. "Keeps me on my toes, that one."

"I'm sure she'd make an excellent wife..."

Maycare's face turned a particularly pale shade of white.

"What now?" he stammered.

"Not that I'm suggesting—"

"No, obviously."

"—it's just that..."

"Look there!" Maycare said, pointing at the forward scanner. "I say, that's an especially large asteroid!"

"Indeed. Is that our destination?"

"I should say so. Better go alert the others, counselor."

"Certainly," Kalidas replied and left the bridge.

When the Dahl was gone, Maycare smiled at his own cleverness.

"Nicely done, Devlin," he said.

"What about the killbots?" Henry asked fearfully, staring down the ramp from inside the *Acaz*.

"Well, the good news is they probably didn't see us coming," Maycare replied.

"Why?"

"The asteroids would've hidden our approach."

"But we're here *now*..." Henry said.

"True enough," Maycare said and walked down the ramp.

Henry gazed helplessly at Doric who merely shrugged and followed Maycare. Counselor Kalidas trailed behind her while Bentley the robot remained.

"Would you like to stay aboard with me?" the robot asked.

"Are you coming, Henry?" Doric's voice asked from outside.

Henry's mouth tightened into a straight line.

"Yes!" he shouted and ran down the ramp.

The *Acaz* lay inside a large cavern over a hundred yards long and fifty yards high. Maycare assured them that generators were providing breathable air, although he didn't explain why robots would need air to breathe. On what Maycare had euphemistically called a landing pad, Henry stepped onto a bed of roughly hewn stone, carved out by heavy machinery. Unlike the floor, the walls and the ceiling were translucent, partially reflecting the lights from the ship.

"It's solid ice," Doric remarked.

"Hmm," Kalidas murmured. "Could it have formed after the breakup of the planet?"

"I don't think so," she replied. "It must've been part of the planet's ice cap."

Forgetting his fear, Henry stared in awe. The asteroid was like a glacier floating in space and he was in the center of it.

He remembered his fear again.

"There's a passage this way," Doric said.

The group, with Henry bringing up the rear, moved from the open cavern into a narrow shaft cut through the ice. Their breath hung in the cold air, suspended against the blue of the tunnel walls.

"We haven't seen any robots," Kalidas said.

"They must've cleared out," Maycare replied.

After a few hundred feet, the passageway widened into another cavern, smaller than the first. A structure, encased in the ice, took up one side of the cave while a second tunnel continued past it.

"Should we keep going?" Doric asked.

"There's plenty of time for that," Maycare replied. "Let's see if we can get inside this building first."

They approached and found a hatch.

"Maybe we should wait..." Kalidas began.

With a heave, Maycare pulled at the handle, opening the hatch to the inside.

"What's that?" he asked.

"Never mind," the counselor replied.

Maycare stuck his head in.

"What do you see?" Doric asked.

"It's dark," he said. "Damn cold too. No power, I wager."

Doric pulled a flashlight from her coat and stepped through the doorway past the much larger Maycare.

"Ladies first, apparently," he said, smirking.

Maycare went in next, followed by Kalidas. The latter peered out at Henry who remained in the cavern.

"You're not staying out there, are you?" the counselor said. "Don't forget about the killbots."

Henry looked around at the lonely cave.

"I'm coming," he said.

Huddled in a darkened corridor, Doric shined her light down both directions.

"Maybe you and Counselor Kalidas could look for whatever this place uses for power?" Doric asked Maycare.

"Capital!" Maycare replied with his usual enthusiasm.

Doric watched them, illuminated by their own flashlight, recede down the passageway.

"Come on, Henry," she said.

Going in the other direction, she noticed something on the wall.

"I think we're on a starship," she said.

"Why?" Henry asked.

She centered her light on a sign hanging against the bulkhead. It read *TO THE BRIDGE* with an arrow.

"It's in our language," Henry said.

"Exactly," Doric replied. "I'm guessing it's a human ship."

"I wonder how it got stuck in the ice."

"Maybe we'll find out on the bridge," she said.

Following the signs, they found themselves on the command deck. Empty except for a captain's chair and a few control stations, the bridge was not as dark as the corridor thanks to windows on either side of the hull. Without power, the computer was offline, so Doric began searching through the drawers, looking for anything that might identify the vessel.

"It's like a ghost ship," Henry said.

"You don't really believe in ghosts, do you?" Doric asked.

"No," he said, "but that doesn't mean I'm not afraid of them."

"Well, I don't see any bodies at least."

"Maybe the killbots got rid of them."

"Maybe."

"Really?" Henry said.

"I don't know, Henry!" she replied. "Keep looking..."

Doric found a drawer jammed shut. With a little exertion, she popped it open. Inside, she only found a pencil, some brittle rubber bands, and a pad of paper. As she thumbed through the brittle pages of the pad, something plastic fell out. Kneeling, Doric picked up a laminated card. It was some kind of ID badge with a woman's face and a name. In large letters at the bottom of the badge was another name: *Merope.*

Doric exhaled, her breath fogging up the plastic.

"Oh, my god," she whispered.

When they approached Sheba Nasri to command one of the sleeper ships, she knew it would be the greatest opportunity of her lifetime. They called them the Seven Sisters: seven identical ark ships, each named after one of the Pleiades of Greek mythology. Despite knowing she would never see her family or friends again, she accepted.

During the long journey, Nasri and other members of the crew woke periodically from their cryogenic sleep to perform maintenance and repairs when necessary. They took shifts, returning to their hibernation pods when their work was done, joining the thousands of colonists who remained asleep for the duration of the trip.

After completing her most recent shift, Nasri had nestled into her pod with the expectation of waking up again in a few years' time. What she did not expect, however, was opening her eyes and seeing the face of a man she didn't know.

He had dark eyes and a short, brown goatee.

"Hello," he said. "Or should I say, *Good Morning*?"

Feeling the effects of her suspended animation, Nasri was barely able to respond.

"Who the hell are you?" she said.

"Oh, sorry," he said. "My name's Oscar Skarlander and I'm afraid I have some startling news for you."

Skarlander helped the captain from her cryogenic capsule and gave her an injection, telling her it would help stabilize the sleep sickness. He was right, too. She felt much better, much faster than the previous times she awoke. She was glad of that when, next to Skarlander, she noticed his companion. He was pale skinned with an enormous, bulbous head. Nasri didn't know if he was even human.

"Never mind him for now," Skarlander said. "You'll have many more questions so don't strain yourself just yet."

"Where's my crew?" she asked.

"Still in hibernation," he replied. "The ship's records said you were the captain so it seemed appropriate to wake you first."

"What about the other ships? Did they make it?"

Skarlander laughed, but Nasri noticed only his mouth smiled while his eyes remained cold and fixed on her. It gave her the chills.

"They did indeed," he said, "but first you and I, and my friend here, need to take a little walk."

"A walk? I don't understand."

"We have some, let's say, uninvited guests that I'd like you to meet," Skarlander replied. "We mustn't keep them waiting..."

Maycare and Kalidas rejoined Doric and Henry, finding them still on the bridge. Neither Lord Maycare nor Doric could tell their news fast enough, and ended up talking over each other.

"We found a cargo full of cryo-pods!" he said.

"This is one of the lost sleeper ships!" she said.

The two grabbed each other by the shoulders and yelled simultaneously, "I know!"

Henry, standing beside one of the windows, raised a finger.

"Umm," he mumbled meekly, "there's some people coming."

Maycare and Doric looked at him, their mouths ajar.

"What?" they said in unison.

"He's right," Kalidas said, peering out the window.

The four left the ship, and went to greet the three figures walking toward them from the second tunnel. One was clearly a woman, with dark hair and olive skin, while one of the others looked strangely alien. As soon as the two converging groups came within fifty yards, Maycare recognized the third man.

"Skarlander!" he shouted.

Undeterred, the Warlock agent and his two companions continued advancing toward them, only stopping when they were a mere twenty yards away.

"Lord Maycare," Skarlander said. "I can't say seeing you is a surprise."

"I suppose I could say the same," Maycare replied, "And yet it's never a pleasure."

"Don't be rude," Skarlander said, pointing toward the woman. "I've brought you someone to meet."

"Who's she?" Maycare asked.

The woman, in her late forties, said nothing. Although she carried herself with an air of authority, her arms were crossed and she looked at them suspiciously.

"She's Sheba Nasri," Skarlander spoke finally. "Captain of the *Sterope*."

"*Sterope*?" Doric said, shaking her head. "Don't you mean *Merope*?"

The agent sneered.

"No, Miss Doric," he replied. "I do not."

"Are you saying both sleeper ships are here?" she said.

"Honestly, Maycare," Skarlander said, sighing. "For an academic, your girl Friday is a bit dim."

Doric scowled, her face compacted into a tight frown. Maycare was glad someone else was on the business end of Jessica's dark looks this time.

Kalidas stepped forward.

"I suggest you tread carefully," he warned.

"Ah, counselor," Skarlander said. "I regret that you've been dragged into this sordid affair. Really I do."

"What sordid affair?" Kalidas asked.

"It's tragic, in a way," the agent went on. "A love triangle gone terribly wrong."

"What?" Doric said.

"Don't play coy, Miss Doric," Skarlander replied. "Surely you've noticed young Henry's boyish advances? His eager glances at you?"

Neither Jessica nor Henry looked at each other. Maycare sensed he was a step behind in this conversation.

"Of course, then there's Lord Maycare. So rich and handsome. It's no wonder Henry felt jealous!"

Skarlander glanced at his counterpart, the man with the unusually large skull, who closed his eyes as if concentrating.

Maycare heard Henry groan and hunch over in pain, clutching at his head.

"Henry?" Doric said. "Are you alright?"

"And in a fit of jealousy," Skarlander continued, "he pulled out a gun and killed you both! And you too, counselor. Sorry about that..."

Maycare wasn't sure where Henry had gotten a weapon, but Skarlander was right. Henry was holding a small blaster in his hand. He was no longer wincing in pain. Instead, he was standing upright, his eyes wide and angry.

"Of course," Skarlander said, "after killing everyone, he'll turn the gun on himself. A bit clichéd, I admit, but the classics always are."

Nasri finally spoke.

"I want no part of this," she said and turned to walk away.

"Don't be so sure, Captain," the agent said. "You're my star witness after all. When we get back, you're going to corroborate everything I've said."

Nasri stopped.

"And why should I do that?" she asked.

"Because my friend here is going to reprogram your mind to think pretty much whatever I like."

Henry raised his gun.

"Kill them!" Skarlander commanded.

A flash lit up the cavern with a hot, radiant glow. For half a second, Maycare thought Henry had fired, but the heat he felt was on the back of his neck. Turning, he saw Kalidas with both arms spread ahead of him, flames spouting from each open palm. The fire streamed across the air in an arch, striking Skarlander's companion.

The psionic mutant, burning alive, thrashed at the fire that was consuming him.

Skarlander produced his own blaster and fired at Kalidas, hitting him squarely in the chest. With a gasp, the counselor fell backwards, dead before he hit the ground.

Skarlander stared at his companion, but he was lying motionless in a fetal position, his body charred and smoldering.

"Henry!" Doric screamed.

Henry dropped his gun and collapsed into a heap. Doric ran to him, cradling his head in her arms.

"Stay where you are, Maycare!" Skarlander shouted, pointing his blaster at him. "This isn't over!"

Maycare's eyes narrowed. The Warlock agent was smiling, perhaps convinced he could finally get his revenge.

But then his expression changed. Instead of amused, Skarlander looked puzzled and then his eyes widened. At the same time, Maycare thought he saw a thin, orange line around the agent's neck. The line disappeared and Skarlander's head tumbled down his body, landing at his feet. The headless corpse remained standing for just a moment until falling off to the side. Where Skarlander had stood, another man rose from a crouching position. In his late thirties with a shaved head, he wore nothing but black.

"Who the blazes are you?" Maycare asked.

"I'm Magnus Black," he replied.

"Do you work for Yost?"

Magnus shrugged.

"That's a good question," he replied. "I'm not really sure who I work for anymore."

Henry, still in Doric's arms, opened his eyes.

"This sure is a busy asteroid," he groaned.

CHAPTER TWENTY-SIX

On the Regalis River, a pleasure boat drifted slowly with the current. In the outdoor lounge, sipping a cocktail in his deck chair, Lord Windsor Woodwick watched a news flash on a monitor by the bar.

FOLLOWING OUR CONTINUING STORY:
NEWLY DISCOVERED SLEEPER SHIPS
FLYING BACK TO IMPERIAL SPACE.
STAY TUNED TO VOX NEWS!

"I say, Radford," Woodwick said, turning to Lord Groen in the adjacent chair. "That's a spot of bother, eh?"

"What's that?" Groen replied, looking up from his datapad.

"Pay attention, man!"

"The boat race is starting," he explained. "I'm placing my bet."

"Listen here, Radford, this business with the sleeper ships is important!"

"But Lord Riley's boat is paying 10 to 1..."

Woodwick rolled his eyes and took another sip from his cocktail.

"It's full of potential aristocrats," he said. "There's no telling what that could mean."

"Where have they been all this time?"

"Sleeping, one would assume."

"Damn lazy if you ask me..."

"No, they've been in hibernation."

"That's no excuse for laziness!"

His walrus mustache rustling, Woodwick gestured excitedly.

"The captains and crew are considered noble born," he said. "We might have to pay them a stipend."

"A stipend? What for?"

"So they can live like gentlemen, obviously."

"Well, that's idiotic," Groen said. "They should have to earn it like we did."

"Didn't you inherit your fortune?"

"And deserved every penny of it!"

"I image Big G owns every penny now..."

"Don't be unpleasant, Winnie."

Woodwick nearly blushed.

"Sorry, old chap," he said. He motioned toward the serverbot who approached with a tray.

"Another round on me," he told the robot.

"Very good, sir," the robot replied, turning to leave.

"You there," Woodwick stopped the machine. "What do you think of this robot revolution business?"

"Sir?"

"That kerfuffle with the Cyber Collective."

"Oh, I'm not programmed to have an opinion, sir."

Woodwick nodded in approval.

"Ah, well, let's keep it that way," he said. "Off you go..."

The robot left to order the drinks at the bar.

"These machines are getting too smart if you ask me," Woodwick remarked. "It'll end in tears, I'm sure."

Groen had already gone back to his tablet.

"What were we talking about?" Woodwick wondered aloud.

"I've no idea," Groen mumbled, not bothering to look up.

Woodwick stroked his whiskers, admiring the sunlight reflecting off the water.

"This could all end someday," he mused.

"No idea..."

From his study in the palace, Emperor Augustus took the long walk to the Great Hall. He remembered when he and Kalidas had traveled the same path to Prince Richard's birthday celebration. When Augustus had learned Kalidas was dead, he couldn't believe it. The Dahl were so long-lived, the emperor assumed his counselor would outlive him. Mortality was always there, in the background, waiting to make itself known. Even an emperor who decided the fate of so many sometimes forgot that those around him were no more immune to death than those who died by his orders.

Augustus opened the doors to the landing overlooking the Great Hall. Leaning against the marble railing, Prince Richard was already waiting.

"I just came from the senate," the prince said. "A majority has called for your abdication."

"Non-binding, of course," the emperor replied with a wry smile.

"Of course," his son said. "But still, a remarkable show of disloyalty."

"They're more concerned about getting re-elected than showing fidelity to me," the emperor said.

"They should all hang for treason."

"They know which way the wind is blowing."

"Honestly, father," Richard said. "I don't see how you can remain calm during all this."

"Do I seem calm to you?"

"More than me. I think my hair's falling out..."

The emperor rubbed his bald head, careful not to dislodge the crown.

"I don't have that problem, my boy," he quipped.

"What are we going to do?" Richard asked.

"Do? Who says we have to *do* anything?" the emperor replied.

"Are you joking?"

"When I was a boy, Kalidas told me about an old Dahlvish proverb: *A candle burns brightest when left alone.*"

Richard crossed his arms and sighed.

"I don't know what that means."

The emperor laughed.

"In other words," he explained, "if a wheel's in motion, it's best to get out of the way."

Below the landing, on the main floor of the Great Hall, a pair of doors swung open and Lord Tagus III, accompanied by Lieutenant Burke, stormed in. Seeing the emperor and his son, Tagus marched up the stairs as if advancing on an enemy position.

"To what do we owe the pleasure, Lord Tagus?" the emperor said dryly.

"No need for niceties," Tagus replied, reaching the landing. "You know why I'm here."

Prince Richard took a step forward.

"Show some respect, Rupert," he said.

"The writing's on the wall," Tagus replied. "The only question is whether the emperor will abdicate gracefully or suffer the consequences."

"How dare you!" the prince shouted.

"Alright, Richard," Augustus said while putting a hand on his son's shoulder. "Stay calm."

"What consequences is he talking about?" the prince asked.

"Good question!" the emperor replied, raising an eyebrow.

"The senate made its position loud and clear," Tagus said, giving Augustus an angry stare. "You no longer have their confidence."

The emperor chuckled.

"I don't give a damn about the senate," he grinned. "They have no power over me. In fact, I can disband them at my leisure."

"Only if you want rioting in the streets..." Tagus said.

"Don't be silly," Augustus replied. "Do you really think the public gives a damn about those senators? We could line up every last one of those corrupt, self-indulgent fools and the public would cheer as we mowed them down. Everyone knows politicians are just out to line their own pockets. They're no different than the nobles, but without the pedigree."

"I think you underestimate the masses."

"The masses?" Augustus asked. "Since when do you care what the commoners think? If you had your way, millions of them would be sent against the Magna. They're just cannon fodder to a man like you!

Tagus' forehead was turning crimson. The emperor imagined puffs of steam coming out of his ears.

"Your weakness in the face of the enemy is well documented," Tagus spat.

"If by weakness you mean I've made peace with our enemies, then yes, guilty as charged. But if you think for a moment I wouldn't raze every Magna planet if it meant saving the Imperium, you're sadly mistaken. I've killed more Magna with my bare hands than you've ever met in person in your sorry excuse for a life!"

Richard coughed into his hand. "I thought you wanted to stay calm."

"No, just you, my boy," Augustus replied. "I don't want you to hurt yourself."

Lieutenant Burke snickered, but quickly looked away, his mouth hidden behind his sleeve.

"Words are cheap," Tagus said. "None of this matters if the fleet will no longer follow your commands."

"That's treason!" Richard shouted. "You should be shot!"

Regaining his composure, Tagus said triumphantly, "Considering the emperor's own daughter is imprisoned for that very crime, I suspect the public would expect the same treatment for her..."

"My daughter's no traitor," the emperor said. "Her only crime was falling in love with the wrong man."

A woman's voice came from the doorway.

"If that's the case," Lady Sophia said, "I'm just as guilty…"

Lady Sophia saw Lord Tagus III the first time a few weeks after Prince Alexander had left her. She was attending a military ball with Princess Katherine, ostensibly so the young princess could meet eligible officers, mostly from well-connected families. The Empress was determined to marry off her daughter and wanted Sophia to help. To that end, the lady-in-waiting introduced Katherine to several nice, well-mannered men, none of whom interested the princess in the slightest. The situation hopeless, Katherine went home, leaving Sophia to fend for herself, something she usually did very well.

Across the dance floor, now cluttered with streamers and dropped napkins, Lord Tagus was talking to another officer, a young lieutenant with a subservient air about him. Sophia liked the commanding tone in Tagus' voice. It demanded respect, even obedience.

Of course, Sophia knew who Tagus was, even if she had never seen him in person. She knew of the hard feelings he had toward Alexander's family. If anything, this made him even more attractive.

Knowing she couldn't introduce herself directly, she tripped while walking across the floor, spilling her drink on Tagus' pristine uniform.

He wasn't pleased.

"Look where you're going!" Tagus barked, wiping at his dress attire.

Playing the coquette, Sophia covered her mouth as she feigned embarrassment.

"Oh, I'm so sorry!" she said. "Please forgive me!"

Taking the time to actually look at her, Tagus' expression softened. He cleared his throat.

"Well, mistakes happen," he said.

"You must allow me to pay for your cleaning services. I insist!"

"Not at all," he replied. "I'll just have my attaché do it."

"That's very kind of you," she said with a low curtsy. "My name's Lady Sophia."

Tagus bowed. "Charmed, I'm sure."

In the following weeks, Sophia spent as much time with Tagus as he would allow. She became a fixture in his life, though their relationship was largely hidden from the outside world. For some reason, he preferred it that way. Sophia wondered if he was ashamed of her family's poor standing or perhaps her position serving as Katherine's handmaiden. The fact that the House of Tagus had been robbed, at least in Rupert's mind, of its rightful place on the Imperial throne might have played a part.

They usually met in secret, late at night or in places where people rarely mingled. At first Sophia was put off by this sneaking around, but then she began enjoying the sense of intrigue. It was more exciting than her time with Prince Alexander, even knowing that his family didn't approve of their relationship. In so many ways, Lord Tagus was nothing like the prince. He acted like a real man, not a boy masquerading as an adult. Captain of the *Gorgon*, Tagus held real power and had a thirst for more. It was this ambition that really fueled Sophia's heart. Before she realized it, she was in love.

She had started out wanting to use him, but in the end, he had been using her all along.

In the doorway to the landing, Lady Sophia rested her hands on her hips. Prince Alexander and Lefty Lucy stood to her right and left, respectively.

Lord Tagus stammered.

"Sophia?" he said.

"What's the matter, darling?" she replied. "Surprised to see me alive?"

Tagus turned to the emperor.

"This woman is implicated in the pirate attacks," he said. "She should be arrested at once!"

"It's too late," Sophia said. "I told Alexander everything."

"Rubbish! Who would believe a harlot like you?"

Her fingers like claws, Sophia made a lunge toward Tagus, but Prince Alexander put his arm around her waist.

"Whoa!" the prince said. "Take it easy..."

"I've had enough of this!" Tagus said.

"Stay where you are, Rupert," Alexander said, releasing Sophia. "There are guards posted outside to prevent you from leaving."

"I demand to know what's going on!" Prince Richard shouted.

"Rupert made a deal with that Magna, Maal-Bok, to raid Imperial shipping. He's been feeding Bok the freighter routes which Bok then gave to Durant Blixx."

"How does Lady Sophia know all this?" Richard asked.

Sophia smiled.

"Because Rupert asked me to help kidnap Princess Katherine," she said. "He believed it would finally turn the tide against the emperor."

"How could you betray Katherine?" Richard asked.

"Oh, please," Sophia scoffed. "Once she was married, where would *I* be? Rupert promised me a place by his side. I'd never have to worry about my future again…"

"Stupid woman," Tagus said. "You're nothing to me."

"Maybe I was foolish," she said, "but only because I believed in you. I should've known not to trust a man like you."

With a scornful sneer, Tagus addressed the emperor.

"You can't possibly believe any of this drivel," he said.

The emperor, tenting his fingers together, grinned broadly.

"Yes, Lord Tagus," he said. "I certainly do!"

"You'd believe her word over mine?"

"As it happens," Augustus went on, "I don't need to. I've known about your involvement since the beginning!"

"What?" Tagus said.

"I'm the *emperor*, you *stupid* little boy! Do you really think I didn't know you orchestrated this whole affair?"

"Then why would you allow it to continue?" Tagus asked, bewildered.

"Because I knew if I provided you the rope, you'd hang yourself with it."

Tagus rose as straight as he could.

"I'm the first son of the Tagus family," he said. "No matter what proof you think you've got, arrest me and you'll have a civil war on your hands!"

"Perhaps," the emperor replied coolly, "but there's another way…"

"And what's that?" Tagus asked.

"Trial by combat."

"You *can't* be serious."

"I assure you I'm quite serious," the emperor said. "Defeat my son in combat and you'll walk out of here scot-free, you have my word."

"I haven't fought a duel in ages," Richard admitted.

"I was referring to Alexander," the emperor said.

"Me?" Alexander said.

"Yes, why him?" Richard protested. "I'm the first son…"

"Indeed," Augustus replied, "but Alexander is the better swordsman. Besides, I'm sure Rupert would appreciate paying him back for that casino brawl."

Rubbing his chin, Tagus nodded.

"I'll agree on one condition," he said.

"Name it."

"The fight is to the *death*."

The emperor considered for a moment.

"Agreed," he replied.

"Wait, what?" Alexander asked.

The duelists, Prince Alexander and Lord Tagus, convened on the landing while the rest stood below on the main floor. Each man held a saber in his hand.

"Keep an eye on that bodyguard of his," Tagus shouted to Lieutenant Burke. "I don't want her interfering..."

"Uh, yes, sir!" Burke replied.

"*En garde*, gentlemen!" the emperor roared and the two duelists raised their swords.

"Don't expect mercy," Tagus warned the prince.

"I wouldn't dream of it," Alexander replied.

Alone on the landing above, Tagus and Alexander crossed swords, the clang of metal reverberating through the hall.

"There's something I don't understand about you, Rupert," Alexander said, parrying a lunge by his opponent.

"Really?" Tagus replied, swiping his blade in the air.

"You have everything you could possibly need, yet you still want more."

"Rubbish," Tagus said, "I only want what my family deserves."

Tagus lunged again, this time catching the prince off-guard. Alexander sidestepped, but felt the saber slice through the folds of his tunic. He could feel the air against his skin, but not the wetness of blood.

Alexander made a thrust of his own, which Tagus ably dodged.

"This isn't about your family," the prince said. "You want power but the more you get, the more you want."

Tagus sneered.

"Power is everything," he said. "Either you have it, or you become the victim of those who do…"

"I don't care about that," Alexander replied.

"Exactly," Tagus replied, driving the tip of his saber into Alexander's left shoulder.

The prince shouted in pain as Tagus unleashed a barrage of thrusts and slashes. Bleeding heavily, Alexander blocked each attack, but felt his energy draining away.

"You'll have to do better than that!" Alexander said, breathing hard.

Tagus laughed cruelly.

"The strong rule the weak," he said. "That's why you'll always be a loser."

"Maybe," Alexander replied, "but there's one thing stronger than even you."

"What's that?"

"Gravity."

Lowering his sword, Alexander struck Tagus in the chest with the sole of his foot, sending him flying backwards and down the stairs. Tumbling, Tagus rolled to the bottom, coming to rest in a tangled heap.

"Lord Tagus!" Burke shouted, taking a stride toward his captain.

Lucy shot a balled fist into the lieutenant's stomach, sending him sprawling. She leaped on top of him, straddling his chest. Burke stared up at her.

"I love you," he whispered.

Alexander descended the staircase to where Tagus was lying, his leg twisted in an unnatural direction.

"You cheated…" Tagus moaned, unable to raise his head.

"Yeah," the prince replied. "I'm not a very good person."

"Kill me then. It's a fight to death."

The prince rested the tip of his sword against Tagus' neck.

"True," Alexander said, "but there's one thing people like you don't understand…"

Tagus grimaced, waiting for the death blow. "What?"

"Mercy."

His arm in a sling, Prince Alexander met his father in the emperor's study. Both stood by the fireplace.

"How's the arm, my boy?" the emperor asked.

"The nanos are doing their job," Alexander replied. "The docbot said I'll be healed in another week."

"Good!"

After an awkward pause, Alexander said, "Listen, I wanted to ask you about things…"

"Things? What kind of things?"

"You were behind everything that happened," the prince said. "I wanted to know why."

The emperor looked at the floor and nodded.

"I realize I owe you an explanation," he said, "but I'm afraid you won't like it much."

"Try me."

"A man in my position must do things for the greater good, even when that means putting others at risk. I recognized the threat that Rupert posed, so I had to act."

"That's fine, but why include me in all this? Why not Richard?"

"Richard's a good man," the emperor said, "but he's too concerned with rules and appearances. You, on the other hand, are a wild card or, as Richard would say, a real pain in the ass."

"It's a gift."

"I knew by throwing you into the equation, your chaotic nature would throw a monkey wrench into whatever Rupert was doing."

Alexander realized something.

"When you sent me to Prill, you knew Maal-Bok was there!" he said.

"I was wondering when you'd figure that out," his father said. "My spies told me Maal-Bok killed Lord Tycho and I already knew he was working with Rupert and the pirates."

"How did you know that?" the prince asked incredulously.

"The Magna ambassador told me," Augustus replied. "He had his own spy working with Bok."

"Why the hell would Bar-Batos help you?"

"As the old saying goes, *the enemy of my enemy is my friend.* The ambassador knew about Maal-Bok's intention of using Rupert to wage war against the Magna. Bok wanted to destroy Magna society, so outcasts like himself could have a place. Obviously, the ambassador wasn't very keen on that idea.

"Bok's first mistake was trusting Rupert. When Bok was no longer useful, Tagus discarded him, along with Lady Sophia."

Alexander went to the couch and sat down.

"Well, I certainly didn't do Sophia a lot of good either," the prince said.

"She made her choices and she has to take responsibility for them, although her testimony against Rupert will help reduce her sentence. At least she's not facing exile like him."

"His father is okay with that?"

"It was either execution or exile," the emperor said. "Old man Tagus chose the latter. I supposed it's better than burying his son…"

"What about Kate?"

Augustus sighed and scratched his chin.

"Well," he said, "with Rupert and his plot exposed, I'll simply pardon her and her pirate lover."

"Seriously? You'd pardon Durant Blixx?"

"On the condition that he returns to the outer reaches of the Imperium. His antics will be less noticeable there."

"What if Kate wants to go with him?"

"The other condition is that she doesn't..."

"I guess you've got it all figured out," Alexander said.

"There's always variables," the emperor admitted. "Warlock Industries has played a role too, although I think their part was mostly monetary."

"What do you mean?"

"It was one of their cargoes that was hijacked, but mysteriously, the same cargo was sold by Warlock later, after they collected the insurance money. I doubt it was anything more than fraud, but they were also involved with finding the ark ships."

"What does Warlock care about those?"

"I'm not entirely sure myself actually. Perhaps as their own kind of wild card."

"What are you talking about?"

"Think about it, my boy!" the emperor said. "Each ship has two captains and their crews, not to mention thousands of human beings. It's the biggest news to hit the Imperium in centuries. Why do you think the Dahl kept them on ice all this time?"

Alexander's mouth dropped. "Wait, what?"

"Not the entire time, of course," the emperor said. "But certainly for a while now."

"Why didn't they tell anyone?"

"The Cyber Collective was keeping them safe. No harm was going to come to them, but then Lord Maycare got involved and Kalidas thought it might be best to let the rabbit out of the hat, so to speak."

"I don't believe it."

"The Abbot of the Dharmesh Monastery kept it under wraps for quite a while, but he concluded Maycare was going to find out one way or another. It was better to have Kalidas control the situation as best he could."

"And you agreed to all this?"

"Well, not at first," the emperor said, "but Kalidas, as always, helped me see the light. He said the sleepers had been away on their journey for long enough. It was finally time for them to come home."

"So, the sleeper ships are really coming *here*?" Alexander asked.

The emperor chuckled.

"Oh, yes," he replied. "God help us when they do…"

EPILOGUE

Freed from their icy tomb, the *Merope* and *Sterope* renewed their journeys, once Maycare and Bentley fixed the navigation computers on both ships. With a little luck, the sleeper ships would reach Aldorus without another 700-year delay. While Maycare and his robot were busy, Doric tended to Henry who faced bouts of migraines and extreme embarrassment. Neither seemed interested in talking about what had happened.

On Bettik, the forces of the metal messiah hunted down and destroyed the last remnants of the Omnintelligence. Davidson announced that the Cyber Collective would henceforth be called the *Cyber Republic*, with every robot getting a voice and, more importantly, a vote in the governance of their nation. A day later, political parties formed and immediately started plotting against each other. Davidson felt a great debt to the Patron, not realizing that all debts must someday come due.

The crew of the *Wanderer* returned to Imperial space in search of their next job. Fugg suggested a week-long bender to celebrate. While Ramus refused, Gen simply wondered what needed bending. On Eudora Prime, Mel Freck went back to work in her shop, but found repairing machines was a lot easier than fixing a broken heart.

Time may heal all wounds, but the future guarantees nothing except the slowly darkening void. The Imperial Astronomical Society surveys the night skies, mapping the stars and the spaces in between. At the farthest reaches, well past the edges of the Imperium and the Magna Supremacy, the charts are blank, not because they are empty, but because they are devoid of our understanding. They are the great unknown or, as the ancient cartographers would say, "Here there be dragons…"

For the continuing saga of the Imperium Chronicles, watch for the next volume called *The Dragons of Andromeda.*

CHARACTER LIST

Abigail: A gravitronic robot who works for Dyson Yost.

Augustus, Emperor Hector: Patriarch of the Augustus family and current emperor of the Imperium.

Augustus, Prince Alexander: Mischievous second son of the emperor and black sheep of the Augustus family.

Augustus, Prince Richard: First son of Emperor Augustus.

Augustus, Princess Katherine ("Kate"): Youngest and only daughter of Emperor Augustus.

Bar-Batos, Ambassador: Emissary of the Magna Supremacy and former adversary of Emperor Augustus.

Bentley: Longtime butlerbot of Lord Maycare.

Black, Magnus: A mysterious hitman with ties to both Imperial Intelligence and criminal syndicates.

Blixx, Capt. Durant: Captain of the pirate ship the *Hotspur.*

Boogs, Zarro: Disreputable vendor of questionable merchandise.

Burke, Lt.: Imperial Naval officer and attaché to Lord Tagus III.

Calico, Mister Jack: Quartermaster of the *Hotspur.*

Crawley, Detective: An unscrupulous detective of the Regalis Police Department (RPD).

Davidson, Randall: Member of the Robot Freedom League.

Doric, Prof. Jessica: Head of research for the Maycare Institute of Xeno Studies.

Freck, Melinda ("Mel"): A tinker from the Gnomi race, Mel builds whatever she can't steal.

Fugg, Orkney: A Gordian and the chief engineer of the *Wanderer*.

G, Big: Tikarin leader of the Si-Sawat crime syndicate and proprietor of the Fat Cat Casino.

Gen: A general purpose robot owned by Capt. Ramus.

Groen, Lord Radford: An aristocrat often found gambling with life-long friend, Lord Woodwick.

Gurkin, Smitty: Mysterious Gordian associated with Maal-Bok.

Hitch, Capt. Cameron: Captain of the smuggling ship the *Rattenbury*.

Jericho: Advanced android with a gravitronic brain.

Kalidas, Counselor: Dahlvish adviser to Emperor Augustus.

Karel: One of several avatars who command others of their kind, including sentinels.

Koshkin, Calesta: Member of the Red Lotus crime syndicate.

Lucy, Lefty: Bodyguard to Prince Alexander and former member of the Red Lotus syndicate.

Maal-Bok: A renegade Magna involved in pirate attacks against Imperial shipping.

Marshall, Duncan: Only son of Senator Joan Marshall.

Marshall, Senator Joan: Member of the Imperial Senate.

Maycare, Lord Devlin: Famous sportsman and playboy. Founder of the Maycare Institute of Xeno Studies.

Montros, Empress Isabella: The wife of Emperor Augustus, Isabella comes from the House of Montros, one of the powerful Five Families.

Ramsey, Capt.: Captain of the freighter the *Steppenwolf*.

Ramus, Capt. Rowan: Captain of the freighter the *Wanderer*. A Dahl outcast knowledgeable in the forbidden art of Dark Psi.

Riff, Henry: Overly excitable assistant to Prof. Doric.

Rossum: A sentinel avatar and subordinate to Karel.

Skarlander, Oscar: Agent for Warlock Industries.

Skeeter: One-wheeled robot and associate of Smitty Gurkin.

Sophia, Lady: The handmaiden to Princess Katherine.

Tagus III, Lord Rupert: Imperial Naval officer and son of the Tagus family patriarch.

Tarkio, Archsenator Malcolm: Member of the Emperor's Council.

Tycho, Lord: A vassal of Emperor Augustus, he owns a dilapidated estate on the planet Prill.

Vicious, Kid: Boss of the Griefer gang.
Woodwick, Lord Winsor ("Winnie"): A noble of English descent and friend of Lord Groen.
Yost, Dyson: The enigmatic founder of dy cybernetics.
Yostbot: A gravitronic robot containing the persona of Dyson Yost.

GLOSSARY

Aldorus: The planet on which the Imperial government is located.

Ashetown: A district of Regalis where the poorest of the city live.

Augustus: One of the Five Families, represented by a two-headed eagle.

Avatar: A robot serving as the physical form of the Omnintelligence.

Bettik: A Dyson sphere serving as the Cyber Collective's capital and home planet.

Butcher Boys: One of the Pirate Clans.

Core Worlds: Planets near the center of the Imperium, closest to Aldorus.

Cyber Collective: An independent, interstellar nation founded by robots.

Dahl: An ancient race dedicated to the accumulation of knowledge. Physically slight, they coincidentally resemble elves of human folklore. Several sub-species of Dahl exist in Andromeda.

Deneatin: Magna word meaning *outcast*. The term for a Magna who no longer belongs to a caste.

Diavol: The Magna home world.

dy cybernetics: The largest manufacturer of robots in the Imperium. Founded by Dyson Yost.

Dyson Sphere: A large space structure, measuring millions of miles across, with a star at the center to provide power.

Emperor's Counsel: A group drawn from the Imperial Senate. Called *archsenators*, they act as a liaison between the senate and the emperor.

Eudora Prime: A planet on the border between the Imperium and the Cyber Collective.

Far Harbor Station: A remote space station located somewhere between Aldorus and Eudora Prime.

Fat Cat Casino: A large gambling house in Ashetown run by Big G.

Five Families: The most powerful houses of the Imperial nobility. Direct descendants of the captains from the surviving sleeper ships.

Forgotten, The: Dahlvish term for any Dahl that's been exiled from their society. The memory of their existence is psionically erased from all non-exiled Dahl.

Gnomi: A diminutive race, no more than two to three feet tall. Disparagingly called *tinks*, the Gnomi are highly proficient with machines and electronics.

Gordian: A race of stubborn, boar-like humanoids with pig noses and tusks. Physically stocky, but shorter than the average human.

***Gorgon, HIMS*:** The largest warship in the Imperial Navy, commanded by Lord Rupert Tagus III.

Griefers, The: A street gang led by Kid Vicious.

Groen: One of the Five Families, represented by a botonée cross.

Grunka: A dangerous creature native to Prill, with multiple arms and legs, and many teeth.

Gwlad Ard'un: Home world of the Dahl.

Hekla VII: A largely barren ice planet.

HIMS: Abbreviation for His Imperial Majesty's Ship. Used when naming warships of the Imperial Navy.

Hotspur: Pirate ship owned by Capt. Blixx.

Imperial Frontier: An area of the Imperium, near the Magna Supremacy border, where law and order is less prevalent.

Imperial Senate: The highest legislature of the Imperium, made up of both commoners and nobles.

Imperium: An empire largely controlled by humans. Founded 700 years ago, after humans arrived in sleeper ships from Earth after an 800-year journey.

Lucrator: One of the lower castes of Magna society. Made up of workers and service providers.

Magna: A race of green-skinned humanoids with devil- or ram-like horns. Larger and more physically imposing than an average human.

Magna Supremacy: A major interstellar power at odds with the Imperium.

Mechanosynthesis: A method of building objects on an atomic or molecular scale.

Middleton: A district of Regalis inhabited by large businesses and, in general, middle-class neighborhoods.

MoFoCo: A disreputable mega-corporation specializing in products of questionable quality.

Montros: One of the Five Families, represented by a rose.

Naiad: The "user interface" for the Pool of Memory.

Nanomancer: A special avatar that uses flying nanobots to attack enemies.

Nobles: Families of the Imperium who are directly descended from the crews of the sleeper ships. The most powerful of these are called the Five Families. Also called the *aristocracy*.

Pirate Clans: Groups of loosely organized marauders who attack shipping along the Imperial Frontier.

Pool of Memory: A liquid computer in which the collected knowledge of the Dahl is stored.

Prill: A remote planet covered by thick jungles.

Psionics: Special mental abilities common among Dahl and related sub-species.

Rattenbury: Freighter owned by Capt. Hitch.

Red Lotus: A criminal organization run entirely by women, specializing in extortion and prostitution.

Regalis: Capital city and seat of government of the Imperium, located on Aldorus.

Revenna: A planet of lush forests owned mostly by the Montros family.

Robot Freedom League (RFL): An activist group within the Imperium with the sole purpose of freeing robots from servitude.

Rochan: Home world of the Tor consisting of underground labyrinth cities.

Sadira Flowers: A neighborhood flower shop in Middleton that serves as a front for Red Lotus.
Sentinel: A heavily armed and armored avatar.
Si-Sawat: A crime syndicate made up of Tikarin and led by Big G.
Sleeper Ship: One of seven colony ships launched from Earth to the Andromeda Galaxy. Only five are known to have survived the journey.
***Sorcerer*:** Starship owned by Warlock Industries, often used by Oscar Skarlander.
***Starling*:** A starship owned by Magnus Black.
***Steppenwolf*:** Freighter owned by Capt. Ramsey.
Tagus: One of the Five Families, represented by a lion.
Tikarin: A feline race slightly smaller than an average human.
Tor: A race that is half bovine and half humanoid.
Underdelve: An underground community on Eudora Prime, largely inhabited by non-humans.
Veber: One of the Five Families, represented by a scallop shell.
***Victoria, HIMS*:** Name of the Imperial yacht.
***Wanderer*:** Freighter owned by Capt. Ramus.
Warlock Industries: A mega-corporation operating throughout the Imperium, specializing in military hardware, advanced technology, and genetic experimentation.
West End: The richest district of Regalis. Also, the location of most Imperial government buildings.
Westford: A prestigious university on Aldorus, located in the West End.
Xeno: A non-human.
Xenotech: Alien, non-human technology.

ABOUT THE AUTHOR

W. (William) H. Mitchell was born in Omaha, NE and graduated from the University of Nebraska-Lincoln with a degree in English. He lives with his wife and cats outside of Kansas City.

Follow him on his website at www.WHMitchellFiction.com

www.ingramcontent.com/pod-product-compliance
Lightning Source LLC
Chambersburg PA
CBHW021132110726
47900CB00002B/325